WIDOW'S RUN

TG WOLFF

WIDOW'S RUN

DOWN&OUT
BOOKS

Down & Out Books
3959 Van Dyke Road, Suite 265
Lutz, FL 33558
DownAndOutBooks.com

The characters and events in this book are fictitious. Any similarity to real persons, living or dead, is coincidental and not intended by the author.

Cover design by JT Lindroos

ISBN: 1-948235-94-3
ISBN-13: 978-1-948235-94-5

For my sons Jack and Viktor.
Life with you is never dull. Thank God.

WHAT A LOVELY
CORPSE YOU HAVE

They buried me today and I had the balls to show up. Here I was, on a sunny day in May, shaking my head along with a hundred other people, wondering how someone so young and vibrant could—*poof*—be gone. I hid in plain sight, loitering on the edge of the crowd. A shit-brown wig in place of my usual chemical blond, matching contacts to camouflage my signature green eyes, and sunglasses plucked from the seventies ensured my face wouldn't catch the attention of the masses. A theater-quality padded suit added forty pounds to my athletic frame and clothes I wouldn't be caught dead in completed the illusion. The people who claimed to be closest to me would see what I wanted them to see, another mourner, lamenting the waste of a good life.

Sunny day in May—yeah, I've always had trouble with funerals being on sunny days. I firmly believe in mourning and expect nature to get on board with it. A funeral wasn't a funeral if the day wasn't gray with clouds so heavy water leaked like tears. Any temperature that didn't chill through skin and muscle down to the bone was an affront to the guest of honor. Stark silence needed to be center stage, the absence of natural sound, the absence of life, then fill it with the guttural cry of a bagpipe.

That's what I call a funeral.

Yeah…that's not what I got. I got the Disney version.

An expansive, pure blue sky stretched from horizon to horizon. Wisps of cotton ball clouds, a decorator's tasteful accent, floated listlessly above. Hardwood trees stood sentry over the church and cemetery, swaying to the rhythm of the breeze. Robins played tag, racing tree to tree, gliding between the branches.

Robins! WTF? There should be ravens or at least crows. Big, black, noisy crows, crying over my dead body.

Well, not *my* body, but let's not split bananas.

So why am I at my funeral? I'm not narcissistic. I'm here for a man. Where is the little turd? Faces floated above the sea of black created as shoulder pressed against shoulder. Everyone I knew. Names ticked off as I searched for the one who went by Black.

The bells on the church rang out. Lemmings marched up the steps, trading the warm sunshine for darkness, ten degrees cooler. Voices faded, leaving only the sound of shoes on the tiled floor. I took a seat in the back on the far aisle, no sign of my man.

The bells called out one final time. The pipe organ picked up and voices joined in. Enter my casket, a cherry box with ornate detailing on the edges and silver hardware. A nice choice. Pall-bearing for me were six men from different sides of life as I knew it. Representing family was my sister's husband and my father. Regardless of what my mother said, her first husband was my father. I've never seen that expression on his face before.

My life as an owner of a four-bedroom, three-bath suburban home was represented by the barbecuer-in-chief of our subdivision who day-timed as a vice cop. He dealt with more shit than a fertilizer salesmen—nothing shocked him—but here he was looking sad for me. Behind him was a social worker who was the carrot to my stick at the youth intervention facility where I worked for the last few years. The man was a marshmallow who loved those kids more than some of their families did.

Pre-suburbia, I put the *boom* in *ka-boom* as a CIA agent, specializing in chemical weapons, working with Enrique Torres.

2

He held his head high as he walked with my casket. When a man covered your back for a fistful of years, he tended to want to see it through to the end. Personally.

The shortest and last role in my life was the most unexpected. In high school, I was voted "least likely to marry." I created the category and spent fifty dollars campaigning for the win. I looked at the Vegas odds on "wife" and bet the under. How did I know I would be outmaneuvered by a PhD and a crooked smile? Now, here was my husband's brother, a man I only met a handful of times, walking me down the aisle. The family resemblance was so strong, I forgot to breathe.

"Why! Why did this happen?"

Excuse the whale birthing in the front row. She's just my mother. Her tummy-tucked, three-day-a-week-trainer, skinny latte-ed ass was wrapped in black silk so tight, you could tell her religion. She would need a crowbar to remove the cock-eyed black hat shellacked on her teased nest of blond hair. Nothing about her was natural or real. Even her crying was fake. Her nose wasn't red. Her makeup still fresh and in place.

The hypocritical bitch didn't have one nice thing to say to me in my thirty-one years on this earth. Not one. But the minute I was dead—*boom*—she squealed like a cat under foot.

"I can't believe she's gone. I can't believe my Annalisa is gone."

Annalisa. My given name. This is the last time you are going to see it. The only one you need to know is Diamond. A name as hard earned as my reputation. Did you know the word diamond comes the Greek word *adamas*, which means indestructible, unbreakable, unconquerable, and prone to blowing things up?

"In the name of the Father...."

The Catholic funeral service—my mother's current religion of choice. She went through churches the way some women went through shoes, always looking for a better fit.

I leaned back to inventory the other side of the church. There he was...my man. The guy with the answers and a sick sense of

3

humor. Picture a small-framed man with absolutely nothing striking about him. A man you would walk past in a hall and swear under oath the hall had been empty. A man ten-out-of-ten dentists wouldn't recognize as their patient. That was Ian Black. One row up, other side of the church. The dipshit looked like he was enjoying himself.

The rear doors slammed against their stops. Instantly a hundred pairs of eyes snapped to the man stalking up the aisle. Leather boots with soles thick enough to walk across hot coals echoed with every step. Black pants and shirt, undoubtedly some ridiculously priced silk-cotton-titanium blend, tucked in and covered with an ass-kicker leather coat trailing behind like a cape. His only color came from his dark mane of auburn hair.

Sam Irish and, if I read the clenched jaw correctly, he was pissed.

"I want to see her." The polish of London blistered under his seething mood, letting the Dublin alleys surface through the festering wounds.

"Sir, you are disturbing a funeral service." Color blossomed from the priest's collar, tinting first his throat, then slowly flushing his cheeks. His voice squeaked when he spoke next. "I must ask you to leave."

"And I must ask you to open the God damn lid."

Enrique and the boys and girls from my boom-boom days moved their hands to their sidearms. Slow. Calm. Practiced.

My father stepped into the aisle.

"Step back. Step back," I whispered. I've seen Sam Irish in this mood. You do not mess with him. My father must have seen it because he stepped back, and I breathed a sigh of relief.

"Open the lid," Irish ordered in a voice honed on cigarettes and whiskey.

The priest stood his ground. "I will not."

Ungood. Very ungood. What the hell was Irish thinking? What was he even doing here? We went back—way back—pre-husband days. More than once, we ended up at the same place at the

4

same time and, well, let's just say we scratched each other's itches.

Being dead created a feeling of impotence I hadn't bargained for. There wasn't one damn thing I could do about the scene unfolding. I just had to stand here, like every other dumb ass rubbernecker, unable to look away from the walking disaster.

"How do you open this fucker?" Irish felt around my coffin for the lid.

"Sir, stop immediately! And watch your language, this is a place of God." The priest lectured but smartly did not interfere. There were more than muscles bulging under Irish's coat.

Then the lid was open.

A collective gasp rose. The church was small and there were no bad seats. Everyone saw everything.

It wasn't pretty.

Why didn't I have myself cremated? If this had just been about me, I would have. But Gavriil, my husband, wanted to be buried, which I did for him. Nobody (apart from my mother) would have believed I wanted to be cremated instead of laid to rest next to my husband. When you're faking your death, the last thing you want to do is give people a reason to look below the surface. They expected me to be buried, so I was being buried.

Irish leaned over her, ur, me, both hands on the lid. His head turned as his gaze swept up and down. "You sure this is her?"

Shit.

"Of course, it's her. Who are you?" My sister pitched forward from her first-row pew. Cass, Cassandra, was three years younger. She was as good as I was...wrong. Her hair, the color of corn silk, was natural. We shared the green eyes. When we cry, our green goes mutant with red, like hers were now. I hated she was paying the price for this mess.

Irish gave her the same scrutiny he'd given my corpse. He let go of the lid. It slammed close, a thunderous bang bounced ceiling to floor and back again. Irish didn't notice; his focus on my sister. "You have her eyes." He raised a hand to cup Cass's cheek.

Her husband gripped the forearm and stopped it several

inches from his wife's face.

Irish glared at my brother-in-law but quickly turned his attention back to Cass. "What happened?"

"Fire." Her voice broke. "She fell asleep with candles lit. One...one must have fallen over."

I wanted an explosion, something truly epic, something Diamond-worthy, but do you know how hard it is to pull off? There would have been a fire investigation and a utility investigation and more questions and more tests. There was just too much risk.

Instead, I had a little pity party on the anniversary of my husband's death. Maybe I had too much to drink and fell asleep on the couch with a bottle in my arms and candles on the table next to me. Were there risks? Sure, but I mitigated them. By the time the neighbors called the fire department, my living room didn't exist anymore. And neither did I.

Irish blinked once, twice, then deafened the saints with a booming laugh. "You're tellin' me Diamond was taken out by a fuckin' candle?"

Shut up, Irish. Shut up.

He was out of his mind calling me by name. A quarter of the people in the church had never heard of Diamond. The half who did knew exactly what kind of man Irish was...if the leather-clad entrance and f-bombs hadn't given him away.

Irish cut off his outrageous laugh and replaced it with cold dominance. "How stupid do you think I am?"

Enrique stepped to the aisle, angling his body for whatever came next. Three other agents did the same. "You paid your *respects*." He spat out the word. "Now it's time for you to move on."

Something between a growl and a chuckle rumbled in Irish's chest. "Diamond! Come out, come out wherever you are." He spun in a slow circle, empty hands flared wide. "Olly olly oxen free." He turned again. "Marco."

Polo, you Irish hot head.

My mother shuffled into the aisle, her dress too tight, heels too high. "She's not here, you idiot! She's *dead!*"

This ought to be good. Nobody called Irish an idiot. Well, almost nobody. Point is, I don't recommend it unless armed with something stronger than Chanel No. 5.

Irish looked like a pit bull and my mother was a juicy steak. He licked his lips. "You're certain this is Diamond?"

My mother rolled her eyes. An expression I lived under all my life. "A mother knows her own daughter. I know her here." She struck her fist to her corseted breasts. "Besides, who else would be wearing her wedding ring? You're in the wrong place. There's no Diamond here. Bah." She dismissed Irish with a royal wave of her hand and returned to her place. "Take a seat or get out. Move it along, Father."

"Married? Diamond married?"

The shock on Irish's face was worth showing up for. He was lucky I was dead, or I would have held it over him for the rest of his life.

Then he was in motion. His long, smooth strides carried him halfway up the aisle when he stagger-stepped. Something surprised Irish, a man who was surprised by nothing. He turned his head and surveyed the gathered, a predator selecting his entrée. I couldn't avert my eyes. Everyone looked at Irish. If I was the only person looking at the casket or the priest or the rafters... well, I might as well have stood on the bench and screamed "Polo."

He was then on the move again. The brief appearance of the brilliant sunlight the only indication he had left the building.

The service continued. The priest. Blah-blah-blah. My mother, this time baying like a donkey. *Hee-haw. Hee-haw.* Finally, the pipe organ began the final dirge and my coffin hung from strong hands.

I kept to my place, leaving with my row, staying in the thick of the line. I kept one eye on Black and the other on lookout for Irish. Impossible? Not when you've had advanced training. Chatter in the ranks picked up as the parade behind my coffin crossed the country road to the cemetery.

Chatter. See what you get with funerals on sunny days?

Do you think there would have been chatter if it were forty degrees? If buckets of water were pounding the crowd? If a flock of ink black crows circled above?

Hell. No!

Freaking Disney funeral.

With no sign of Irish, I closed on Black. Quickening my pace, I matched his stride. He cut me a glance, then dismissed. Fat chicks were not his type.

"So...uh, are you a friend of the family?"

Black cut another narrow glance. "Old friends." He walked faster.

So did I. "Old friends? Like college?" When he didn't answer, I kept going. "Older? High school? Was she the prom queen? She always seemed like the prom queen type."

"A prom queen? Sister, you have no idea."

"Yeah, Ian, I do."

He tripped over a crack in the sidewalk.

"Smooth as ever." I lengthened my stride, making him give chase.

"Diamond?" His bland face reappeared at my side with amusement in a crooked grin. "Loved the corpse. It gave the event a certain...generic say pa." A linguist Black was not. "Nice funeral. You plan it?"

I shot mental daggers at the little birds who played follow-the-leader overhead. "No. What do you have for me?"

Weeks before I killed myself, I contacted Ian Black for information. He was a broker, trading in facts, figures, names, and dates. I hadn't talked to him since my husband's funeral, but he pushed all in when I called. It began when a woman emailed me with a shaky video and a story. The hit-and-run accident in Rome that killed my husband wasn't an accident. She was there, a few feet away. When the *polizia* dismissed her account, she sent the video to me. I played it straight, making the calls, tugging on old relationships. Reality was a cold slap in the face. The authorities didn't want to hear from a grieving widow with a conspiracy theory.

I didn't want Mrs. Gavriil Rubchinskaya to die. They killed her when they took the last scrap of her sanity and squashed it like a bug. Fortunately, I had Diamond. Using the information Black had, I was going Spanish Inquisition on anyone who spoke to, looked at, or thought of Gavriil those last days.

Hell hath no fury, etc., etc., etc.

Black's gaze raked over me like a TSA scan. His face contorted as if he'd gotten a whiff of month-old gym socks. "You really let yourself go."

"You got my information? You don't want to cross a dead woman." I pulled up short and let him feel my point...in his soft underbelly. So, I went to my funeral armed? A woman needs to be prepared for all circumstances.

"First time I see you in a year and you insult me." He eased away from me, amusement wiped off his face. "Yeah, I got it."

"Give."

"Jesus, Diamond, it's not on me. You think I'm going to walk into a funeral with it in my pocket? Keep walkin'." He paced next to me as we stayed with the crowd. "I have it. But there's a catch."

My hand was on his arm, ready to break it if the situation demanded. "A catch?"

"I need you to flush out game for me. One hour. Two at most." Black reached into his pocket and retrieved a blue Post-It. His gaze took my measurements again. "If you're not up for it..."

I slapped him upside his medium brown hair. "It's a padded suit, you pig. I couldn't have people recognize me. What were you thinking picking my funeral for the drop?"

He didn't answer, instead smoothing his hair back in place, his relief visible. "Lose the fat chick suit, Diamond. I need a slut. A sophisticated slut."

The crowd reassembled under a white tent, forming a loose

circle around my coffin. Black stood next to me, his hands folded and chin to his chest as the priest began to read again. The words droned on as in some other world. It reminded me of the old Peanuts cartoons, the way the adults sounded. *Wah wah wahwah wah wah.*

I didn't want to stand here, listening to whitewashed words of a man who didn't get my life. Who would never get my life. I wanted the file Black put together. I wanted to get out of here and do what I hadn't been able to do for a year—learn what really happened to my husband.

The blue square in my hand held an address. No name. No phone number. "When?" I said quietly when everyone else said "Amen."

Black draped an arm around me. Anyone looking would only see a man comforting a woman. "This afternoon works."

"I'll need an hour to change."

Black's gaze pierced my cheap sunglasses. "Take two."

A member from the funeral home wandered through the thin crowd, handing out white roses. Real roses, not wannabe carnations. Somebody gave a damn and a few bucks.

"Let's get out of here." I took a step toward the open air outside the tent.

Black held me in place. "Keep it together, Diamond. We leave now, all eyes are on us."

Guilt mated with determination and their love child was anger. I directed it at Black. "We don't leave now and you're the next body in the ground."

He shook his head, woefully under intimidated. "A few more minutes."

I didn't move because the pain-in-the-ass was right. Unless I wanted to feign being inconsolable—oh, wait, my mother's already doing that—I was stuck 'til the end. My mother revved up and went into a rendition of a cat in heat on a hot summer's night. I planted an elbow in Black's ribs as the priest opened his arms wide, embracing the crowd. "Why the hell did you pick my funeral for the drop?"

Again, he didn't answer but stood stoically at my gravesite, his head bowed.

The priest spoke into the space grief created. "At this time, I invite each of you to come forward and offer your parting words."

The parade started anew. Focus. Catalog names and faces. Who else thought enough of me to give up a day of golf...

Mother. Blah-blah-blah. More fake tears.

Cass entwined in her husband's arms. "This can't be real."

My father. "Give 'em hell, baby."

Enrique Torres. "It's hard to believe you're really gone, Diamond. I always thought you'd go out in a blaze of glory. Not this way." He choked up, swallowed it, then a smug twist graced his mouth. "Figured you'd take a dozen bastards with you." He tossed the rose onto my casket.

My section chief before I retired. The man taught me everything I knew about playing by the rules until the rules got in your way. He threw the rose in. "You were one hell of a woman, Diamond." A high compliment.

A few more CIA coworkers who didn't let a little thing like a few years keep them away. Good people, no matter what their resumes said. Neighbors from the cul-de-sac where I played suburban grown-up. Good barbecue. Good times. More good people. A group of teens and early-twenty somethings moved with a herd mentality. My kids and their chaperones, my coworkers. After I retired from field work, I took a really dangerous assignment, mentoring the troubled, dangerous, razor-sharp youth of DC. Every one of those kids should have been tempered by the dangerous neighborhoods, the hard lives they'd been born into. Instead, they paraded silently by my hole in the ground, faces tainted by grief. The caboose of the line, a skinny punk in sagging denim and a black t-shirt, glanced my way. His gaze caught mine; his eyes widened. I feigned disinterest when I wanted to slap his hairless face. The girl in front of him said something, distracting him, and I stepped behind Black, impossible for the kid to see.

Black stepped forward and I was up close and personal with my husband's head stone. I had seen it every day from when it was installed until two days ago. Subtly, I blew him a kiss.

Allow me to do the introductions. Gavriil, meet the world. World, this is the love of my life, Gavriil Andrei Rubchinsky. Born April 28, 1979. Died May 14, 2018. One year to the day from the date that will be carved on my side of our headstone.

I placed my hand on my casket, palm flat, fingers wide. Who's inside? Don't judge. It wasn't like I picked some innocent, productive member of society. She's past her problems, lying on a bed of silk, next to my husband, wearing my wedding ring.

My wedding ring.

It had been days, but my finger still wore the imprint. I was never naked until I took off my ring.

A hand settled gently between my shoulder blades. "It is always hard to say goodbye. Take comfort. She's gone to a better place." The priest, doing his job and keeping the show moving along, guided me to standing.

I cursed myself using words unbecoming for the priest. A smart woman didn't lean over her own coffin, jealous of the body within. A strong woman wasn't caught off guard by a man of the cloth she didn't know and words of comfort she didn't want. A sane woman didn't rebuke kindly blue eyes or turn consolation into an accusation.

"Better place? Where she's going, the devil don't dare look." I tossed the rose sidearm. It hit one of those stupid, happy birds who chose *that* moment to fly through the tent. The rose and the bird fell, a satisfying thud punctuated the ending.

The priest's gaze followed me, consolation gone from the gaping mouth, replaced by confusion and a healthy dose of apprehension. I lifted my chin as I turned away from him, power coursing through my body as I embraced my true self.

I strutted away, transforming with each step into a sophisticated slut. Striding from the cemetery as fast as my chub-rubbed thighs allowed, I headed to the powder-blue Prius I had borrowed from the parking lot next to my building. I broke into a giddy-up run to get ahead of the pack. Starting the Prius was a matter of touching the right wires together, and she was humming like the day she was born. I threw her into reverse and pulled out behind a dark crossover.

Faster than you can say "oh shit," said crossover fishtailed, drove over the high curb, and came to a cock-eyed rest across the only exit. The driver staggered out. He leaned heavily on the car, considering the doors and tires as though he couldn't remember what they were used for.

Oh, hell, I knew what was coming next.

PUMP THIS, JACK...
OR IS IT PUMP THIS JACK?

Alexei Rubchinsky was drunk, but that wasn't the problem. What my brother-in-law knew about automotive maintenance fit on the head on a pin. I heard the stories and was surprised he still had all his fingers. One thing was certain, he thought a lug nut was a type of dessert.

If you want a job done right, blah, blah, blah.

I got out of my car. I wasn't worried about Alexei recognizing me. I hadn't seen him since Gavriil's funeral, and I was incognito. "Seems like you have a little problem."

He swayed subtly, his eyes glassy and blurred. "I do not know what happened. I dropped my phone and the next thing, she is flat." His empty hand ran through his dark hair. "I should call the car rental, they will send help." He always had a close and personal relationship with his favorite vodka distiller, a man who counted on Alexei to marry his daughter. It seemed he'd taken some bolstering for my funeral.

"That will take too much time and you're blocking the exit. I can change it for you."

He frowned, a big, sad, upside-down horseshoe. "No. No, you are woman, and this is not right."

I rolled my eyes, dismissing the insult. "I've changed tires on every continent but one." A fact, albeit not a proud one, and

14

not the continent you'd think. "Pop the hatch."

He pressed a button on the fob and the SUV hatch silently raised. The trunk being empty simplified the process. The small spare was hidden under the false bottom, complete with the jack. I got to work. Like a NASCAR pit crew, I wanted my man back on the road before the field knew he'd pulled off.

"I should do something?"

The car was already in the air. "No. This is a one-woman job." I glanced at him, only to find him studying my face. "Is there something wrong?"

"You look very much like my brother's wife." He blinked twice, then narrowed his eyes. "It is in the shape of your face."

I lowered my head, obscuring his view. "I'm her cousin. Family resemblance." It was an explanation his brain could wrap around. Alexei lived in California. Though he and Gavriil spoke several times a week, we'd only been face-to-face a few times. Out of nowhere, he called shortly before my death. He was coming to DC and wanted to stay with me. I was on a tight time table at that point with zero room for collateral damage. I told him my house was infested with bed bugs and he told me he'd stay in a hotel. We had plans for dinner the evening after my death. I expected him to leave after I died.

"You are big, sturdy woman, like your cousin, yes?" He pronounced cousin "kuss-sin," enunciating all three s's.

I'm five feet nine inches and while I won't blow over in a storm, I am not, nor will I ever be "sturdy." That may be a compliment in some parts of the world but not in the good ol' US of A. Cursing him, I worked on breaking the lug nuts because I didn't have time to break his. The suit worked against me as I struggled for the right angle over my latex blubber. The padded tits didn't help. There was no place to put my arms where they didn't get in the way.

"My brother very much loved your cousin. I am glad he is dead. This, her death, would have killed him."

Swallowing hard, I focused on the work at hand and refused

to listen.

"I would never have believed anything would be more important to him than his research. Knowledge and the laboratory were always his first loves." Alexei took a deep, noisy breath. "Until he met her. She was his...I do not know a word for it in English."

My throat tightened to the point of suffocation. I was a victim of my own anatomy. Close your eyes, you can't see. Close your mouth, you can't taste. Hold your breath, you can't smell. But you can't not hear, you can't not feel. The pain of a thousand knives pierced my heart through my ears.

"Yes," I said, my voice cracking. "She felt the same way."

"That is why it surprised me when he sent the key to me."

Errrrk.

My brain screeched to a halt. I blinked a few times and got it jump started. Then thoughts raced into my head, the scene resembling a bumper car pit. I shoved the emotional baggage out of the way and tamed my thoughts with a crack of a whip, letting one coherently form. "Gavriil sent you a key? Before he died?" Like he could have sent it after. Yeah, I was real coherent.

"The envelope was in his handwriting. It was buried mistakenly within papers for my own research. My graduate assistant recently found it." He pulled a small key from his pocket. "It is foolish, but I carry it everywhere." He shrugged, not pulling off nonchalant any better than I did coherent. "It is from my brother. Is the tire fixed?"

"Nearly." Footsteps approached. I needed information before we had an audience. "What does it open?"

"A box in a bank. The note said this was insurance and to give it to his wife if anything happened to him. That is why I make this trip, to give the key."

Gimme gimme gimme.

Oh fuck, I'm dead.

"Hey buddy! You need a hand?" Enrique Torres strode across the blacktop with the confidence of a well-armed man. "Hey. I know you. Don't tell me...I never forget a name or a face."

The spare was on, just needed to tighten the lug nuts. One minute more.

"Alexei, right? I'm Enrique."

Alexei turned to Enrique, unconsciously sheltering me with his body. "Yes, yes. I remember. From the cookout after they bought the house. You are good?"

"Good? Maybe another day, but not this one. I can't believe my girl went out like that."

Glancing up, I could see part of Enrique's face over Alexei's shoulder. Enrique was too close, and he was too good to rely on makeup to hide my identity. Play time was over. Time to make like a tree and leave. "The man who stomped in, he was of the same mind, yes?" Alexei asked.

Slowly, slowly, slowly, I lowered the car. With nowhere to go but in, I opened the back door. The crossover SUV had room enough for me to curl up behind the driver's seat. Alexei wouldn't see me once he was in the car. I covered my head with his black suit coat. With the tint of the windows, I was invisible to all but direct scrutiny.

"Yes. I thought for a minute we'd have to go Molotov cock-tail on his ass, you know? Opening the casket like that...but it's hard to believe Diamond was taken out by a candle." There was speculation in Enrique's voice.

Sometimes, it didn't pay to have a bad reputation.

"Do you know she tickled a volcano once?" Enrique asked. "We were working a faction of weapons dealers who set up shop on the volcano. She was a rookie, there to learn only. Things got hot, our inside man got made. Diamond fought fire with fire. She set off a detonation that had the bad boys thinking the volcano was erupting." Little chuckles grew to a familiar belly laugh. "They raced down the mountain screaming from their windows as this nasty black smoke rose up. Down at the bottom, our men and the local government forces waited. She saved the agent's life and took down a multi-million-dollar-a-year black market. I was the first one to get to her. Found her sitting inside the volcano rim, laughing at the chaos around her."

I shouldn't be smiling under all this latex and makeup but talk about running like rats. Those big bads were all tough when they had rocket launchers on their shoulders but shake the earth a little, and they were little boys running for their mommies.

"I squatted down next to her. I remember shaking my head and saying 'You are one hard woman. Gorgeous but hard. Come on, Diamond. You're on clean up.'"

"She wouldn't answer to anything except Diamond that day forward." A new voice entered the conversation, my ex-chief's. "She was one of the best. Remember the time..."

New voices entered, and the stories flowed, all at my expense. And they were total bullshit. It was not true that explosions followed me across the continents and I so did not tip the scales of a certain Central American coup. If the general got the wrong idea, you can't blame me. He asked me what I was there to do. I told him straight out I was there to blow the shit out of him and his asshole friends. He told me to get to it. I did. It might have registered as a small earthquake. You see, I—

"What in the name of all that is holy is going on here! This is a funeral, not a traffic jam." My mother's voice, melodic as fingernails on a chalkboard, cut through the reverie.

"You, Alexei." My mother snapped like a mousetrap. "You've been in this country long enough, haven't you learned to drive?"

"Oh, ur, yes Mrs. Allerton."

"Mrs. Ridgeway. My marriage to Allerton was annulled." Her reply had the arrogance of a woman who expected everyone to keep up with her daily Facebook, Instagram, Twitter, and billboard postings.

I dug my nails into my hand, fury barely contained. Leaving my father wasn't enough; she annulled him. As if with the snap of fingers, fifteen years never happened. She wouldn't let me see him. We fought over it. That's when she dropped the bomb.

18

Edward Allerton was not my biological father. But he was Cass's, she couldn't annul that. I didn't really know the current Mr. Ridgeway and never would. I'm sure he's a perfectly nice man—wait, no he's not. He married my mother.

Point to the curious...why wasn't *he* here today? Mommy dearest probably left him tied up on the porch. Hope she left a bowl of water for him.

"Mrs. Ridgeway. My congratulations and condolences," Alexei said.

"Huh?" my mother said. I snickered. Alexei probably thought she killed her officially nonexistent first husband. "All of you, get. You don't have to go home, but you can't block the driveway. Get out of the way, Alexei."

"Mrs. Aller—Ridgeway. The tire is flat." In his moment of silence, I held my breath. "But...where is the cousin?"

I didn't move. This was make or break time.

My mother squawked again. "Close your trunk and move your ass."

I swallowed a twisted laugh as I cheered my mother on. No one ruined a good time like her.

The rear hatch closed, then the driver's door opened. The car shifted as Alexei's weight settled into the front seat. He muttered in Russian as he brought the engine to life. A left out of the parking lot, a right onto the main street. We were clear.

Still, I stayed hidden. I wasn't trying to give Alexei a heart attack and end up wrapped around a telephone pole. It wasn't part of my plan to die leaving my funeral.

His phone rang, the one he was searching for when he surfed the curb. It was wedged between the center console and the driver's seat. I knew because the light from the screen blasted my eyes. Alexei flailed wildly, as if the phone would sense his hand and jump to it like Thor and his hammer. The groping hand landed on my head. I freed the phone and held it out. If he had turned around, he would have seen the phone floating above his coat.

But he didn't. The scavenging hand brushed against the device and then locked on. "'Ello? Alexei Rubchinsky here...Yes, Mr. Winston, I read your email...Excuse me, Buford..."

I sucked air like a Dyson, getting carpet dandruff, lint, and weird rental car seeds in the bargain. Buford Winston was the head of an agricultural conglomerate called AgNow! and Gavriil's arch enemy. I can't tell you the number of nights I listened to Gavriil nerd rage over some scheme Winston was selling.

Screw Denmark, something was rotten right here in DC. Alexei was a medical researcher. There was no reason for him to be emailing with Buford.

"I tell you I will look, so I will look. That is all I can do. My brother has been dead for a year. I am sure his wife would have claimed what was his."

Hell, yes. Everything important to Gavriil miraculously escaped the murderous fire. No one would find it. Least of all Buford Winston.

The click of a turn signal warned me, but the turn was sharper than I expected. My face bounced off the carpeting, saved from rug burn by my disguise. Latex, it's not just for jowls anymore. Sitting back on my haunches, I shoved the coat aside for air. The shocking truth was revealed. Those weird little rental car seeds were really...quinoa!

I hated quinoa!

Gavriil conducted research on starving populations and was convinced quinoa—pronounced *keen-wa* for those without a Whole Foods nearby—was adaptable to challenging climatic conditions.

We had eaten so much of it, I was sure my lower forty was still cultivating a crop partial to red wine, dark chocolate, and medium-rare steak. I rummaged through Alexei's pockets and found his hotel key, an EpiPen, three individually packaged mints, ten jeweler's baggies of quinoa seeds, and folded sheets of paper. Gavriil's handwriting! It was in Russian, which meant he was agitated when he wrote the pages. When he was wound up, English eluded him, especially the written word.

"I have appointment shortly at university with my brother's assistant. I will see what she has. Perhaps she will know the meaning of the key."

"No!" Buford's response was so emphatic, they heard him throughout Virginia. "Do not tell anyone. You just do your looking quiet like."

"Yes, yes." Alexei capitulated, his voice without confidence. "I will call later." His cell phone landed on the passenger seat with a small thud. He nearly elbowed me taking a go-cup out of the holder. He sipped and answered with a moan that could follow a woman but never coffee or tea.

As the car slowed to a stop, I peeked out the windshield, seeing the traffic light turn red. He replaced the go-cup in the holder and sighed. This was my chance to come out without killing either of us. Before I could act, metal slapped against the driver's window.

"Get out of the car, muthafucka, you bein' jacked." The voice was so deep it likely originated in the man's ankles. Despite being sourced from Urban Dictionary, it had a smooth polished tone of rhythm and blues and didn't belong with grand theft auto. I waited for the deep bass to say "gotcha" and let me get on with my day. Instead, he said, "I'll take your money and your car. Out before I get mad."

"What? The car is not mine. You want money? I have money." Alexei's hand groped around my head again.

"One...two..."

The crossover went into park and the driver's door opened. "Okay. I am listening. No need for the gun."

A big weight dropped into the car and then we were flying. Right turn. Left turn. I braced my back again the rear seat, trying to keep my feet under me, so to speak. The ride was wild. A ménage à trois between X- Games, the rodeo, and *The Fast and the Furious.*

The deep voice laughed. "It's King, wanna go for a ride? Be

there in ten."

The hell we were. Time to hijack this carjacking.

I rose slowly, peering over his left shoulder at the road ahead. We were on a narrow side street with cars randomly parked in front of houses. The road in front of us was open.

I sprung up now, barring an arm across his collarbone and holding on. The car bucked wildly left and right, like a prize bull. We clipped a parked car, rode up a curb, turfed the one patch of grass in the neighborhood but never stopped. I hung tight, using my legs and barre hold to keep my seat. Ghetto bull riding! What a freakin' rush!

I laughed with the thrill of the ride while the bass voice sounded like a tornado siren.

"Quiet," I ordered. I pressed the EpiPen into his thick neck "You want to live, you shut up now. You hear me?" My voice was calm and professional.

"What did you do? What was that?" His voice cracked as it went up an octave it couldn't reach. "Did you kill me?"

"I injected you with a powerful neurocontroller. Mind control. *Your* mind is under *my* control. Listen to my voice. You will do what I say, or you will feel extreme pain. Do you understand?"

"I don't wanna die!"

I hate working with amateurs. "*Extreme* pain. Do you understand?"

He whimpered once, then remembered he had balls. "Yeah. I understand."

"Slow down. Drive the speed limit." He complied, letting the car coast down to the posted limit. "What's your name?"

"King."

"You're real name. Not your gang banger."

"Just King. When you got a name like mine, don't need another. You got one? A name?"

"Diamond. Now that we've been introduced, we're going back to pick up the man you borrowed this from."

King didn't balk but drove like a YouTube video on safe

driving. Hands at eight and four o'clock, speed one mile an hour under the speed limit; he used the turn signals as we circled back to Alexei. He stood on the corner, unsure if he should sit, stay, or roll over.

King pulled over and lowered the passenger window. Alexei bent down, twice as bewildered as he had been.

"Get in," I yelled.

Alexei inspected the length of the car. "But, what happened? The rental car company will charge to my credit card."

"I'll fix it. Get in."

He opened the door this time and eyed the situation. King sat behind the wheel, twitching as though he didn't quite have full command of his faculties. Me in the back seat, the lion tamer in control of her pride. "Cousin? You were there and then you weren't."

"And now I'm here. For the last time, get in." Finally, he did. He grabbed his go-cup with two hands and poured it down his throat. Liquid clear as water escaped the corner of his mouth. I gave King directions to Alexei's hotel. "You have thirty minutes to answer my questions. You went to the bank box. What did you find?"

"It—it was full of packets of seeds. The quinoa my brother loved so. Different varieties, I think, different colors. There were notes." His gaze flashed to King, an antelope waiting for the lion to strike.

"Don' worry 'bout me. She shot me with mind control juice." King hit the brakes hard to let a panel van merge in front of us. "Without the juice, I'da sliced the muthafucka for cutting me off."

Alexei wasn't comforted. "The pages had dates and notes from conversations between my brother and that man Buford Winston. He had circled some. The last date was three days before he died."

"The letter with the key, was it dated?"

He nodded gravely. "It had the same date as the last entry."

The day before Gavriil left for the conference in Italy. I pictured those last days, searching for a clue he thought something was wrong. It wasn't the first time I'd tried to "watch" those last moments. Each time, I saw nothing but my own problems. How self-absorbed I was! "Did he say why he didn't leave the key with my cousin? Why send it to you and ask you to give it to her? He could have handed it to her over morning coffee."

The fact he chose his brother over me hurt. If it was so freaking important, he should have left it with me. Gavriil was lucky he was dead because we would have had one hell of a fight over this.

"I think...I think he hoped it was nothing."

King butted in. "So, this dude put a bunch of seeds in a bank and then mailed you the key before he died?" He shook his head. "Bad news. I don't know what kind of shit y'all are messed up in but keep me out. I don't do bad news."

"You don't do bad news?" Alexei's brows pressed together at the incredulous declaration. "You carjacked me! At gun point!"

"Well, yeah but, that ain't nothing."

"It is to me!" One minute, Alexei was searching frantically, the next he pointed the business end of the gun at King. "How does it feel, being on this end. Does it feel like nothing?"

"No!" My shout was swallowed by the explosion of the gun. I screamed at Alexei, I know I did because I felt my mouth moving but the fucker deafened me by pulling the trigger.

Alexei dropped the gun like a hot potato. His mouth was open in terror, his eyes equally wide. King faced Alexei, his hands pressed over his ears, his lips moving in a flurry.

I was glad I was deaf. They were making a hell of a racket.

King patted himself for wounds instead of keeping his hands on the wheel. The car played pinball between the parked cars.

We got tossed like a salad.

"King. Hands on the wheel." My voice bullied past the ringing in my ears. I used the tone honed on inner-city kids to keep the big man hopped up on a double dose of adrenaline under control. "Alexei, give me the gun. Now." He picked it from his lap and shoved it at me. I engaged the safety and wiped it down. I couldn't have a dead woman's fingerprints on it.

"Give me some of that brain juice!" King's voice was strained but his hands were steady. "I need it. Please, Diamond lady. Just a little hit."

"You're doing fine. Take the next right." Police weren't going to be far behind.

"Damn, I'm glad you shot me up. If it wasn't for the numb-numb juice, I would have shit myself."

"Don't pull something patting yourself on the back. Just drive. Sanely." We drove for a mile. Sirens came, then lights. They raced past us, and we let out a collective sigh of relief. King began to laugh. The deep bass was contagious, infectious, sounding like something exotic and melodic.

"You have a beautiful voice," Alexei said. "You sing?"

Embarrassment crinkled his eyes, reddened his cheeks. "No," he said...but he wanted to.

"King, when I say 'Barry White' you sing. You won't feel shy or embarrassed, just confident and joyful. You understand?"

"No...I don't think—"

"Barry White."

"Keep yo' hand on that plow. Hold on." Notes as full and rich as the history of the old spiritual permeated the car, reaching through muscle and bone to the soul. Time suspended. All the bullshit of the carjacking and the gunfire lifted with his voice. I didn't notice the buildings speeding by or the sounds of a city. There was only the pure beauty of King's voice and the message he delivered. "If you wanna get to Heaven, let me tell you how, just keep yo' hand on that plow and hold on."

Verse after verse wove a veil of peace, covering the world of violence and deceit in serenity. Silence brought me back to the car.

Alexei was wiping his eyes. "So beautiful and right on this

day, when my brother has his wife by his side. What is this song?"

"A negro spiritual. It's called 'Hold On.' My gran's favorite." King's smile revealed the kind and gentle man within. "What now?"

"I am to go to the university and meet with Professor Liu," Alexei said.

Right. Forgot that detail. "Why are you meeting with her and what does Buford Winston have to do with it?"

"His name and number were in the bank box, so I call him yesterday after my visit. I was hopeful he would know more. He is eager to know Gavriil's work. They collaborated on work."

Maybe. If collaborated is spelled s-t-o-l-e.

"Did Winston tell you to talk to Professor Liu?" Quili Liu became chair of the department after Gavriil's death. It was the opportunity the quiet woman needed to take the reins. As his assistant, she was the natural choice to continue the promising research. "What does he want with her?"

"He asked me to meet, this is true. He does not trust her. He does not say this, but I hear it behind his voice."

"Did he say why?"

"Intimated. The work, my brother's work, is not moving and she is, um, stalling him. Yes, putting him off."

Typical Winston. It's all about the dollars. Someone finally stood up to him and he cried foul. Typical bully move.

"I go," he continued, interrupting my mental rant, "because it is my brother's work. It was everything to him and if I can help it to move forward, it is what I must do. You see?"

"Yes, I see." I didn't trust Buford farther than I could throw him—about two feet—and was curious what the understudy was doing with the role of researcher-in-chief. "Call her and tell her you are going to be late. Blame it on the funeral." I scrawled my voicemail number on a receipt shoved in a cup holder. "After you meet with her, call this number and leave a message with a summary."

He took the number, tucking it into his shirt pocket. I expected questions, they were there in the piercing set of his dark eyes, but he didn't voice them. We neared the hotel. It was time for action. "Circle the block. We'll drop you off, King, and then we'll park the car. You come from the back of the lot, get in, and we'll drive away. Alexei, you'll go to your hotel room. Wait two hours, then come back down and report the car stolen."

King circled and pulled into a fast food restaurant behind the hotel. He parked and turned to Alexei before he got out. "Sorry about the jacking and all. You were right. You ain't nothing. You something." He offered Alexei his hand but in an urban style, putting their hands at an angle to each other.

Alexei imitated a dog who just heard an interesting sound. "So! Like television." He placed his palm in King's and pulled his carjacker in for a hug.

King patted the older, smaller man on the back, then opened the door. "Gettin' me a milkshake then I'll be seein' you." He walked to the fast food restaurant, singing to announce his presence. "Keep yo hand on that plow. Hold on!"

Alexei left the passenger seat for the driver's, going out and around. When he slid onto the leather, he was humming the music of another people, from another time. "Is a good song, yes?"

I closed my eyes, trusting Alexei to drive around the block without getting lost or carjacked again. I still needed to get to Black and do his deed to get my file. Buford Winston just got himself added to my list as Suspect #1. The engine turned off. I opened my eyes and moved into the gap between the front seats. "Call Liu and stall. Take a shower, work, do whatever you need to buy us a few hours, then report the car stolen. Got it?"

He nodded, calm and determined. "I am glad to have met you today, cousin. I wish you luck." He stunned me by cupping my face in his hands and kissing one cheek, then the other. Then, with hurried movements, he opened the door, dropped his phone on the ground, followed it out, and closed the door.

The keys were still in the ignition. Oops.

I watched Alexei until the automatic doors swallowed him. He moved much like his brother. Seeing him made the ache better and worse. The driver's door opened, and I swung the gun toward the invader.

"I got you chocolate 'cause ladies are always lovin' on the chocolate." King passed a tall cup to me. "Where to, Diamond lady?"

If he thought anything of my reaction, he didn't let on. For me, I was pissed at myself. I needed to get these feelings back in check. I blamed Black. My head wouldn't be so effed up if he hadn't picked my funeral as the drop. "My castle," I snapped, then gave him directions to my neighborhood. He figured out I was done talking and turned the radio on. Bass thumped out, cheering on a rapper who smeared the women stupid enough to sleep with him.

"That the way you treat your women?" I collected the detritus from the floor and shoved it back into the coat Alexei left behind.

"Naw. King's a lover of the ladies." He changed the station. "And the ladies love me back."

I slurped down the last of my milkshake as King pulled into the parking lot next to the building he didn't know I owned.

"Okay. Do it." King had his arms braced against the steering wheel, his face in a tight grimace.

He had me. "Do what?"

"The mind control antidote."

"Ri-ight. The antidote. Well, King, I'm afraid the antidote expired last year, and the drug company can't make more because the DEA bought the last of the supply and shut the factory down."

"Fuckin' DEA." He punched the steering wheel. "Am I gonna to be under mind control for the rest of my life?"

"'Fraid so. Here's what you're going to do. First, get rid of this car. Wipe it clean and do whatever you were going to do with it. Give me your hand." I picked the pen off the floor, then copied a contact from my phone to his hand. "Second, you're

28

going to call this man and sing for him. He tries to brush you off, you tell him Diamond's cashing in a marker. Then you listen to him. Period. Finally—"

"How much you think I can remember?"

"Finally, have a good and happy life, King. I order you to." I left the car.

He leaned across the center console. "What about you, Diamond lady? What manner of trouble you gonna make?"

"The multifaceted kind."

WANTED: SOPHISTICATED SLUT, MUST HAVE THREE-INCH HEELS

The stiletto heels of my knee-high boots clicked as I stepped onto small islands of concrete adrift in a sea of rubble. The city long ago forgot this patch of nowhere existed, leaving it to reclamation by feral beasts of all species. My target was the squat building wearing a mish-mash of sixties, nineties, and Y2K renovations. Looked like everybody ran out of money before the job was done. Still, the building stood when others had fallen, surviving the urban apocalypse like a cockroach without the good sense to die. Around the joint, an ad-hoc parking lot took over the space demoed buildings left behind. Crushed glass sprinkled across the parking lot like sugar on a donut, glistening under the happy-ass afternoon sun. The Hideaway.

Yeah, it was hidden...like a zit on the tip of a nose.

The plywood front door was painted black and had a pull handle covered in God knew what. Inside was a cave for nocturnal humans, offering cover from the offensive light of day.

My eyes were blinded by the darkness, but my nose picked up the scent of the dregs of humanity. Cheap booze was the drink of the day with a good portion of it spilled on the floor and left to season. My eyes adjusted quickly. The place was as pretty as it smelled. A long, narrow bar with salvaged stools making their final stand. Five square tables, all empty. The

30

patrons eschewed them for the battle-weary bar. Seven pairs of eyes focused on me. The only pair looking at the daytime crap on the television belonged to Ian Black.

Black turned his attention to me when I was two seats away. His gaze raked up and down, a clinical assessment of my wardrobe. My designer dress cost more than most of the cars in the parking lot. I wore it spray painted on, showing off a rack that didn't need bodywork. The skirt ended a few inches south of Treasure Island, then a nice length of leg ran into knee-high boots.

"You're skinny." Black turned back to the television, raising his beer to hide his mouth. "Not used to you without hair."

First, I'm fat, now I'm skinny. Men!

When it came to my hair, he wasn't the only one not used to it. My own reflection still surprised each morning. I traded long hair—wild, full, and highlighted blond—for short, sexy, and my natural dark chocolate. A color I hadn't worn since virgin days. "You're not going to be seeing me long enough to get used to it. Get on with this before I walk from this STD incubator."

He snorted derisively. "You're not walking. We both know it. Sit down."

Pulling out the stool next to him, I leaned my weight against the battered wood frame. "Nice place. You come here often?"

"Too often." When the bartender drifted down to our slice of heaven, he ordered a beer for me, passing on the optional glass. "The guy to your right."

Since I no longer had hair to throw over my shoulder to steal a glance, I stood and turned to hang my purse from the seat back. The eyes I looked to were watching mine. I let a slow, steamy smile grow as though I liked what I saw. Black nudged my arm, and I shot a displeased glare at him before winking at my mark and sitting like a lady. "Story."

He drained his beer, pushing it away as the bartender placed cold ones in front of us. "Disability scam. You are flirting with Montgomery Rand. Employed by my client for eighty-eight days—two less than the probation period—when 'an accident' made him unfit for work."

I looked over my shoulder again at the man-child sitting six chairs away. In his mid-twenties, he hadn't outgrown the baby fat. Dark wheat hair flopped on to his forehead. Light brown eyes showed intelligence, despite his current choice of venue. He probably shaved once a week. You don't need a blade when you don't have whiskers. "I'm guessing Mr. Rand wasn't going to make the cut."

"Nope."

I turned back, looking at Black in the mirror behind the bar. "What's the deal? Why do you need me?"

"I've been on him for two weeks. He's either good or the luckiest bastard alive."

"Any chance he's actually hurt?"

"No witnesses to the accident. The scene was a little too good, according to my client. He moans and groans, walks like the Tin Man but it doesn't reach his eyes. You hurt like that, it shows in the eyes."

Yeah it does. I pulled a Tin Man a time or two. You get to a certain point and pain wasn't put away in a drawer. It permeated your life until you were the asshole who made the deli girl cry because the extra lean corned beef wasn't lean enough. I stole another look. Rand pecked at a tablet with his thick fingers. His brows were furrowed, his tongue repeatedly swept over his lower lip. Concentration. Determination. But no pain. "Painkillers?"

"That shows, too, when you know what you're looking for."

"Which we do. Okay. Classic play? You want me to get him into a compromising position, so you can snap your dirty pictures."

"It's a classic for a reason." Black turned to me then. Anybody watching would see his attention fully on me when it was really on his quarry. "How do you want to do this?"

I leapt off the stool, sending it crashing to the floor behind me. "You son of a bitch! You're cutting me off? Half of the shit is mine. I worked hard for it."

Black came off his stool after me. "You call spreading your legs working hard? A washing machine works harder than you and it's wetter, too."

I slapped him. I didn't pull it. The crack cut through the heavy air like a chain saw. Some men stared, some snickered at the poor loser's predicament. "You limp dick asshole. Don't you dare—"

"Bitch!" He came at me, grabbing my dress but the tight fabric had no give. I slid under his arm and pushed him away.

"Entertaining as this all is," the bartender said, a baseball bat in his hands, "it needs to end."

Black jabbed his index finger at me. "You haven't heard the end of this." He kicked the stool, sending it sliding across the grimy aisle, then stalked to the door and hit it with the flat of his hand. A blast of white light assaulted the bar. Arms hastily covered eyes as the vampires recoiled with a hiss, ending Act One.

Act Two was all on me and completely improvised. With all the grace of a sophisticated slut, I turned back to the bar, ran my hands over my breasts down my stomach to smooth my dress, then finished my beer.

"You dropped this." Rand's head appeared in the mirror over my shoulder.

I turned around, tits first. My purse dangled from his hand. "Thank you. It's nice to know there are still a few gentlemen in the world." I accepted my purse, withdrew my lipstick, then repaired my undamaged mouth. I cocked my head, letting my gaze roam from the wide-eyed stare to the faded T-shirt, to the more faded jeans, to the sandals. "What's your name?"

"Monte. You?"

"Diamond." My gaze back on his, I pursed my lips as if considering, then smiled invitingly. "Are you in the mood for a little fun, Monte?"

His eyes glistened with hope. "What did you have in mind?"

Opening the wallet I snatched from Black's pocket, I withdrew a credit card. "An early dinner, a little wine, and then who knows? Wine always makes me...a little crazy. My car's outside."

He didn't hesitate. I walked as quickly as the heels allowed. Thought I might get lucky and have him break into a run. Black would have his eyes on us along with some high-speed film. A little trot out of Monte and my part of the deal was done.

"You have great legs," Monte said. "I like the boots."

I looked over my shoulder to where he shuffled along. His gaze went from my ass to my eyes, and back to my ass. Appreciating the view, he lacked the motivation to run. I quickened my pace, but he kept his. I tripped, my heel sliding off one of the concrete islands. His hand shot out to mine, but his body did not. Something held him in reserve.

Black was right. Either Monte was a platinum club con man or the luckiest bastard alive. I reassessed the vintage nerd vibe he gave off...nope. I wasn't buying it. He wasn't half as slick as he gave himself credit for.

"Where are we going?" he asked.

"To burn a little hole in this black credit card."

I drove to a part of town a sophisticated slut would frequent and a restaurant with a six-week waiting list for prime-time dining. At this time of day, Monte and I walked in. Well...almost.

"Stop fussing. The jacket looks good on you." My index finger danced suggestively around the lip of my wine glass. He ran his hand inside the collar of the borrowed suit coat, stopping at my direction. His gaze again and again swept around the well-appointed room. Each time, his tongue licked his lips as though savoring the taste of the good life.

"I don't like wearing other people's clothes." He glared like a belligerent child but stopped tugging at the coat. "So...your boyfriend's gonna be pissed you swiped his card."

"What's his is mine, etcetera, etcetera." I waved my hand like the king himself.

We small talked through appetizers washed down with a hundred-dollar bottle of wine. Monte didn't like the taste of the wine, but he liked the price, the class, so he drank without complaint. By the time the most expensive dishes on the menu were served, he'd relaxed, convinced himself he belonged in this place. He ran his hands down the borrowed wool, smoothing the fine material over his soft chest.

"I noticed you walk with a limp." I sipped my wine. "Is there a story behind it?"

"Industrial accident," Monte said without pause but didn't expound.

I linked my fingers and rested my chin on my hands. "Ooo, I'm intrigued. Tell me more."

He shrugged, looking about the restaurant, measuring the worth of the few diners. My timing had been off. He wanted to see himself as a man with the coin and standing to be at this restaurant with a woman such as *moi*. He didn't want to be a warehouse fork lift driver.

"You don't want to tell me what really happened? I'm okay with that. Tell me *your* story."

His eyes widened in surprise, then his gaze drifted to the upper right. He wasn't looking at something but rather concocting his story. I watched his face, his body, further acquainting myself with his mannerisms.

He drained his glass and then refilled it.

"I worked as a manager of a warehouse for a big tech firm. Like, BIG." Monte sighed then, shaking his head. "You would be shocked at the type of people we get in the warehouse. Losers. Burnouts. Ex-cons. Everyone has a story to sell. What I could do with a handful of *intelligent* human beings." He waved his hand, bringing himself back on topic. "We had been training this new guy on the forklift. It's as simple as they come but the guy's got two left feet. He'd already pierced a shipping container. He turned ten grand of inventory into trash in under two minutes. The guy was on his last chance. I had him moving a few pallets to make room for an expected delivery, as basic a job as I could give him. About ten minutes in, I go over to check

on him and don't I see crates stacked way past protocol and teetering like a Jenga tower. Without thinking about what I was
doing, I ran to the guy, pulling him from the forklift seconds
before…" He set his elbow on the table, hand in the air and let it
fall to the table with a clumsy thud. "We got clear but…my
back." He winced, the first I'd seen any indication of discomfort.

I plastered care and concern on my face. "Bad news?"

"The worst. It may never be right. I can't work like this.
Look at me, I can't move." Monte rotated five degrees to one
side, five degrees to the other. "I can't move, I can't work."

He was so full of shit his eyes were brown.

"Well, that's disappointing." I pouted, full bottom lip out.
"So, you can't…" I wrinkled my nose as I held up my fork and
let it fall until it dangled limply from my hand.

His brows furrowed in a V. "No. No, it's not…like that."

His depravity did have limits. Screw the company, no biggie.
Imply he can't screw, biggie.

"Good," I said, layering my voice with relief. "Because I
thought we'd take dessert back to your place."

"My place?" For an instant, the smallest instant, he looked
embarrassed. "Why not yours?"

I rolled my eyes. "Obvious reasons. Look, if you want to end
it here, just say so. I thought we could keep the good times roll-
ing, but if you're not up for a party…" I shrugged like it didn't
matter. I raised my hand for the check.

"I didn't say that." He looked around to see if he could be
heard. "You think I can keep the jacket? I kinda like it."

"On you…it's one of a kind." I handed the waiter Black's
credit card. With a swipe in a handheld device, we were free
and clear.

Well, almost.

"Here's the plan," Monte said, leaning forward in conspiracy.
"We get up, walk to the door, and then run like hell to your car."

It worked for me. "Run like hell" sounded like a photo op.

"One problem." I straightened my legs to show off three-inch heels. "I don't run. How about this…I leave now and pull the car around. Then you run like hell and jump into the car."

He nodded like a bobble head. "Let's do it."

I stood, picked up my purse, and walked out the door with haute sophistication. As promised, I retrieved the car and waited at the end of the valet canopy. I didn't see Black, but the man could disappear in broad daylight.

The doors were thrown open, and Monte burst out like a pudgy bull of Pamplona. He ran stiffly, arms circling, hair falling in his eyes, a braggart's grin on his face. The doors flung open again and the elegant maître d', in his black suit and fitted vest, leapt through the air, catching my guy in a flying tackle. Monte's eyes were wide as he was felled.

The maître d' came up first, planting his foot on Monte's neck while stripping the finely woven wool from his back. I laughed, enjoying the unfolding scene, knowing Black was getting every frame.

In a minute, it was over. The maître d' and the jacket were back inside the halls of the *trés* chic restaurant and Monte poured himself into my passenger seat.

"He was stronger than he looked." Monte examined his elbows and his knees. "Fast, too."

I pulled into traffic. "You win some, you lose some." My phone rang. I dug blindly into my purse and came up with a screen with a black square. I accepted the call. "You got it?"

"I didn't get it." A litany of curses followed.

"How did you not get it?"

"Equipment malfunction." Background sound moved to the foreground. Heavy breathing. A door slamming. A motor starting. "Take him to his place and keep him on the ground floor. Use the bedroom. I can get a clear shot if the shade is up. You gotta buy me fifteen minutes to get into place."

"I'll give you one more chance. You blow it and you're on your own." I disconnected before he could negotiate.

"Was that your boyfriend? You sound tough." Monte

winced as he picked sidewalk sand out of his knees and elbows.

"I am tough. No other way to survive in this world. He needs to learn to appreciate a woman like me." I didn't listen to the crap I spewed, but Monte did, nodding because he wanted to lose his virginity. I glanced at the clock. Nearly four. I needed to create Black's fifteen minutes. "I need gas." Taking the side roads, we wandered a mile out of the way to a station.

"Nice neighborhood," he said.

The hundred-year-old homes with their four bedrooms and three baths, their two-car garages and three-point-two kids with optional dog were just part of the landscape. "Nice enough. If you like that sort of thing."

Another turn and we were back on a commercial strip opting for function over form. Two traffic lights and we pulled into the gasoline oasis. Twelve pumps, no waiting.

Monte opened his door, wrapped his hands around the frame, then pulled himself out. "I'm going to run inside. You want anything."

And to think I thought he was going to be a gentleman and pump the gas. Did I want anything? Time. "A bottle of water and mints."

"Cool." Pregnant pause. "You got any cash on you? Hate to use a card for a few bucks."

I flipped a twenty across the trunk, knowing I wasn't seeing any change. I should have given him Black's credit card. Ten-to-one he'd have bought a c-note's worth of Ding Dongs and Ho Hos.

The pump finished in no time, which is what it took to dispense five gallons. I leaned against the car waiting patiently for the loser. Of all the gigs Black had to pull, seducing a post-acne twenty-something with a hormone-to-sense ratio of one-hundred-to-one sucked. Real work waited. I didn't have time to dick around playing Catholic school teacher.

Monte came out sucking down a Red Bull. I got my water and mints. No change. Business done, we headed across town, passing the restaurant twelve minutes after we left it. I stayed within the posted speed limits, which was akin to pulling my fingernails out one at a time but bought Black the rest of the time he wanted.

Montgomery Rand resided in a twelve-hundred-square-foot colonial with paint curling from the wood and packed dirt where grass should have been. I leaned down, scoping out the structure. It wasn't hard to pick out the spots likely hiding Ian Black.

Monte mimicked my pose. "My uncle owns it. He lets me stay here in exchange for taking care of the place."

"Looks like you've been doing a stellar job of it." Once begun is half done. I opened my door and moved the game forward.

Monte pried himself out of the car and lurched ahead of me. He moved stiffly again, as though something prevented him from moving freely. He pitched his body sideways to the stairs and stepped up one at a time. A practiced move. "If I'd known I was going to have a guest, I would have cleaned."

Great. Black owed me.

The house was decorated in old lady, except for the media system. A fifty-five-inch flat screen sat in front of a couch patterned in red and purple flowers. A coffee table a cat used as a scratching post was cluttered with gaming controllers. The house was as neat and clean as any apartment occupied by five twenty-year-old guys and their pet goat.

Disinfection was on tap for the third half of the day.

"Cozy." I made myself at home, memorizing the layout of the living room...dining room...kitchen...condemnable half bath... and—bingo—bedroom. "Come here, Monte."

"We can go upstairs. With just me, I don't go up there much. Just to shower but, you know, I don't use those rooms, so they are—"

My mouth on his stopped his running babble. My hands on his torso, I felt the brace making him move like the Tin Man.

I pulled my head back but kept my fingers running seductively along the edges of the Velcro bindings. "You need this? Wouldn't you rather feel me? My skin on yours?"

Monte grabbed the ends of his T-shirt and stripped it. The white, medicinal girdle squeezed his doughy breasts up a cup size. His gaze on me, he yanked the binding, the Velcro crying out. "Oh, man, this is really going to happen, isn't it?"

"Yes, Monte, this is really going to happen."

"I knew it. As soon as I saw you walk in, a cougar on the prowl." He let the girdle drop and then went for the button on his fly. "Steve and Wilson are not going to believe this." He pulled out one leg, then the other. "Can I take a picture?"

I backed him up until the rumpled bed took his legs out from under him. "Not a chance. But don't worry, I'll leave you with sex dreams to last you the rest of your lonely, horny life."

"Fuckin' awesome." He lifted his head. "Wait...what?"

I straddled him, grinding against the tent post in his navy-blue briefs. His head fell back, groaning with pleasure. I gave him the belly-dancer routine—hip swivels, pelvic rocking, slow, fast, light speed.

Reaching behind, I unzipped my dress. It was one of my favorites and wanted to protect it from slobber. Monte popped up and buried his face in my cleavage. I wrapped my arms around his head, ran my fingers through his hair. He did have nice hair, thick and soft.

While Monte worked on freeing my breast, I looked toward the window. There were no telltales, but I knew somewhere a high-powered lens focused on me. Monte was into me, but he hadn't done anything acrobatic enough to call his bluff.

I needed him on top.

"Hey big boy..." I threaded my hand between our bodies, stroked his rigid cock. Once...

"Shit."

"Will you give me what I want?"...Twice...

"Yeah. Anything. Everything."

"Get on top."...Three times...

"No!" Monte's arms clamped around me, his cock jerking

beneath the blue cotton blend. "No. No, no, no."

Another equipment malfunction. This just wasn't my day.

He fell back on his bed, the crook of his arm over his eyes. "Damnit," he sobbed, then hit the mattress with his fist.

"I take it as a compliment." No, I don't. "I'll get us some drinks, we'll play for a while and you'll be back in the game. With twice the staying power." Which gave me a full minute to work out Act Three.

"Yeah?"

"Abso-yeah." I leaned in and bit his lip. "I'll be right back." I dismounted and exited the room. What were the odds the kid would prematurely lift off? Pacing the kitchen in my spectacular bra, panties, and boots, I needed another plan. Monte had been playing the game long enough—he wasn't going to blow the gig easily. The brace kept him in check in public and in private, well, if he'd been sloppy, Black would have gotten the job done by now. How could I flush the guy out?

An idea blossomed. A wickedly hot idea.

The setup took a matter of minutes, which included fixing Monte the promised drink. Can you call opening a can of Red Bull "fixing"?

Hips swaying, I reentered the bedroom where he was propped up on pillows like some pampered prince. I handed him the drink, walked to the window in my bra and panties, and opened it. The screen had two long tears in it, as though a cat been dragged down the length. Eight feet below was the ground.

"You are really beautiful." Truth rang in Monte's voice. "Women like you, they don't look at men like me."

I turned to face him, resting my bum on the sill. "Men like you?"

"You know...geniuses. I have an IQ of one-fifty-three."

My gut reaction was lie, but I had an ear for falsities. This had the same ring of truth as his compliment on my looks. "Don't take this the wrong way, Monte, but if you have an IQ of one-fifty-three, what the fuck are you doing here?"

He pulled the blanket over his body, picked at the little pills of fuzz. "You have no idea what it's like. From the time I was in kindergarten, my parents pushed and shoved. Extra lessons. Extra studies. 'You're going to make something of yourself, Montgomery. A doctor. A researcher. Find the cure for cancer.'" He snorted. "No pressure. Just find the fucking cure for cancer."

"You showed them," I said. "You quit."

"Quit? I like to think I found other uses for my talents. Can I tell you something?" He patted the bed next to him. When I complied, he leaned toward me and whispered. "I know who you are."

A decade of undercover work had schooled my reactions. I let a slow, feline smile grace my lips. "Who am I, Monte?"

"I don't know who, but I know you're with him. The guy in the bar."

I rolled my eyes. "Everybody knew I was with him. That was then. Now, I'm with you."

He shook his head. "I know you work for him."

My turn to snort. "I do *not* work for him." Easiest truth I ever told.

"He's been trying for weeks to prove my injury isn't real. Dropping shit and asking me to pick it up. Following me." His gaze measured by cup size. "He's upped his game. I like it."

"If you believe the bullshit you're spewing, why tell me? If I was gaming you, I'd be smart to walk away after a revelation like that."

"I told you, I'm a genius. You're not walking away from me without proof, one way or the other. I bet you're the best at what you do." He propped up a pillow, leaning against it, arms crossed behind his head. "I hurt my back, on the job, just like it said in the report. I understand if you need to, uh, verify my story."

"You want to hear my version of the story?" I stood back up, picked my dress from the bed, then started putting it on. "Once there was a twenty-year-old genius who didn't know jack shit about the world. He thinks he's smarter than everyone around him. He pulls off small-time scams but doesn't net enough cash to buy a real glass of scotch and lives the high life in a hand-me-down Granny home from family too soft to put him out on the street. One day, this genius pulls a con on a guy with smarts who knows a pile of horse shit when he smells one. So, the guy with smarts hires a guy with skills and the guy with skills blackmails a woman on a mission. Now the woman on a mission doesn't give a rat's ass about the genius, he's just a speed bump in her day." I crossed to the window, pushed in the tabs, and released the screen, letting it fall to the ground. Monte sat on the bed, his jaw unhinged and gaping. "There's a fire on the other side of the door. This window, with a wide-angle lens focused on it, is the only way out." I picked up my keys and phone.

He stared at me, a player deciding to raise or fold. His yawing mouth closed into a deep frown. "That's a pretty speech, but it doesn't do a damn thing for my broken back."

His gaze went to the door, his bravado as limp as his dick.

"One way to know for certain." I waved my hand toward the door, inviting him to call my bluff.

He climbed out of bed with the grace and speed of a ninety-year-old. He walked stiff-legged to the bedroom door, performing for the camera. He opened the door and looked into the hallway.

Hell looked back.

A monster with a raging hunger, the fire ravaged the wall and licked at the hardwood floor. It growled and crackled as it devoured lead-based paint and the detritus of past generations.

He slammed the door, propping it closed with his back. "My house is on fire." His gaze flashed to his phone. He was easy to read. His plan was to call the fire department and stay put.

I beat him to the phone and threw it out the window.

His voice went fourteen-year-old girl. "Are you insane? You're going to kill us both."

"Not both." I went to the window, straddled the sill. Landing in the three-inch heels was going to be a bitch. I'd rather have jumped barefoot, but the ground below was a collection of forgotten stone and dying plant. Sunlight reflected off abundant materials not organic in nature. My boots were staying on. "I'm leaving now. You have a choice: stay, die, and you don't collect the disability. Leave, come clean on the scam, and use your big brain to build a real life." With those words of wisdom, I swung my other leg out the window and hang dropped to the ground. I managed to do it without spraining an ankle or breaking a heel.

Monte appeared in the window pulling on a T-shirt. "Don't leave me." Fear tightened his voice.

"I'm right here." Calm. Cool. "Do you have shoes on? Your wallet?"

"Shit." He disappeared into the darker interior then reappeared. He sat on the sill. One leg. Two legs…almost, his heel caught on the sill. "It's too far."

"Bullshit. If I could do it in Donna Karans, you can do it in your sneakers. Get your leg out the window."

His leg freed, he clung to the side of the house, holding the window frame like it was floating lumber from the Titanic. "I don't think I like you very much."

"I don't give a shit."

"The fire is eating the door." His legs bicycled uselessly against the clapboard.

"Fire will do that. You're three feet off the ground. Let go."

He did. He landed off balance, fell backwards, and did half a somersault. Downside up, his legs pedaled like a bug stuck on his back. Falling to his side, he pushed up until he sat on his butt.

Black better have his money shot because this shit was over.

I reached down and helped Monte to his feet.

He looked up through the window to the room now basked in red. "What happens next?"

"Withdraw the claim and nobody has to see the pictures. You have two hours." Sirens called in the distance. "It was nice doing business with you, Montgomery Rand."

I left him standing in his driveway, a stupefied look on his face, as I backed into the street and raced away. My phone chimed. I put Black on Bluetooth. "Tell me you got it."

"I am a professional."

I snorted. Enough said. "I gave him two hours to end it on his own."

"Long as I get paid." The sirens echoed in stereo, coming from behind me and through Black's call. "Meet me in fifteen minutes." He named a park a few miles away.

"You jerk me around and you'll be the next body found in the creek." I disconnected but not before I heard him chuckle his lack of concern.

The patch of green he selected was narrow but did the job to separate where people lived from where they worked. A winding drive through seventy-year-old trees ended in a long parking lot. There were runners and dog walkers and mothers with kids. The place wasn't crowded, but it was still public. I parked away from the trail-using population and kept the motor running.

Black pulled in next to me and then climbed into my passenger seat. He handed over a thick file. "Everything I found plus what you'll need. I used photos from two years ago. Didn't know you ditched the blond."

I let my fingers walk through the pages. Police reports, interviews, still photos, conference registration list. "Did you—what are you staring at?" It wasn't a creepy leer, but I still didn't like the intense facial scan.

"The hair still. You don't look like you." The staring didn't stop. "When did you sleep last?"

"I'm dead. I don't sleep." I pulled out a passport for Celina Matta. She had the blond hair I sported until my untimely death. Next was a plane ticket. "I'm going to Rome."

"Tomorrow. You have reservations at a small hotel run by friends. Be nice, I want to keep them. Gavriil's notebook isn't listed among any of the reports. Do you have it?"

I shook my head. "It wasn't in his things I brought back

45

from Rome. He didn't leave it at home, and it wasn't in the boxes from his office."

"You didn't pack his office. Someone at the university did it. Could they have kept it?"

Confession time: I might not have been clinically sane for a few weeks after my husband died. I didn't think I was crazy at the time. Looking back, I realize I can't quite remember the details. It's like I wasn't there in person but maybe Skyped in. Those weeks were the only time in my life I let people do things for me, big things, like packing my husband's office. "Could someone have kept it? Sure. I didn't realize it was missing until I got that email."

"Is it possible he was killed for it?"

"He wrote in it constantly. New ideas. Tweaks. Anything he didn't want to lose. And you know Gavriil, he had a lot to lose."

The careless façade Black wore faded as if my words struck a chord. "Yeah. Yeah, he did. It could have been valuable, in the right hands."

The right hands. Fucking Buford Winston. The name shown before my eyes in red, neon letters, the no-good, cheap, dirty bastard.

Winston lived in Oklahoma and had his tentacles in a dozen states. "Why am I going to Rome?"

"Read the file. There's a lot of questions. Where is Gabe's notebook? Who was this Russian woman? Why was Gabe outside the hotel? We need to start at the beginning."

Gabe. God, I hated the nickname Black had given him. It just didn't fit. My husband loved it, saying it made him feel American. Who would have thought the professor and the purveyor, for lack of a better term, would become poker buddies? A chance meeting. An insincere invitation. An unlikely friendship between two men who lived by their wits.

"There are other ways to do this," Black said. He reached for my hand, then thought the better of it. "You don't have to put yourself back out there. I know how much Gabe meant to you, but you mean a lot to a lot of us."

An idea bubbled. "This is the third time I'm asking you, and this time I expect an answer: why did you pick my funeral for the meet?"

He turned, facing me square. "I know you think you lost everything when Gabe died—"

"Don't tell me you know, Ian. You don't know shit—"

"I know you. And I know Gabe. He wouldn't want this for you, Diamond. He loved you. All those people there today love you, too. This whole idea of killing yourself is...it's bullshit, Diamond."

"You think I wanted to kill myself?" Emotion was a flamethrower to my throat. "All I wanted was the fucking police to look at the video, to look at Gavriil being pushed in front of that fucking car and investigate. I didn't even expect them to find the bastards, you know? I know the game. I know the odds. But they wouldn't even try, Ian. They nailed his coffin shut every bit as much as the asshole who pushed him and the murderer who hit him. I tried to play it straight. I tried to go by the rules, but no, Gavriil wasn't important enough, not to them. He was everything to me." My voice broke. I swallowed, squelching the flames, pulling the hurt inside, locking it away. "Annalisa Rubchinskaya played by the rules and look where it got her. A dead end. So, fuck the rules. And nobody fucks the rules like Diamond." Her power washed through me, burying the grieving widow. I dug my nails into her confidence, her determination, her complete resolve to see Gavriil's killers bleed the way his wife did. I closed the file. "I'm going back to the beginning to follow every line, every thread until I find the place where the son of a bitch messed up."

I hadn't expected this from Ian Black, a guy who would sell bricks to a drowning man. In my line of work, friends weren't luxuries, they were liabilities. In the confines of that car, he felt like a friend. He didn't speak but scrutinized me the way he might a grenade with a pulled pin.

I leaned into him, a feral hunger curling my lips. "Don't look so worried. I'm going to do what I do best."

"That's what I'm worried about." He cupped the back of my neck, pressing forehead to forehead. "I want to see the bastard bleed, just as much as you do. Understand me. This isn't business, it's personal. You need anything, you call me. You end up dead at the end of this and I'll fucking kill you myself."

I grabbed his neck, mirroring his pose and grinning into his dirt-brown eyes. "Don't worry. I've got a plan."

FIRST STOP, HELL

Rome made sense as the place to start. Sure, I wanted to go for Buford Winston's throat, but too many mistakes had already been made on this investigation. If the Italian police had only— nope. Not going there. Like they say, if ifs and buts were candies and nuts, we'd all have a Merry Christmas.

With the information from Alexei, the certainty big agriculture was the root of Gavriil's death rose to eighty percent. I'm woman enough to admit twenty percent was fact-based and the balance gut-checked. Big ag was called big ag for a reason—it wasn't limited by inconveniences like oceans or borders.

Gavriil worked here in the States, but his research took him to the four corners of our spherical world. When he traveled, he rarely resided in the spaces made famous by Michelin. When your field of choice was feeding starving populations, you went to spaces made famous by violence, drought, social unrest, ethnic strife, and natural disasters. My husband went in willingly, his idealism buffed until it glowed like the North Star; his ammunition was his laptop and his treasured quinoa.

It'll take a little time to drive back to my place. Indulge me in some backstory...

In my pre-marriage days, I was the poster child for a happy, successful, professional woman. I had the life beyond what I dreamed of, jetting around the world in the high-stakes game of chemical weapons—buying, selling, arming, disarming, arresting, entrapping, yadda yadda. The CIA recruited me before I finished grad school. I had all the credentials: fluent in four languages, master's degree in chemical engineering with a specialization in explosives, and what turned out to be my biggest assets—tits and ass.

I loved my job. Let me make this clear. This is not a sob story of someone who never quite made it to the top, who had her hair messed up when she smashed against a glass ceiling. This is a story of an agent who got to get up every morning, wheeled and dealed in international justice, and went to bed each night knowing—absolutely knowing—the world was better off than when the sun rose.

I. Loved. My. Job.

Were there downsides? Depends on your point of view. I wasn't there for those sentimental family dinners where you (me) were reminded how you were incapable of doing anything correctly. (Bonus.) I wasn't there for the accident my mother caused by paying more attention to her lipstick than the concrete median, then needed to be driven around for the next six weeks. (Double bonus.)

I kept it real with my sister and father. They traveled to me a few times and we talked, emailed, texted enough. It was hard, but they understood. My life was simple in some ways, complex in others, but, ultimately, my own.

Until three years ago.

I was in Washington after completing a successful mission that sent an unspecified regime's chemical weapons program back to the Stone Age. Each day seemed to have a new reason for a never-ending meeting in a windowless room with bad coffee and tasteless sandwiches. Any moment I could, I was outside. One day, the meeting ended early thanks to a little something-something in the chicken salad, which I was not responsible for but did appreciate. To celebrate my foresight to choose yogurt and fruit salad, I went for a run. You just never know when the difference between a good and bad day comes down to stamina, training, and moving just a little bit faster. I was in a park with a hundred other people who escaped work early, enjoying the feel of real air on my skin, the sunshine on my face, the pavement beneath my feet. Then he ran into me. Literally.

Gavriil, which is pronounced similar to *Gabriel*, came around a bend on the wrong side of the path and *POW*. Just like in Batman from the nineteen-sixties, the word leapt between us, putting me down hard on the coarse surface.

The asphalt took the skin off my knee when I rolled. I ended up in a very un-professional, un-athletic position. I was about to go Hulk smash on the dumbass when I got an unimpeded view of Professor Bambi on ice. Hulk backed off at the total confusion in those big chocolate eyes. I got to my feet. "What the hell were you thinking?"

Gavriil's foot kept shooting out from under him, the grass beneath was slick from a hard morning rain. I gripped his arm and pulled him toward the path, arms and legs learning to work together again. On his feet, his eyes several inches above mine, he cocked his head like a curious bird. "I was considering the effects climate change would have on nutrient-limited populations."

Not what I was expecting. And he just kept going, limping after me when I would have left him, grass and blood coloring his legs. He was like a determined puppy who spoke in big words. What could I do? I took him home.

He was smarter and kinder than any man I had met. He was incredibly absentminded about what he considered the trivial details of life (socks) but obsessive about emerging challenges of our times (feeding already-starving populations). Our first date was Chinese food while I administered first aid to our knees and elbows, after which he rearranged my apartment to make it more efficient.

Weird, but it did work better.

We weren't an obvious couple, the agent and the professor, but it worked. In all departments. Gavriil ran as an excuse to think. Nobody talked to him when he ran. Nobody asked questions. The running fed a prolific researcher but also developed stamina, which he put to good use along with the springs of our mattress. I accused him once of reading a book on sex because no brainy professor should know as much as he did. He had read a dozen books, he corrected, and had plans for me.

Days turned into weeks. Gavriil and I saw each other every day. He got my sense of humor. I got his obsession for answers. We talked, and we laughed. We shared a passion for fro-yo and nineties music, and tacos.

I was happy, but I knew I was living on borrowed time. I'd been in the States for two months, the longest since I'd gone out on assignments. It couldn't last. Sooner or later, an assignment would come, and I would leave. I backed away emotionally. It was a survival instinct more than an intellectual choice.

Gavriil's temper had a fuse a mile long but was connected to a nuclear bomb. It detonated one Sunday after I explained what we had was fun-and-games, and it was time to move on. When the dust cleared, we were engaged, and I had put in for a transfer. Six months later, I was Mrs. Rubchinskaya, we owned a little slice of suburbia, and I was part of a pilot program keeping the sharpest, hardest kids in DC in line.

Life was good, in a different way. I thought I would miss being an agent. How could being a suburban house wife satisfy my need for the thrills, the pace, the intellectual challenge? Holy crap was I naïve. Reality was I didn't have time to miss the life. My husband invited me into the world of chemical formulas capable of sustaining people rather than killing and maiming. My day job was in the poorly named "Youth Prevention Facility." Most students lived at home and came to the YPF six days a week as a condition of release. To qualify, kids had to have genius-level IQs and a rap sheet. You know what happens when you combine wicked smart and few moral boundaries? Yep. *Moi.*

Every day I reaped what I'd sown. Those kids challenged my ass from sun up to sun down and were as devious as the high-stakes world I'd left behind.

When I changed my life to make one with Gavriil, I gave up nothing and got everything in return.

For two years, I juggled marriage and chemistry, court appearances and barbecues. I could write a book about it, but it would be boring. Nobody wants to read a story about how happy someone is. Please. We all want to read about hardship and pain. We want to know other people's lives are worse than ours. We all appreciate a good underdog story but only after the dog has been kicked, stepped on, and lied to.

And so, you'll be happy to hear, we are at the point where my life went over a cliff.

A year ago, Gavriil had been invited to be the keynote speaker at an international conference on population growth. He was so excited, he called everyone he knew and a few he didn't. He wrote his speech and rehearsed it to the point he recited it in his sleep. He held me hostage when he couldn't decide which of the five brown suits he owned to wear. I loved him most when he geeked out. We were flying out together. I would have a little vacation in a city I adored while he razzle-dazzled big ag from around the world. The night before we were to leave, one of my kids was arrested. Andrew Dixon. Everyone has a favorite and Dix was mine. With my husband's support, I delayed leaving for a day. The next morning, I was at the hearing, at Dixon's side, when he was charged with hacking into the Taco Taco Taco network and repricing beef tacos to ten cents. He owned the crime but argued extenuating circumstances. He was hungry, and he only had a dollar. I loaned him the money for the fine, which he would earn with a part-time job at said Taco Taco Taco. Everyone was a winner.

While I was at home packing for my flight to Rome, Gavriil was in her streets dying.

The call came from the Rome police. They were sorry to inform me my husband had been killed, a victim of a traffic accident. They said Gavriil stepped into a busy street without looking. He died in surgery, his chest crushed.

I didn't question the conclusions. I considered handcuffing Gavriil to me when we walked through DC because his attention was everywhere except in front of him. I felt guilty, of course I did. If I'd been with him as we planned, he couldn't have stepped in front of the car. The one day I thought wouldn't matter made all the difference in the world.

I did get on the flight to Rome with nothing but my travel documents and a shattered heart.

The next half year was hazy. I'm sure I woke and dressed and ate. I had to have gone to work and paid the mortgage. I must have grocery shopped and cleaned the house and done every other part of daily life, but I can't recall a detail. Then I opened an email.

November 9, 2018. The short note was written in broken English. I nearly tossed it in the spam folder, expecting a long-distance cousin was secretly prince of the UAE and interested in practicing trickle-down economics if only I could send him twelve hundred dollars to bribe customs officials.

It wasn't about economics.

"He was pushed. I spended many hours looking to tell you. I telled the police but they no interested. I am hoping I am doing right. Annette Lambert."

The attached video was three minutes long. The first minutes were of a busy Rome night. Tall, stone building flanked a street with cars jockeying for position like in a Mario Kart game. People hurried along the sidewalk. The ground was glossy, reflecting the lights above. It had rained recently. A woman laughed, the one who recorded the scene.

Then he stepped into the frame. My Gavriil. He wore a buttoned-down dress shirt and his favorite brown pants.

The camera stepped down, into the street. A quick *toot toot* had the camera jumping back to the sidewalk. The image shook, but it captured Gavriil lurching forward, tumbling into the street at the same moment a yellow vehicle crossed through the same point in space. He was there and then he simply wasn't.

The camera angle fell until only shoes were visible. Shouts in Italian called for an ambulance, for the police. Calls sounded out to help my husband and many answered. Many tried.

Yeah, well, the fuck lot of good it did.

I contacted the Rome police, spoke to the investigating detective. I sent him the video and presented the evidence. I am fluent in Russian, French, and Spanish but not Italian. Still, I pieced together the vocabulary and calmly showed proof my husband did not enter the street out of poor judgement.

I did not scream like a hysterical wife.

I did not throw out baseless allegations.

I did not make mountains out of mole hills.

My career had been law enforcement. Knowing how the game was played, I professionally laid out the evidence, asking his case be reopened. I obsessed over checking voicemail, email. I slept with my phone next to my bed and even took it into the bathroom.

A week after I initiated contact, I received a short email.

Signora Rubchinskaya, thank you for the video you submitted. We have reviewed and determined our original findings are correct. Signor Rubchinsky, regrettably, stepped into a street and was struck by a passing vehicle. We continue to search for the driver and vehicle as time and resources allow. Respectfully, Inspector Luigi Marconi.

I followed up with Inspector Marconi and then his superiors but to no avail. There was sympathy for the widow but no real consideration of new evidence in such a simple case. Every door slammed in my face.

So, I opened a window.

Four months before my death, I contacted Ian. After months of no contact, he could have told me to pound salt. Instead, he went all in for Gavriil. He called in a friend of his own who interviewed Annette Lambert. She lived outside Paris and had been on vacation with friends. He extracted details not clear from the shaking video, including a partial license plate number. Another of Ian's friends spoke with *poliziotto* who shared the copy of the final report and a forgotten detail. Gavriil had had a lady caller at the hotel. The hotel staff indicated the woman, who spoke with a Russian accent, visited my husband both days he had been in residence. The police suspected the two were having an affair and it was perhaps because of this woman my husband died. Had he been looking at the street instead of his mistress, they speculated, he would be alive today.

The next day, I decided to kill myself.

Before Gavriil, I was a different person. I reveled in skills and resources, brains and a loose enough moral code to take advantage of said assets. While it may not have been my body in the grave, Gavriil's wife died with him. Now? I'm just the woman who's going to set the story straight.

My husband was murdered. Somewhere, someone holds a clue, someone knows something to point me to the next something and so on and so forth until...*POW*. It was about the details of crossing the t's and dotting the i's and the patience and determination to find the place where the killer screwed up and crossed the i's.

With Ian's file in hand, I could get down to my own details—what the hell? My phone just lit up like the sky on the Fourth of July. The ground alarm at my place had been triggered. The gas pedal down, I wove through traffic, racing to the brick shit house I bought and customized. The neighborhood I lived in was a few notches up from The Hideaway but still warranted extra measures. I installed a wrought-iron gate outside the open cage of the rear stairs. An electronic fob was needed to open the gate. Rig it, pry it, climb it—like someone just did—and I know it.

Stopped at a red light, my phone flashed yellow. The perp passed the second-floor landing. Only the first two floors in my three-story building housed civilians. The third floor, with its three apartments, was mine.

My phone flashed red, the light turned green, and I left rubber on the road. The perp was now on my floor. Two apartments overlooked the street. One I lived in; the other I worked in. A third, empty apartment faced the parking lot. I didn't need the space. I needed the privacy.

Only one mile to go, but a mile in the city was like the last two minutes of a basketball game. I hit every fucking light as if the traffic gods were getting off by slowing me down. Stopped at another blasted light, I swiped across the phone, opening an app showing an elongated dot in the empty apartment. The infrared image indicated a single perp. Who?

Irish was my first thought. I'd been careful setting up the cover. There was no way Sam Irish could find me four hours after he knew I was dead.

Except it wasn't impossible. Irish was that good.

What did Irish want with me? What was the scene at the funeral about? He and I concluded any unfinished business years ago. Okay...technically I owed him one but, come on, can't a dead woman catch a break? This just wasn't like Irish. He was all business and no business would bring him to my door after three years.

Finally, I whipped into my lot, feet on the pavement before the engine was off. A glance at the app showed the soon-to-be-dead man was in my apartment, lingering in my kitchen.

The cocky bastard was in my refrigerator!

Not Irish. This was too, well, unprofessional. Whoever this asshole was was about to get a lesson in breaking and entering. My hands breaking his neck, my boot entering his ass. I skirted close to the yellow brick, invisible unless the son of a bitch stuck his head out the window. Around to the gate, a quick swipe of the fob, and I was in. I traded the phone for my 9mm and silently climbed the stairs. The ancient, cast-iron steps were as temperamental as an old dog. I invested serious time learning the bitch's moods and sore spots. Skip step three. Step on the right edge of step six. Slowly, methodically I crested the third-floor landing. I consulted the app. The perp sat at my kitchen table.

The two front apartments have rear doors off the kitchen to a common hallway. The hallway led to a door and the rear landing, where I now stood. My perp had picked the useless hundred-dollar electronic lock I'd installed but was considerate enough to leave it open for me.

Weapon drawn, I proceeded up the hall, ready to make Swiss cheese of anything that moved. I reached the set of twin doors. The one on the right, to my work space, was intact. The one on the left, to my living space, was ajar.

With a wave of my fob, I entered my work space and then reengaged the lock. The kitchen in my work space had as much to do with food as a cow did with a ladder. This was my laboratory. Behind the vintage nineteen twenties cabinet doors were the latest in chemical engineering tools and materials. Some of my shit was so new, it hadn't been invented yet.

I checked the app. The son of a bitch was back at my refrigerator. What the hell kind of bottomless pit asshole was in my house? The spot lingered, it fucking lingered at my refrigerator, then it drifted back to the table, only to pong back toward the refrigerator and veer off to the right.

He was in the bathroom.

Seizing opportunity, I stripped off my sophisticated slut boots to slip across the hall on bare, silent feet. Gun raised, I entered my apartment. The bathroom was directly opposite, door closed. I slipped through the door immediately to my left and took a low position inside my bedroom.

My heart pounded loudly in my ears. I counted the beats, willing my pulse to slow. The dress wasn't meant for surveillance, squeezing the breath from me. I hitched up the short skirt, trading modesty for mobility.

The toilet flushed, but no water ran in the sink. The bathroom door latch clicked as it was freed from the door frame.

I peeked around. A tall, lanky bastard strutted into my kitchen like he owned the place. I struck like a cat, silently, fluidly. A surprised cry went up and then his face pressed in my floor, my gun pressed to his head.

"Give me one good reason why I shouldn't put a hole in your head a bus could drive through!" He was a good six inches taller than me but the body below mine was thin, nearly hollow.

"I...I didn't finish my sandwich."

I shook my head, trying to get the words to make sense. "Your...what?"

"My sandwich."

That's what I thought he said. I looked at the face communing with my waxed floors. Unbelievable! Pushing to my feet, I dragged the teenage bag of bones with me. "Andrew Dixon, what the fuck are you doing here?"

Six feet two inches, one hundred sixty pounds of trouble goggled at me with eyes as big as sandwich plates.

"I knew you weren't dead." Dix moved like an overgrown puppy, not sure whether to spin, leap, or pee. "I knew you weren't!" He clapped his hands and pointed at me. "That was you at your funeral today. Right? I thought you were like, your fat sister."

"How did you know I wasn't dead? How did you find me?"

"I just sort of sensed it, you know. It's like, you know the difference between when you really lose something and when you just can't find it? Yeah. I couldn't find you, but you weren't lost."

Having worked with Dix and a dozen like him for a few years, I'd developed an ear for teen-ese. There were rules and a logic to the speech. I found it best to ignore everything between the commas.

"You just had a feeling." I slid the safety on the gun and secured it in the kitchen drawer designated for "specialty" cutlery. "Did your feeling bring you here?"

"I followed you here like a month ago. Maybe more. You

know, when you started acting weird. After today, well, I don't know, I like, needed to see for myself. When I saw the body in the casket—who was that anyway?"

Shoving the kid toward the table, I sat down opposite him and ignored his question. "Eat your sandwich. Jeeze, Dix, how much turkey did you put on it?"

He flopped into the chair, rocking it on the back legs. "There wasn't much left." He opened his maw and happily filled it.

"It's a full pound. I just bought it yesterday." One slice of whole grain bread floated a good six inches above the other, surfing on alternating waves of deli sliced turkey and baby swiss. My jug of whole milk sat on the edge of the paper towel fronting as a plate. "Don't tell me you're drinking from the bottle."

At least he had sense enough to blush. And not to talk with his mouth full. Silence hung as Dix chewed and I wrestled with what to do. It was embarrassing that some punk juvie found me four hours after I was put in the ground. Kinda pissed me off.

I studied the kid as he ate, wrestling with a circumstance I hadn't anticipated. He knew. Once someone "knows," they can never "unknow." Not while they lived. Alternatives. There are always alternatives to every situation. I could—wait.

There was more color to Dix's face than rosy cheeks. I lifted the veil of black hair obscuring half his face.

"Nice shiner." The butterscotch coloring of his mixed-race heritage was sullied by an explosion of reds and purples. His cheekbone was swollen to twice normal size. I got an ice pack from my freezer and wrapped it in a towel. "Put this on it. You walk into a pole while texting?"

He shook his head, his gaze on his sandwich. "Dickhead gave it to me as a birthday present." Dickhead was his old man. "I shouldn't have complained last year when he forgot it."

Dix was completely matter-of-fact about getting beaten on his seventeenth birthday. Most of the kids in the program came from homes where poverty and violence were as commonplace as Cheerios and American cheese. His face sickened me. They coached us not to get involved in these kids' personal lives. Bull-shit. You had to be inhuman not to be outraged at what these kids endured.

Dix would grow into a handsome man. A few years under his belt, a couple dozen pounds on his frame and, yeah, Andrew Dixon was going to be a heartbreaker.

"Do you think I can crash here tonight?"

"Here?" My turn to impersonate a mouse.

"Yeah. Maybe on the couch? I won't make a mess and I'm quiet." Dixon prattled on, making his case to stay. It was pathetic. Sad and pathetic.

"Couch surfing isn't the answer."

He shrugged. "I got plans. I'm gonna get me my own place. I just need somewhere to crash 'til I make my move. Can I stay?" Cue pathetic eyes. "Please, Ann—"

"Call me Diamond." Shit. This was not in my game plan. "One night."

Dix leapt to his feet, jarring the table, and slopping milk out of the carton. "Sweet. Sweet, man. Let's get going. If we're lucky, he'll be passed out by now."

I shook my head but didn't make the connection. "You fast forwarded on me. Go where?"

"To hell. I need to get my stuff." Dix shoved the rest of the sandwich into his mouth. "'ome on."

Twenty minutes later we rolled passed houses two nails away from condemnation. Bed sheets covered windows webbed with cracks. Lawns were a patch work of broad leaf weeds and dirt with outposts of shrubbery along shabby porches. This street was once something more, a hub of the middle class with a parade of mature oaks and maples on the tree lawns. It had taken the triple hit of white flight, economic downturn, and urban decay.

"That's me. The one with the beware of dog sign."

Dixon had named his house "hell." I'd have named it "junk pile." I turned into the driveway, pulling the borrowed minivan nose-to-nose with the gate and said sign. "Do you have a dog?"

"No, just the sign." Dixon leaned into the dash, staring at the house as if to use X-ray vision to see inside. Bass thumped out of the house. "AC/DC. Not good. Come around back with me."

"What's bad about AC/DC?"

"Dickhead drinks too much and relives his glory days working security for bands. He was a champion head smasher. I'll go in through my window and hand you my stuff. He cranks the music up so loud, he'll never know we were here."

The house wasn't much. The small Cape Cod couldn't have more than a thousand square feet. Dixon stared at it, his eyes wide, his face colorless except for the tag on his cheek. He licked his lips as he faced his hell.

"Let's just walk in front door. We go in, get your shit, walk out." It would be my pleasure to handle the man who handled Dixon.

Dixon withdrew subtly, shoulders curling in, and he leaned back against the door. "L-let me just go in through the window. I do it all the time. It'll be easier."

I disagreed but wasn't going to force it. "I'll leave the car running."

"I'll open the gate. Pull back past the house. He can't see you then." Dixon moved hurriedly to the gate. He walked hunched over and on the balls of his feet, his gaze on the house. He opened the gate slowly, more slowly when it squeaked. He cleared the driveway and hurried me through with a frantically waving hand.

I let the car roll forward, under a window, past a door to a blind spot with my tail lights at the corner of the house. By the time I had it in park, Dixon was standing on two inverted five-gallon buckets and had a window lifted high. Hands pressed to the window frame, he jumped and disappeared into the house. I left the comfort of the van to stand in the fenced square of competing weeds.

"Take this." A thirty-two-inch flat screen came out the window.

I took it, setting it down carefully. A second one came and then the desktop computer and a box with a keyboard sticking out of the top. Then came a leg.

"Dixon!" I snapped his name in a whisper.

His face appeared over his knee. "What?"

"Clothes."

"Oh, yeah." The face disappeared, and the leg retreated. I got busy settling the electronics into the van. The monitors snuggled into the floor mats of the rear seat. The tower and box of accoutrements went in the back.

"What the fuck are you doing here?" Shock blanched the slurred speech.

"Nothing. I'm not here." Dixon spoke too high, too fast.

Racing back to the car, I retrieved a set of handcuffs and my 9mm.

"You're stealing from me!" There was a crash, heavy and dull. "You worthless shit." Another crash, and Dixon cried out.

I removed the safety as I sprinted to the side door. Five steps up and I was in a small hallway. Ugly, violent words blasted from the room to my right. Dixon laid on the floor, curled into a ball while two hundred plus pounds of drunk, ghetto trash kicked him in the ribs.

The calculations happened in an instant. It took me twice as long to execute, but then the senior Dixon was on the floor sucking up whatever crap littered the soiled carpet. I planted my boot on the outstretched hand, enjoying the crunch. "How's life on the receiving end?" Dickhead cried out. Dixon was still curled in a ball. I couldn't get to him to see how bad the damage was but needed him on his feet. "Dixon. Get your stuff. Dixon!" He lifted his head then, and I saw the boy battered, bullied, broken by the man who should have been his hero. I centered my sights over said man. "He's never going to touch you again."

Maybe it was the calm truth in my voice, but Dix clamored to his feet. He upended a tin Redskins' garbage can and stuffed in clothes from the dresser.

"Wh-who are you? Po-lice?" Dickhead craned his neck. His teeth were stained pink with his own blood.

"Yeah, I'm the po-lice. You have the right to remain silent." I kicked him in the balls. He waived his right. "Anything you say can be held against you. You beat your son? You like beating on a kid?"

Dickhead cuddled his swollen nectarines. "He's a waste of air. Worthless. He needs discipline."

A geode Dix had sitting on a shelf fell and landed on the old man's ear. Oops. "You almost done, Dix?"

"Yeah, sure." He shoved a fist full of T-shirts in the can.

"Take your stuff out to the car."

He nodded and went to the window.

"Dix, we're using the door." I moved around the old man, giving the boy the room he needed.

The can filling his arms, Dix leapt over his father as though he were fire, then he ran out of the house. When I heard the back door slam, I crouched close to the old man.

"People like you sicken me. You don't feel like a man unless you're beating on someone weaker. You don't like your life, that's your problem. You take it out on a kid, you've made it mine. Me? I'm a problem solver."

The door slammed again, and Dix landed in his room, leapt over his father, then moved a pile of clothes from the closet floor to an empty box. He ran the box to the car and returned. He then pulled his pillow out of the case and filled it with trinkets from the room. Including the rock sitting next to his father's head. "I'm done."

The floor was cleaner without piles of clothes. The table working as a desk was empty except for a stack of textbooks and binders.

"Take the school books and get in the car. I'll be right there."

Dix started to argue on the need for the books but then his gaze focused on the nose of the 9mm and where it was pointed.

"What are you going to do?"

"Bad things happen in bad neighborhoods." The poundage beneath me began army crawling across the carpet, raking a hundred pounds of fat over the coarse fibers.

"Let's just go." Blood dripped from Dix's nose, his long hair dragged it across his face. He trembled, a dog running from a fight. "He's not worth it."

Dickhead made progress by inches, aiming for the gap under the bed. I put the cuffs to good use, then bound his legs using a belt. "He's not but you are. He's your boogey man, the thing under your bed. You're not going to be free as long as you're afraid he's going to come after you."

Dickhead kicked his feet, teetering on his lump of belly fat. "You want to live on your own, think you can do better without me? Get out. You ungrateful shit. After all I gave you—"

"Gave me?!?" Dixon roared. He stood taller, thrusting out his thin chest. "Like the time you gave me a broken rib? Like the time you made me lie to the cops about falling down the stairs? It's no wonder why Mom left, it's a wonder she f-fucked you in the first place." He loomed over his pater, fear transformed to anger and then...it dissolved. Like sugar in a glass of hot tea, it was there one minute, gone the next. A smile grew across his face and then he laughed. "Let's go, Diamond."

Dixon made the key to his prison and walked out a free man. We left like normal people leaving a normal house. Dickhead? I left him on the floor, hands cuffed behind his back, legs bound. Sooner or later, he'd work his way out. Or he wouldn't. The neighbors would come, maybe the cops. Didn't care. In the minivan, we cranked the radio until the windows vibrated. We sang at the top of our lungs, leaving one life behind and racing into a better beginning.

Happy birthday, Andrew Dixon.

With his business was taken care of, I could get back to mine.

GRIEVING WIDOW
SEEKS HUSBAND-SEDUCING BIOTCH

Spring had taken hold of Rome. Beneath my window, I watched Italians walk leisurely along the narrow street before the midday break, basking in the warm, bright sun. Tourists did the same but pointed out sights to each other and stopped to window gaze. Their cameras and bags hung across Rubenesque figures, bisecting breasts on men and women alike.

I yawned, which reminded me I'd been awake for—shit—longer than I could figure. It would have been smart to sleep after I got Dix settled. Instead, I pored over Ian's file like syrup on pancakes. Speaking of food, Dix nosed his way in, crunching on an apple. The kid was like an overgrown lap dog. It didn't matter how many times I slapped his nose, he just kept coming back for more. I thought of his father and stopped pushing him away. When I wouldn't talk about my work, he started talking. He had plans and plans for his plans. It got to me, knowing it was the last time I'd see him. I left him with a restocked refrigerator and enough cash for him to make his start. I hoped he would make it.

A bird swooped close to my window, drawing me back to the here and now.

I called my voicemail and there was a message from Alexei. The stress in his voice mixed anger, frustration, and insult into a

Russ-lish rant. I had to listen three times to get the whole picture. Short and sweet—Quili saw him for ten minutes. She claimed the work in the lab as fully and solely hers and dismissed my husband's contribution. Alexei promised a lawsuit and to give her crops the equivalent of the Russian evil eye so they would wither like her heart. I hoped he was talented like that.

Sitting on the wide windowsill, I laid my head against the window frame and closed my eyes. I had been in Rome a half-dozen times; never as a tourist. Only the last one haunted me. Refusing to be tormented, I invited the memories in. Blurs of light and color raced by as if moving at a hundred miles an hour. My first hours as a widow. Focusing, focusing, cobble-stones formed beneath my feet. I had heels on and couldn't walk evenly on the rounded stones. Proof I wasn't in my right mind. I knew better than to wear heels in old cities. Nameless people encouraged me along, but I wasn't fast enough. They pulled away. Fear of being alone swamped me. I took off my shoes and began to run. There was no ambient sound. No under-lying rhythm setting the tempo for life. My own heartbeat pulsed in my ears. Through a door, into a building, and then I sat in a waiting room, on a chair upholstered in worn, red velvet. A woman spoke to me in a language sounding more like music than conversation. I didn't understand a word.

I hadn't been in full command of myself the last time I was here. Maybe if I had been…well, I've never been one to dwell on maybes. I fucked up not bringing Ian with me the first time. He barreled through bullshit the way pigs went through slop. He wouldn't have accepted the ready explanation and called them on their bullshit. I wouldn't have either if I'd been sane.

I wouldn't make the same mistake.

I had two hours before my meeting with the event coordinator at the hotel hosting the conference. Ian had established my cover as Celina Matta, a junior investigator for an insurance company. The interview was standard company protocol to verify the details ahead of a very large payout on a life insurance policy.

Ian had arranged the meeting with the event coordinator and a translator to assist. With the event coordinator's help, I would know every movement leading Gavriil to walk out those doors.

Flopping down on the bed, I ordered my brain to turn off. For Gavriil. Just turn the fuck off.

Brring ring. Brring ring. Brring ring.

My pitching hand found the damn phone and air mailed it to the room next door. It bounced off the wall as I came to my senses. Rome. Meeting. Gavriil. The phone rang again, the tone muffled by the carpet. Cursing myself, I rolled off the bed and played fetch. "Hello?" The thick, husky voice didn't resemble my own.

"*Signora* Matta? This is Carlo Giancarlo." The voice sung to me in broken English, a pitch too high for a man.

"Seriously? Is this some kind of fucked up game, Carlo John Carlo?" I got out of bed for this?

"This is no game, *signora. Signor Nero*, uh, Black, *signor* Black said to meet you here at three."

The clock on the bedside table showed three on the dot.

"I need a few minutes," I said and hung up.

A hot shower had me firing on all cylinders. Opening two cases, I transformed into Celina Matta. Rose-scented lotion. Blond with caramel streaks. Blue eyes. Delicate makeup. An insurance investigator isn't one to slather on the sex paint. Business attire. Beige skirt, white blouse, simple shoes. Flats with rubber soles. Perfect.

My costumed ass sashayed down the stairs into the hotel foyer. Ian knew what he was doing. The family-owned hotel was close enough to the beaten path to be convenient, far enough away to be discrete. The only man in the foyer was a twenty-something Italian leaning on the registration desk flirting with the girl behind it. He was under six-foot but his long, lean lines gave the impression he was taller. His hair was chocolate brown and curled at the ends. The eyes matched the hair, even the curl at the end, giving him a devilish appearance in the way every girl dreamt about.

"Carlo."

He immediately dropped the girl's attention when work called. "*Buon pomeriggio, signora* Matta." He came toward me with a toothy smile and an extended hand.

I held up my hand. "English and call me Celina. Let's do this."

Carlo bowed his head, recalling his hand but keeping the smile. "Of course. Our appointment is at four o'clock. We should arrive comfortably." He led the way into the streets of Rome, pointing out buildings and sharing interesting tidbits I couldn't have cared less about. A few minutes on the constantly changing streets and we were at the subway—*la metropolitana.* Sounds nicer in Italian. Ten minutes later we surfaced on a street identical to the one we left. Identical. Until we turned the corner.

I staggered, tripped over my own corporately cultured feet when I recognized the street I had stared at for hours through a stranger's lens. The day faded, and the night rose like a monster from the shadows. I saw the blue awning stretching over the sidewalk, bright lights illuminating *Il Leone.* The lion. From the mouth, I saw Gavriil walking down the sidewalk, coming to me. He was unmistakable in the rumpled brown suit I had threatened to burn but couldn't bring myself to.

An arm caught me around the waist. Carlo's arm. I made a fist, ready to help Romeo understand where my personal space and his pain began.

"Careful, Celina. The traffic may not be heavy, but it is fierce." He forced me to take a step back before dropping his arm.

My feet were inches from the curb's edge. How easy it would have been to fall into the street as Gavriil had.

He pointed to the stone façade looming over us. "We are here. The Lion is one of Rome's most exclusive hotels."

I'd done my homework. "It's hosted dignitaries, celebrities, more than a few presidents. The queen. What were a group of ag geeks doing in a place like this?"

"Shall we go inside?" Carlo led the way, nodding to the doorman who granted us entry. He spoke in rapid Italian. I caught a word here and there and the name of our target. Isabella D'Onofrio.

D'Onofrio embodied the opulence and luxury of *Il Leone*. She had a gravity-defying figure. Her impressive chest, swaddled in antique lace, entered the room well ahead the rest of her. The dress hugged her narrow waist and graciously flared to accommodate hips built to cradle a man. She was in a class with Marilyn Monroe, Anna Nicole Smith, and Sofia Vergara.

Her face. Yeah, she had a face but, yikes, the body. I'm straight and I had a hard time keeping my eyes off her. Carlo? He tripped over his tongue on the way into her office.

"*Buon pomeriggio, signora Matta, signor Giancarlo.*"

Carlo turned the charm to high and the two were off in a rhapsody of fluid Italian I couldn't decipher. D'Onofrio left her desk for one of three full-size filing cabinets. This woman was old school. Sure, there was a computer on her desk, but the drawer of the file cabinet she pulled out was full. This was a woman who believed in print. Back at her desk, she opened the file and began reading. Carlo glanced at me. He saw it, too. D'Onofrio continued her monologue as she extracted a thick manila file.

I stood up, drawing D'Onofrio's attention to me. "*Parle inglese?*"

I crammed in a few phrases in the sleepless hours on the plane. Where is the bathroom? Do you speak English? Did you kill my husband? Just the necessities.

"Yes, of course, *signora* Matta. I understand your company is interested in the Feed the World summit we hosted last year." D'Onofrio smiled, humoring me.

I hate being humored.

"I'm interested in Mr. Gavriil Rubchinsky. He had a large policy with our company and our protocol is to thoroughly investigate the circumstances of all unnatural deaths. Is that your file on Mr. Rubchinsky?" I pointed to the opened folder with my chin.

D'Onofrio pulled the file closer, a selfish child determined to keep a toy for herself. "No, not of him specifically. I keep a file on each corporate function. It helps to tailor our services upon their return."

"Such an elite venue for a summit on world hunger." The juxtaposition of a meeting to solve third-world problems in a place where a cup of coffee cost twenty dollars smelled fishy.

"Thank you, we do try." D'Onofrio sat taller in her chair, folding her hands over the file as she graciously accepted the compliment I didn't give. Whatever. As long as she told me what I needed, I didn't care.

"*Scusi,*" Carlo said, fading into a corner on a pretense of taking a call. He turned in a slow circle as he spoke, discretely photographing the room for future reference.

I kept D'Onofrio's attention on me. "Did you coordinate the event?"

"The CEO of a sponsor, AgNow! made the request personally with our president and we were happy to accommodate. Mr. Winston is a frequent guest, a generous man."

Buford Winston. Again! My fingers itched to give the old cowboy a lesson in how to choke a weasel. D'Onofrio preened as she spoke about Winston, making me wonder how generous blow hard Buford had been with the generously proportioned D'Onofrio.

"Sounds as though this was an important conference for you." A soft growl rumbled in the back of my throat.

D'Onofrio sighed. "It was. Such a shame."

It wasn't a sigh of grief or sympathy. It was self-serving regret associated with having one's personal plans inconvenienced by a little thing like a man's death. My upper lip curled, exposing my canines. "Gavriil Rubchinsky's death didn't fit into your program?"

D'Onofrio's face stilled as her hazel eyes locked on mine. She instantly appeared a decade older and twice as formidable. Or maybe it was her hands curling into claws. "*Signor* Rubchinsky was out on the street and carelessly stepped in front of traffic. Easily explained. But Francisco Thelan, his death was distasteful." She shook her head, returning to her cultured façade. "But he is not your concern. What can I tell you about *signor* Rubchinsky? I apologize for rushing you but pressing issues must be seen to."

My tablet was readied for notes. "Mr. Rubchinsky attended a reception here on the night of his death."

"Yes. AgNow! sponsored a grand reception. A popular band played. Tickets were sold with proceeds going to a charity led by Mr. Winston. Mr. Rubchinsky attended, as did most of the scientists and leaders attending the broader event."

"Did Mr. Rubchinsky stay for the entire event?"

"No. The security film showed he left near nine in the evening. The band was soon to take the stage and a crowd had gathered, but Mr. Rubchinsky was seen leaving on his own."

"What happened after he left the hotel?"

"I am afraid all I have is speculation. We know he exited to the right on foot. Shortly after he was out of the camera, ambulance and police arrived."

"When did the other man, Francisco Thelan, die?"

"He has a policy with your company? No?" D'Onofrio stood. "I have other commitments I need to attend to. I hope my answers have been useful." With the skill and dexterity of a politician, she had us out of her office, down the hall, and standing in the public atrium, shaking her hand.

Carlo and I stood under the fresco ceiling in silence as D'Onofrio hurried across the atrium, disappearing through French doors.

"Oops," I said, fingertips to my cheek. "I left my purse in

her office."

"I will wait for you here." Carlo took a position leaning against an embroidered Queen Anne chair with a clear line of sight to those French doors. "Women and their purses."

With the same casual demeanor, I returned to the hallway, to the office. The middle cabinet, second drawer, was ruthlessly organized. The file I wanted was labeled AgNow!

When you have limited time to accomplish a task, the key isn't to move fast. It's to move precisely and efficiently. A drowning man who flails about only drowns himself faster. It's the man who can stay calm and put energy to work for him who survives.

Using the tablet, I photographed every page. D'Onofrio was blessedly OCD. The file included the police reports for both Gavriil and Francisco Thelan. Handwritten reports from hotel security staff and witness statements. Newspaper clippings. Sure, all were in Italian, but I had Carlo John Carlo.

The closing leaf of the file had a thumb drive clipped to it. The Italian scrawl on the sticky note was easy enough to decipher— security footage. I returned the rest of the file and closed the drawer, keeping the space neat. I trusted Carlo to keep D'Onofrio away, but shit happens. Better to be prepared.

The middle desk drawer contained a rubber-banded stack of identical thumb drives. It was the work of five seconds to pocket the original and replace it with a blank.

The door handle turned.

"*Isabella? Dov'e'*—" The uniformed man frozen in the doorway was still waiting for his pubes to grow in. I turned on the waterworks. The long hair of the wig veiled my face as I *sobbed* with grief. Remember my mother? At my funeral? Nailed it.

"*Scusi. Scusi.*" He froze in the doorway. A deer in headlights.

I sniffled like a pig rooting for truffles. "I...I j-just need a moment. *Un momento.*"

"*Certamente...scusi...*" And he was gone.

Luck shined on me by sending a man. A woman may have felt the need to console me. But a man? Tears make them run faster than the bulls of Pamplona.

Sucker.

Leveraging the "distressed woman" cover, I snatched a tissue from D'Onofrio's desk and left the office with my head down, sniffling and dabbing my face.

Carlo had his own cover. His lips were locked on D'Onofrio's. He dipped her low, so low she had no choice but to wrap her arms around his neck to keep from falling.

I walked toward the door, crossing Carlo's line of sight. A twitch of his brow acknowledged me. He didn't rush the kiss, but then maybe it was an Italian thing. They didn't rush meals. They didn't rush down sidewalks. Why would they rush kisses?

Carlo brought D'Onofrio upright, holding her when she swayed. Her cheeks were flushed, her lips swollen, her eyes wide with, ahem, admiration. She threw herself onto Carlo. His mouth belonged to her as he staggered backwards, his hand finding purchase on a high chair back.

Hot damn! I swallowed a shocked gasp. I couldn't see Carlo's face, but his wide arms and broad stance said he'd been blind-sided.

I cleared my throat. "Mr. Giancarlo? I believe you are on my time."

D'Onofrio lifted her head. The eyes of a hungry cougar bore into me, but she released Carlo. He turned to me and I had to bite my tongue to stop from laughing. His eyes were so wide that white surrounded the chocolate middle. His lips were sunset red, her lipstick color, matching the flush in his cheeks.

He regained his composure and returned his attention to D'Onofrio for a gracious ending. Taking her hands in his, Carlo kissed her knuckles. He said something, and she smiled. He stepped away and she began to take a step forward, but Carlo held up a hand, staying another assault.

He spun and left on wicked fast strides, grabbing my elbow

as he passed.

I made it around the corner before I broke out in belly laughs. Tears made walking impossible. A glance at Carlo's face increased the intensity. He appeared...affronted. Insulted. Accosted. "I, uh, really appreciate you taking one for the team."

His brows quirked at the Americanism.

"What you did back there. Letting her eat you up. Did she leave bite marks?" I tugged at his collar. "Yep."

Carlo slapped my hands away. "She did not leave marks." He ran to a window and pulled his collar down. Three red lines streaked from under his jaw to his collar bone. His head snapped to me, his eyes wide with shock, his mouth in a perfect O. "She marked me."

Carlo was obviously used to being the seductor rather than the seductee. His expression brought on a new bout of laughter. He scowled because he knew I wasn't laughing *with* him. I was laughing *at* him.

Errant chuckles escaped as I tried to get on with business. "I need a computer and a printer."

"I have a small office I use."

"Perfect. We can stop at a pharmacy and get some disinfectant for those scratches."

Carlo muttered in Italian as he led the way. Once and again he pressed his fingers to his throat, staunching the thin lines of blood pressing to the surface. "Black owes me."

Carlo's "small office" was a closet in his apartment. Size aside, it had a new laptop with a large flat screen, a commercial-grade printer, and all the accoutrements I needed. He connected my tablet, downloaded the images, and sent them to print. I was intimately familiar with the report on my husband. I took the time to make sure every word, every line was identical to the one I'd received and had translated. This one was old news.

I collected a small group of pages, stapled them, and handed them to Carlo. "Read the report on Thelan."

"Francisco Thelan. Age forty-two. Next of kin is a wife and

two children." Carlo read the facts with the same enthusiasm he would a grocery list. "Colleagues noted he complained of not feeling well after the band started. About nine-ten to nine-twenty. A maid found him dead in the bathroom the following morning."

The photos were brutal. Thelan died with his pants around his ankles in a pool of his own blood and feces. My best guess was he fell off the throne during a bout of diarrhea, smashing his head on the corner of the counter next to him. It wasn't a pretty way to die.

Carlo flipped back and forth between two pages. "He was poisoned."

I leaned over his shoulder, but the report was nothing but alphabet soup with a double helping of vowels. "Were they sure?"

"*Si*. A lethal dose of..."

He held it out for me to read. "Organophosphate." English didn't add sense to the fifteen-letter word. With my chemistry background, I understood what it was by classification. As far as what it did? I knew it didn't go boom. "What is it?" I mused to myself, but Carlo took it as a question for both of us.

He brought up the internet and typed it in. The search engine returned hundreds of thousands of hits, but the front page told us enough. "Insecticides. Herbicides. Nerve agents." He read the results as he changed the webpage language to English.

"What are the symptoms of poisoning?"

Carlo clicked on the third entry. "Moderate to severe symptoms include chest discomfort, heavy sweating, loss of muscle control. Involuntary urination and bowel movement."

I straightened up to pace. "We have a man at an ag conference killed with an insecticide. Did they figure out how he was poisoned?"

Carlo returned to the printed pages. "It was in his drink. He must have carried it up to his room. Do you think Rubchinsky's death is related to this man's?"

"I don't know. I mean, I wasn't expecting there to be a second death. How could they be related? Rubchinsky was pushed into the street long before Thelan was killed."

"Before he was found," Carlo corrected. "The time of death set near ten. The notes indicate he likely ingested the toxin between eight-thirty and nine-thirty."

"Which sandwiches the time Gavriil died. We need to watch the video, tracking both men."

The thumb drive contained video feeds from five cameras. Two covered the main atrium. Two covered the exterior entrance. One covered the interior entrance. Carlo arranged all five feeds on the large screen, took them all to seven o'clock, then set them in motion.

The night of the event, the opulent atrium was the place to be. Away from the business of guests checking in and out was a long buffet, four portable bars, and a dozen graciously spaced high-top tables. Signs pointed to the same French doors D'Onofrio has disappeared through. This was where the band had played.

"There's Gavriil." My husband stepped out of the elevator in his favorite brown suit. A woman stepped out with him, smoothing her skirt over her legs. He said something, laid a hand on her shoulder. She beamed at him.

Pardon my French but...who the fuck is the bitch with my husband?

Leaning in, I got close and personal with the woman. Over thirty. Dark hair. Nose too big for her face. She wore a black dress and black shoes. I looked for something remarkable about her because when I found this woman, I wanted to be sure I was kicking the right ass.

"Can you zoom in on the woman?"

"You're in the way." Carlo shouldered me aside. He froze all the images and maximized the one I wanted.

She had a small mole on her left cheek, under the corner of her eye. She wore a necklace with a charm. Her hand was covering it.

Undoubtedly a habit.

Carlo set the screens back. "Who is she?"

"I don't know yet." I didn't take my eyes off my husband. He wound his way through the clustered crowd to a group near the bar.

"There is Thelan." Carlo pointed to one of the men in the group, drink in hand. Gavriil now stood next to him with the woman on his other side. Even with the two cameras, we couldn't see all the faces. There were eight in all. Gavriil and the woman. Thelan. Four men. A small Asian woman a head and a half shorter than the rest. Her I recognized—Gavriil's assistant at the university, Dr. Quili Liu.

The characters jerked like marionettes as the feed moved quickly through time. Drinks. Laughter. More drinks. More laughter. Appetizers. Enter a big man.

I slapped a hand on Carlo's arm. "Slow it down. What's blow hard Buford doing?"

Carlo mirrored my posture. "He is speaking to Rubchinsky. Neither is happy."

Both were pitched forward, two alpha males, unwilling to back down. The rest of the group shifted, glaring at Buford with narrowed eyes, tight mouths. They didn't like what Buford was spewing, but no one said a word. The woman laid a hand on Gavriil's forearm. His posture instantly stilled. His mouth moved one last time, then my husband turned his back on Buford. Buford made a parting comment before walking out of the camera shot. The group closed back in, but the easy, congenial body language was gone.

A waiter entered from the bottom of the screen, carrying a tray with drinks. He excused himself and handed one of the drinks to Gavriil. My husband spoke to the waiter, who shook his head and left to deliver his remaining drinks. Eight, then ten minutes passed. The characters in this little play all looked uncomfortable. Lots of heads down. Not much laughter. Liu spoke to Gavriil. He shook his head, set the drink down, and ran his fingers through his hair. I wished I could hear what was said.

The mystery woman put a hand on Gavriil's arm and spoke to him. His hand went into his coat pocket and pulled out a room key. Oh, no he didn't! He handed it to her! Son of a bitch! The woman walked across the foyer and was swallowed up by the elevator. She returned minutes later wearing a coat and carrying a canvas bag like you would use for groceries. She returned Gavriil's key, and he walked her out the door. Center stage of one of the exterior cameras, he kissed her forehead. She said a few words and left.

Gavriil returned to his friends. The group was smaller. Liu was no longer present. They were also down a man. One of the men greeted him as he returned. Gavriil gestured with his hands in response, the way he did when he agreed or conceded the point. Liu reentered the scene, a pained expression on her face. My husband leaned down, bringing his ear closer to her mouth. He shook his head, they spoke briefly, then he left the table. She left at nearly the same time, going in the opposite direction.

"You keep your eyes on Thelan. I got Gavriil."

Gavriil didn't hurry. His gait was notably casual, relaxed. He exited the building. The camera angle limited the view to twenty, maybe thirty feet. Seconds after he left the frame, the people in the video abruptly turned. Gavriil was dead. Again.

Carlo pointed to the screen. "Celina, he's drinking it."

Tears burned my eyes. I couldn't see the screen any more. "Keep your eye on him." I spun out of the chair and paced the room, breathing in, breathing out.

"Thelan went into the concert. I'm fast forwarding it." People zipped in and out like ants on speed. "Here he is again. He's staggering. Is he drunk?"

"His arm is around his belly like it hurts. What's the time?"

"Nine and a quarter. He is going up in the elevator."

My phone chimed, pulling my attention away from the screen. "You might as well stop the video. He's not coming down."

A text came in. *I know who she is. Call me.*

A dead woman has no friends, so who the fuck was texting me? I paced Carlo's shoebox apartment, studying the seven digits behind the familiar area code. You might guess it was Ian Black calling, but it wasn't. He would have left a message on my voicemail with a secure number for a return call. He did not have this number. He would not have texted.

And thus ended the short list of people who could have contacted me. Or did it?

A knuckle rap to the contact and...

HOW DO YOU SAY
"BUSTED" IN RUSSIAN?

"Dixon." It was the resigned statement you used when a kid straight up beat you at your own game.

"Hey Diamond." Chips crunched in my ear. "How's Italy?"

"How'd you get this phone number?"

"I called myself from it last night." A bag crackled in the background.

"When and where was I?"

"When you went to the bathroom. You said make yourself comfortable."

I wasn't gone three minutes, not three minutes. "And you took it as an invitation to steal my phone number?"

"You know, for emergencies and stuff." Either he had shoved another fistful of chips into his mouth or he had wadded up the bag into a ball and was gnawing on it.

"Dix, you put one more chip in your mouth and I'm going to swim across the Atlantic and give you a chip bag colonoscopy."

He laughed. "That's something old people get, right? Something like a camera up the butt?"

It's hard to physically intimidate someone who lived day in, day out with violence. You know. Been there, done that, got the black eye. The one he'd gotten for his birthday still had days until it would fade.

"Yeah, Dix. I hear it comes with good drugs though. So, who is she?"

This time he glugged liquid, finishing it with a sloppy lip slap. "Who is who?"

"You know who."

"Do who know you?"

I pinched the bridge of my nose. "Dix, you're making my head spin. You texted me you know 'who she is.' Tell me who she is while I'm still young enough to care."

"Oh. Her. Ilsa Dumanovskaya. I'm not making it up either. Musta sucked to spell her name in kindergarten. Least her parents gave her a short first name."

I leaned against an ice-cold plaster wall, prepared to commence head pounding. "Why should I care?"

"Because of Doc." Doc. That was the nickname the kids at the YPF gave Gavriil. He liked the stories I brought home and showed up one afternoon. It wasn't even "take your husband to work day." I found him arguing with the science teacher over a chemical equation. They got past their chalkboard differences, created a bouncy-ball polymer, then had contests to see which formula bounced higher. The kids loved it. Gavriil came in once a week for lecture and the occasional spontaneous laboratory experiment.

"She's the woman he met in Rome."

My chin snapped up. My heart beat in double time. I had her face, now I had her name. I signaled Carlo for pencil and paper. "Give it to me."

"She owns a bookstore. I have the address for her store and her apartment. Do they call them flats?"

"No idea. Give me the address." My mouth watered with the taste of deep-fried quarry.

"Three-twenty-one valle Didochachiata."

My pencil stayed still. "That can't be right."

"Maybe I'm not saying it right. Three-twenty-one Vya Deed-oshakiata. Better?"

"No. Carlo? Can you figure out this address?" I handed over the phone and recommenced pacing.

Carlo alternated between speaking and listening. Then he laughed. Of course, he and Dix would understand each other. Gibberish was an international language.

I took Carlo to dinner at one of family restaurants dotting the streets of Rome. We sat in the window of the twelve-table dining room, which was snuggled into the corner of a square also housing a bookstore specializing in Russian-language books owned by Ilsa Duma-whatever.

What a coincidence. It's such a small world.

The restaurant was clean and modest. Wooden tables had seen years of scrubbing and elbows and plates, leaving once-polished tops worn to virgin material. The chairs had been refurbished at least once. The wood legs and back showed age against the younger, padded seats. The woman running the front of the house was the spitting image of Gavriil's grand-mother. He had a photo of him with her when he had been a boy. She was a sturdy woman, built to endure harsh winters, cook for an army, and dispense hugs to remedy every ailment. Yeah, I said she was sturdy. She had muscular limbs made from hard work, a don't-fuck-with-me attitude the smile didn't hide, and she was Russian. Nothing like me. At. All.

I ordered in Russian. Gavriil and I spoke the language in our home. It started as a way to "eradicate my embarrassing accent" and ended up being one of the threads binding us tightly together. I hadn't spoken a word in his native language since I kissed him goodbye. Today, it rolled off my tongue without hesitation.

Carlo leaned back, rocking his chair on two legs as he regarded me as though seeing me for the first time. "Your friend Dixon, he calls you Diamond."

The kid talks too much. "He calls me Diamond, I call him Dumbass. It's a game we play."

"I once heard of a Diamond. She was a legend is some circles. I understood she died."

Tucking my chin, I let the real me surface. "Are you telling me you believe in resurrection, Carlo?"

The chair fell noisily to the ground. He wiped his dry mouth, glanced over his shoulder for ears that might be listening. "Of course. Tell me—" He shut up to read a text. "Dixon got us a license plate."

I pointed with my chin toward the bookstore. "For her?"

He shook his head. "For the car that struck *signor* Rubchinsky."

The waiter returned to our table, setting two small glasses of crystal-clear spirits. I poured mine down my throat. Did the same with Carlo's.

Carlo's eyebrow quirked, and, in Italian, he asked the waiter for two more. With the waiter discharged, Carlo leaned across the table, speaking low. "This is good, no?"

Yes, it was good. Of course, it was good. But how the fuck did a seventeen-year-old smart-ass get a license plate number when a year's worth of goddamn police work yielded nothing but scapegoats, dead ends, and closed cases?

My skin was too tight. My fingers itched for action. I couldn't sit still, and I couldn't think because thought after thought rammed into each other like vehicles on an icy interstate. How and when and what the fuck!

"Can you run the plate?"

"*Certamente.*" Carlo placed a call. He chattered, I ordered for both of us. He covered the phone. "How much are you paying?"

"What's the going rate?"

Carlo named a price.

"Add another fifty to forget he ever heard of us." I planned while Carlo finished the deal. I had toyed with the idea of approaching Ilsa Duma-whatever tomorrow, but the game had changed. Tonight, I hunted. Before dinner, Carlo had encouraged me to return to the hotel and change. I didn't want to waste the time, but Carlo dismissed my argument. Thanks to him, I was ready for the sudden change in fortunes in sensible shoes, black pants dosed with Lycra, a fitted black-and-white shirt in a geometric pattern hidden beneath a windbreaker loose enough to conceal the gun provided by Carlo via Ian Black. Damn, he thought of everything.

Even now, by Rome's standards, we were early. The streets, like the restaurant, were just filling with people. The night was young.

"He will tag me when he has it." What Carlo really said was "He willa taga me whanahe has it," but that's just too hard to read. Just add an "a" or "o" to each word and say it like you're on a roller coaster, then you'll hear what I'm hearing. "How long has Dix worked for you?"

"Seems like only yesterday." I sipped my water, an excuse to stop talking.

The waiter delivered two steaming platters. One held two red peppers swimming in a sea of a chunky, savory tomato sauce. The other held a stew made of thick beef chunks and potatoes in a lighter gravy. White dinner plates with a delicate blue scrawl around their edges were set in front of us. Carlo served.

"The glass Francisco Thelan drank out of, the poisoned one, was it the one recovered from his hotel room?" I knew the answer based on my translated version. I asked for two reasons. First, I wanted to test the accuracy of the translation. Second, I wanted to see if Carlo came to the conclusion I had.

"*Sì*. It was the same glass Thelan carried into the ballroom. The same one he picked up after Rubchinsky set it down."

The minute the tender beef entered my mouth, I felt as though I hadn't eaten for a week. I chewed slowly to keep from mounting the table and rending the meat with hands and teeth. Work was the order of the night. I had no time for a food coma. "He could have gotten another drink in the ballroom."

Carlo considered and then shrugged. "He could have but he wasn't in there long. The type of glass was the same. I'll take another look and see if the level went up."

"But you don't think it did."

He considered, shook his head, then took a bite of the stuffed pepper.

"We agree Rubchinsky was the target. What do you think the odds are a man narrowly escapes a fatal poisoning, only to trip into traffic and die?"

"The odds? It is a long shot. Possible? Mathematically, yes. In real life?" Carlo shook his head again.

That was my take, too. "How much time can you give me tomorrow?"

"I am at your service for as long as you are in Rome. *Signor* Black made arrangements."

"Track down the plate. We're going to pay a house call tomorrow." I studied the bookstore. Twilight settled into the square, the lights from the bookstore became a beacon, calling me. I dropped my napkin on my plate. "I'm going to do a little shopping."

A dainty bell suggested my entrance. It wasn't bold and announcing. It was soft, as if worried about disturbing the patrons inside. English. French. Italian. Russian. All books smelled the same. A husky combination of aged paper and tanned leather punctuated with the sharp tang of ink. Impregnated with knowledge new and forgotten, the store was a sexy temptress to a man like my husband.

"*Buona sera.*" I didn't follow the words after, spoken by a young woman with full lips, a broad nose, heavy-lidded eyes, and olive complexion. Roman features.

"*Parle inglese?*" See? Cramming came in handy.

"Yes, of course." She smiled graciously. "Can I help you?"

"Just browsing. Your store was recommended by a friend. Gavriil Rubchinsky."

The smile faded to a frown. "I'm sorry, I don't recall the name."

"He's Russian. You're not, are you?"

She shook her head. "I am studying Russian at university. I thought it would help to be immersed."

I switched to Russian. "It does. Speak it every day and she will become your lover, wrapping around your heart, filling the recesses of your mind."

Her eyes grew wide and she giggled, blushing like a woman under the heat of an erotic image. "Ilsa says the same, only differently." Her Russian was stilted, like mine had been. A language borne of textbooks rather than experience.

"Ilsa? Is she the owner?"

"Yes."

"Perhaps she knows my friend. Is she here?"

"Oh, yes. She is in the back. A moment." The woman hurried off, leaving me to pace among Russia's greats.

Carlo had searched the internet and found Ilsa Duma-whatever's website with her photo. She had blond hair and dark eyes, details not captured on the hotel surveillance. She hadn't jumped aboard the social media train so there were no embarrassing photos or posts with too much information.

I wondered what her relationship was to Gavriil. The green-eyed monster whispered in my ear, but I shut him down. I had faith in my husband, and it wouldn't do me any good to act the jealous wife. This was a murder investigation, not reality TV.

The young woman burst through the door marked for employees. She fell more than burst, as if a boot planted on her ass had been her motivation. "Ilsa is on a phone call. She will be out shortly. Is-is there anything in particular I can show you? In a book, I mean?" Her casual friendliness was gone. Instead she was jumpy, as if she expected a skeleton to explode out of the closet.

Oh, crap.

Bolting down the aisle, I shouldered the woman out of my way, blasted through the door, and landed in the store room just as the back door kissed the frame. The narrow street behind the store wasn't wide enough for one of the ridiculously tiny

European cars and yet apartments and businesses opened to it. Twilight made monsters out of mice, casting shadows and trickery across the ancient stone. People milled about, to and fro. Only one ran and I ran after her.

The streets were a chaotic jumble of knotted spaghetti. Turns happened randomly and at odd angles, cutting the map into triangles, octagons, parallelograms. Who laid out this city? Pythagoras?

Yes...I know he's Greek. It isn't *that* far away. He coulda had a gig here.

I turned another corner, hurdled a small motorcycle, then spun around a woman carrying groceries. What the hell was I doing? I stopped, planting my hands on my knees and sucking wind. I pulled out my phone and brought up an app.

Darkness settled around me, a dear and trusted friend. Many people are afraid of the dark, afraid of what lurks beyond their senses. Vivid imaginings turned squeaks and cracks into monsters with voracious appetites.

For me, darkness brought clarity. Without all the bullshit of the day to distract me, I could breathe. I could think.

The door opened. A slice of lemon-colored light cut through my beloved darkness.

The safety on the gun was off. "Welcome home, Ilsa." I spoke in Russian. From her overstuffed chair, I didn't have to lift my hand to have her in the gun's sights.

She was alone. I put odds at three-to-one she wouldn't come home until morning and, if she did, she wouldn't be alone. But here we were, two women with a dead man between us. Ilsa's hair had escaped the binding at the nape of her neck. Her dark eyes were wide with surprise and fear. She was petite, maybe five-foot-two. Barefoot. A pair of heels hung from her hand, one with a broken heel.

I waved her into the room with the barrel of the gun.

"What do you want? Why did you chase me?" Her chest heaved, catching all the breaths she lost leading me on a tour of the city. She tossed the broken shoes in a corner. "I had to take them off. Cobblestones were not made for fashion."

This wasn't coffee with the girls. "Why did you run? You're a business woman. I'm sure you don't normally run when some customer asks to see you."

"But then, you are not some customer, are you?" Ilsa melted onto her couch. "I'm sitting. My feet are killing me. Shoot if you want."

I turned on the table lamp next to me, shedding light on my disheveled host. More than her hair was a mess. Ilsa's blouse was half untucked and she'd lost an earring. Her stocking was torn at the knee and she had a raw, red scrape. Blood had risen to the surface and run, only to be caught in the silk.

"You're going to want to put some ice on it." I wanted to talk, not shoot, so I set the gun down. Safety still off. Still within reach. "My name is Celina Matta. I work for an insurance company and am investigating the death of Dr. Gavriil Rubchinsky. We understand you were one of the last people to see him alive."

Her hand went to her throat. Her gaze slid to the door, to the window. This woman's instincts were to run.

"Ilsa. I saw video of you attending a reception with Gavriil Rubchinsky at *Il Leone* on the night he died. We have reports of you visiting him both days he was here." I took a deep breath, one she unconsciously copied. "I'm not interested in anything you two may have had 'going on.'" Yeah, I used air quotes. I needed her to move past the flight instinct to get to the tell-what-I-know part. "I'm not the police. My report isn't public record."

Ilsa gasped. "No! Oh no. Gavriil was married. He loved his wife. I could tell the way he told stories about her."

Breathe in. Breathe out. Not the moment for an adrenaline spike. "You were friends."

"Acquaintances. I grew up in the same town and went to school with his sister. When she learned he was coming to Rome, she remade introductions."

I hadn't met Gavriil's sister. She lived in Australia and couldn't come to our wedding. Gavriil never said much about her. Not in a bad way. She just hadn't been a part of his daily life for a long time. They emailed. A phone call on birthdays, etc., etc. It was plausible she connected Gavriil with Ilsa.

"You met him at *Il Leone* the night he arrived?"

"Since I knew my way around, it was easier. We found we both had a love of books. Once we started talking, it seemed we couldn't stop. I brought him to my shop on the next morning. He spent hours in my racks."

I ignored the euphemism. "The party at *Il Leone*, you didn't stay long. What happened?"

Ilsa rose from the couch, wincing when her knee didn't bend. Gingerly, she crossed the small apartment and retrieved a mini tray of ice from the apartment-sized refrigerator/freezer. She divided the ice between two glasses and a clean dish towel. Both glasses were filled from a clear, unmarked bottled. I accepted one without asking questions.

She fell back into the couch, setting the ice to her knee, wincing again. "Gavriil was very generous, including me in such an event. I have never been inside *Il Leone*. It is..." Ilsa looked around a home furnished by hard work. The trim wasn't gilded, and the chandelier didn't glitter, but there was nothing to be ashamed of.

"Overdone," I said.

She bowed her head slightly. "None of his friends spoke Russian and only one spoke Italian. They were all very kind, but I felt...I felt I was holding him back. He was there for work, not to babysit his sister's friend. I collected the books he had borrowed from my store and went home." Ilsa sipped the vodka, long and slow. "I didn't know he had died until two days later. When I unpacked my bag, I found I had Gavriil's notebook."

Ding ding ding ding ding

"You have Gavriil's notebook?" I dug my nails into the chair to stop from coming across the woman's lap. "Here?"

She nodded. "I went to *Il Leone* to return it. It was in the lobby I discovered he had been hit by a car and died. I'll never forget. This big man with no neck leered over *il poliziotto*." Ilsa used her hands to draw the figure of the hulking beast burnished in her memory. "He barked like a big dog. In English. I didn't understand what he said. He spoke very quickly and my English…" She shrugged. "Washington, DC. Basketball. California. Jazz."

Her English was as good as my Italian. A small laugh escaped. I hurried to cover it, but she caught me. "Spaghetti. Pizza. Roma. Mozzarella," I said with my American accent.

Ilsa smiled, tentatively and reserved but she did smile, and it broke the tension.

I raised my glass, reaching across the table separating us. "To Gavriil."

"To Gavriil." She tapped my glass. "You aren't with an insurance company, are you?"

"Would I lie?"

"Yes. Why would you?" Ilsa set the towel filled with ice one the couch. She stood again and hobbled to a set of bookshelves lining her longest wall. "The big man, he said Gavriil's name. He is what got my attention. I did not like a man who would shout at the *poliziotto*, shout Gavriil's name."

"How? How did he say his name?"

Ilsa's face tightened as though she'd bit a lemon. "With anger. Big, loud anger on a tomato red face. He was the one Gavriil argued with at the party."

I drew out my phone, quickly navigated to the web and pulled up a picture of Buford. "Is this him?"

Her brows pressed together and then disappeared under her hairline. "Yes. Yes, I am certain. It was then I asked one of the bellmen and he told me two of the scientists had died."

"The big man was Buford Winston. The other man who died was Francisco Thelan."

"Yes. I had met him. He was the one who spoke some Italian. He was kind and told funny stories about cows and chickens and lentils." Ilsa's back was too me as she spoke. The fingers of her left hand stroked across the book spines.

I didn't want to spoil the memory by telling her Thelan likely hadn't been telling a joke. Some scientists doted on their subjects the way some women doted on cats. On the surface, it's good and nice...but down a floor or two, it gets weird.

Ilsa selected a book and brought it to me. "Will you see Gavriil's wife receives this?"

I didn't need to touch it to know what it was. "Yes," I said, my voice failing me. Put it away. I demanded it of myself. Emotional bullshit was a waste of energy for the living and useless for the dead. I drove my nails into my palm, focusing my attention. Ilsa was a witness. I needed to treat her like one.

"Did you recognize anyone else when you went back?"

"Two others Gavriil introduced to me. After so long, I can't recall their names. The woman, his assistant. She sat on a couch, holding a magazine upside down but watching the big man. There also was an older man with a white beard. He said something sharp to the big man but stepped back when the big man answered. I didn't understand what was happening, so I left. I went to the *polizia* a few days later but they wouldn't tell me anything."

Been there. Done that. "Tell me what you remember of that night. You had gone to Gavriil's hotel room."

Ilsa nodded. "He had been interested in scientific books on plants. We had talked through many topics the day before. Then I remembered there was a box in my storeroom from the estate of a botanist. I hadn't had time to sort and shelf them. I brought several to Gavriil. We were late to the reception because we were reading. His assistant called. If she hadn't, he would have missed the whole event."

It was so Gavriil. He had a long history of working through social engagements, including ones with me. "Do you remember who was buying the drinks? The group you were with gathered around a high table."

She nodded. "Gavriil bought wine for me and himself. After Gavriil argued with that man, somebody sent a drink to him."

I stood then, needed to move my body to keep my brain under control. "Somebody? Did you see who gave it to Gavriil?"

"A waiter delivered it. Gavriil went to pay, but there was no bill. He said an admirer sent it."

"You understood what he said?"

"The waiter said it in Italian and then English."

"Did you ask Gavriil what he and Buford argued about?"

Ilsa inhaled deeply. "He said 'profit versus planet.' It sounded like an old argument."

I knew those words. Gavriil used them like a blunt weapon to criticize Buford.

"Gavriil was a happy man," Ilsa said, choking on emotion for the first time. "He said he would call if his schedule changed. He kissed my cheek and then, and then he died. If...if I had thought he would die, I never would have left him."

I understood what she felt, but it wasn't Ilsa's "shoulda," it was mine. I shoulda gone to Rome. I shoulda been at his side. I shoulda saved him.

Ilsa's eyes were on the floor, a child contrite after admitting a poor decision. She was finished. Ilsa had done what she could and now wanted to be alone with the consequences.

I got it.

"It's not on you. Not then, not now." I shot the rest of the hundred-proof vodka. I took my wallet from my jacket pocket and set a hundred euros on the table. "For shoes."

The narrow staircase kept me upright as I descended three floors to the cobblestone street. The vodka worked its magic, disassociating my head from my shoulders, my feet from my legs. I glided along on the wings of spirits, past nameless faces and pastel lights. Lyrical Italian from altos, basses, and sopranos faded to the background, putting the noises of the city center stage. A motorbike engine started. A camera shuttered rapidly. A horn blew long and clear.

The ground rocked as though I had little boats on my feet and I was walking across rough waters. I came to a main street and hailed a taxi. I had come to Rome to find out what happened to my husband but never expected to find so much of him. Vodka and exhaustion undermined the wall I had built until I stood exposed. Every image, every reminder slashed my psyche bone deep.

I needed to get to my hotel. I needed solid sleep if I was going to get to the bottom of the classic question...

WHERE DOES AN ELEPHANT HIDE THE EVIDENCE?

Under the scalding, beating shower spray, my brain worked on the progress made the prior day. I made this trip because I believed Gavriil had been pushed. I had a trainer tell me beliefs were for churches. We dealt in fact, in knowledge, in knowing, but sometimes all you had to go on was faith. Today, I knew Dr. Gavriil Rubchinsky was the target of assassination. Cross the Francisco Thelan evidence with the hotel surveillance, corroborated by a credible witness, and you've moved from the church to the courtroom.

Today I would focus on the how, which would point me to the who and why. Which brought me to my next thought. Shower off. Towel on. Phone up. "Dixon, how did you find Ilsa?"

"Hey, Diamond. Didn't expect you to call."

I don't do chitchat before coffee. "How did you find her?"

"I accessed Doc's email. I know he liked emailing better than texting so I figured, if he was meeting someone, he'd, you know, have an email. I was right."

Maybe my ears didn't work before coffee either. "Did you say you *accessed* his email? His university email? It hasn't been used for a year."

"Well, just because you don't use it doesn't mean it goes away. An e-trail is forever. Like infinity. Or until the technology

95

changes and the system it's on isn't supported anymore. Even then, it doesn't go away. It's more like the door is locked and the key was, kind of, lost."

Thank God I only listened to every third word. "How long have you been hacking?"

"I don't know. Maybe…five years."

"Since you were twelve?" Yeah, I sounded old, talking in the top of my register, glaring at the phone like I could see through it to the slickster at the other end.

"Something like that." Dix was matter-of-fact. Me going school teacher on him didn't have more than a ten-second effect. "Once I got settled in my place, I got bored. So, you know, I took a look around."

"A place? You got a place this fast?" I expected to kick him off the couch when I got back.

"Uh huh. I read a bunch of the Doc's emails, but most didn't make sense. I knew he was smart, but he's like Sheldon smart."

"Any from Buford Winston?"

"Yeah, Buford. I remember Buford. Buford."

Apparently, Buford made an impression. "How about Francisco Thelan?"

Silence hung for a moment. "I don't remember him."

Adrenalin jolted my little gray cells. "I want to read the ones from Buford. Let's start there."

"Who is Buford?"

"A son of a bitch from the biggest agriculture lobby called AgNow! He and Gavriil were always at each other's throats."

"Huh." Keys on a keyboard clicked. "They used a lot of big words, but I don't remember no threats."

Dix was still young. "The threats are veiled. Buford's not stupid enough to put in an email he was going to kill Gavriil. Can you get the emails to me?"

Dix snorted. I could picture the eye roll with it.

"On to the license plate. How did you get it?"

"Oh! You'll like this. I was thinkin' about how to get the

tag. My friend Ru— uh, this guy I know is kick ass with, you know, pictures. He used this program using math and statistics to figure out the most likely answer." Dixon got off on this stuff. The more he spoke, the faster he went. "It wasn't perfect, but we could make out a few of the numbers. Then I tapped into the traffic camera system. That's my area of expertise." He said it like a cocky—but justified—bastard. "They say they only keep the loops for a week but, like I said, e-trails live forever. I looked at cameras on streets close to the hotel and caught the fucker. Ha! Suck on that!" His triumphant tone changed to reticent. "Uh, not you, Diamond. The fucker driving."

The energy of youth. You couldn't do anything but shake your head, be happy you outgrew it, and be happier it was on your side. "I knew what you meant. Carlo ran the plate. We're going to pay a visit to the driver this morning."

"What can I do? There has to be something else."

The same trainer told me no one could do it all alone. Anyone who thought they could was an idiot. Dead or alive, I was no idiot. "I want to see copies of Gavriil's work. If he was killed here, at an agriculture world summit, we have to consider he was killed for his work. He had a grant to study modifications to improve the crop yield in water-poor environments. He focused on quinoa."

"Keen-wa? Sounds like a Chinese toilet bowl cleaner."

"It's a very balanced and nutritious food. Aztec warriors used it in their diet. I'm going to upload some security video to you. I want you to dissect it like a frog. I want to know the to-and-froms of every person who had contact with Gavriil."

"K. I'll send you a secure link. I can do, prob, um, another hour or two."

Damn time zones. I checked the clock on my phone. "What are you still doing up at two in the morning?"

"Reading Doc's emails. I have school tomorrow, but I'll skip it."

"Don't skip the YPF. Hear me? We don't want that kind of

attention."

Dix yawned. "I just sent you the link. I don't mind skipping school."

"Sleep, school, then help me find a killer. I'm counting on you, Dix."

"Yeah? On me?" I heard it, he felt important, needed instead of tolerated. "Sleep, school, dissect videos."

"Good. Call me tonight."

Carlo and I zipped through the countryside in a car one model size up from the toddler toys of my suburbia days. The electric blue two-door fit Carlo, me, and enough air to keep us alive until we reached our destination, Hugo Franzetti. Like any good Italian man in his late twenties, Hugo lived with his mother. With his spotty employment record, it was probably all he could afford. The only asset to his name was a Fiat. A quick search of the make and model revealed a bumblebee masquerading as a car. Hugo liked going fast. Not a surprise. He's Italian. There was a chain of tickets through May of last year. Then nothing. A few months ago, the plate expired.

My gut wasn't liking the way things were setting up, so I dressed for trouble. Good fitting clothes engineered to move with me. Boots I could run, climb, or kick ass in. Leather jacket hiding the gun I borrowed from Carlo. I had a knife at my ankle and one up my sleeve. I kept the blond hair and tinted eyes of Celina Matta. It was her ID in the bag at my feet.

Pieces were coming together. Ilsa. The videos. Now Franzetti. I couldn't help being anxious, wanting to know how he fit into the picture. "How much longer?"

Carlo glanced at dashboard. "Not long. Enjoy the view. Spring is very beautiful in Italia."

"Save it for the tourists." I opened the file Carlo provided. The driver's license photo showed a man in his prime, years before the paunch and disillusionment set in. Hugo had high cheek bones and hollowed cheeks. Brown hair, thick and rich, was a sexy mop of curls. "You send this to Dixon?"

"*Si*. To Dix." Carlo took a sweeping exit ramp putting us onto a smaller road. Hills rolled lazily along, basking in the Mediterranean sun. Small houses on large properties dotted the road, set apart by fields newly planted. Carlo downshifted, letting the car roll into a driveway that was more grass than gravel. This was a road less traveled. Much less traveled. He parked in a cleared area, avoiding the flowers blooming with the full glory of late spring. Carlo dug in a black duffle on the back seat. He handed a name badge to me. I'd buy it was official.

If I was blind.

Oh, things were going to get interesting.

I clipped my badge to my jacket. "You know I don't speak Italian."

"You don't need to speak. Just look, what is the word?" Carlo snapped his fingers. "Tough. Just look tough."

"Alligator meat, shoe leather, and me."

Carlo took the point, knocking on the front door. A dog answered. As we waited for a human, I tried to picture the man who killed my husband living here. The flower beds bordering the house were mature and well attended. Roses bopped their heads, dancing to the rhythm of the wind.

Where the flowers had been doted on, the house had been neglected. The roof needed repair, as did a shutter and the wood trim of the windows.

A woman opened the door who had once been over five-foot before receding a few inches. She stood with shoulders square, her white hair piled on the top of her head. The wrinkles in the corners of her eyes had been carved by laughter and bronzed by the sun. Light brown eyes, ringed in a darker brown, twinkled in welcome. A mutt of a dog, plump and happy for company, competed for space in the doorway.

"*Buon giorno*."

Carlo ducked his head, bowing quickly. "*Buon giorno, signora*

Franzetti?" I didn't follow anything he said after. But then, I didn't need to. The soft smile slid from Mama Franzetti's face. Those twinkling eyes darkened, saddened. She opened the door wider and, with a sweep of her arm, invited us in.

The house was a tapestry for the nose. Wood fires. Fresh bread. Simmering tomatoes. Carlo spoke as we followed Mama into a communal space between the living and dining rooms. Carlo's tone was firm but respectful. It was the same lilting Italian he used to sweet talk the panties off the hotel party planner. The reaction from Mama Franzetti was very different. (Thank God.) Mama put one hand to her throat and planted the other on the back of a sturdy dining chair. She shook her head, as if she couldn't accept what Carlo said.

"No," Mama said. Then it was her turn to speak in the same flowing manner as the hills surrounding us.

Carlo made a *tsk tsk* sound. Apologetic. Then he gestured to me.

The bad cop.

I crossed my arms under my chest and gave him a deadpan glare. "Mr. Giancarlo." I spoke in English. There was no point running a bluff I couldn't back.

"*Un momento. Un momento.*" Carlo held his palms out to me, asking for time.

I turned away with a dismissive wave of my hand and began to assess the scene. The living room was only slightly bigger than my hotel room. It was neat, clean, comfy. No television. A fireplace was swept clean but had seasoned the room and conjured images of campfires and s'mores.

A doorway tucked into the corner lead to a narrow hallway. The hardwood floors were polished by generations of lives lived. Four doors opened to the hall. Two open, two closed. Open, a small bathroom. Fixtures, stained with time, were polished until they shined as much as they could. Open, a small bedroom furnished for a woman with a thick quilt covering the bed and small trinkets dotting a low dresser. Lined on the back edge were framed pictures of a laughing, growing boy. Hugo.

Closed door. The room was colder than the rest of the house. It must have been closed off, but dust had not taken up residence. A twin bed was pushed against one wall. A dresser, a chair, and a chest suitable for Blackbeard's quarters. Hugo's room.

The lock on the chest was familiar. I used to pick them for fun. Wham. Bam. Open ma'am. Inside were all the mementos you'd expect a good boy to have in his bedroom. Skin mags. Five mail envelopes filled with bodies in compromising positions. Two guns. Three knives of varying blades and lengths. A small collection of wicked throwing stars.

I spared a minute for under his bed—nada—but under his mattress was the key to a PO box, clearly marked for the absent-minded blackmailer. An educated guess. The dresser was nothing but clothes. Good-quality clothes.

Last closed door. The bedroom Mama had shared with Papa. Their wedded room was fresh as a daisy, like the couple had just left for the day. In fact, if I didn't know Mama slept in the bedroom next to the bath, I would have thought she still used this room. And maybe she still did. The rocking chair next to the window held a sweater in progress. A glass with water sat on a coaster in front of a radio.

At the end of the hall was a door to the rear yard. The green thumb had been at work here. A garden rivaling the size of the house bathed in the morning sun. A cat daintily stepped across the rows, unconcerned with my presence. The beauty Mama Franzetti infused in her home ended about fifty feet from the house. Beyond, nature ruled.

If Hugo was in his late twenties, Mama Franzetti would be in her fifties or sixties. Nah. She looked more like seventies. A good seventies but still seventies. Grandmama Franzetti?

Beyond the garden, the wind ran through the grass, providing a fleeting image of a path. Of course, I followed it. Down a shallow valley, not far but completely hidden from the house, was a small wooden structure. Smaller than a garage, larger than a shed. No windows. The same rookie-class lock held the door shut. This one took an extra two minutes. Weather had taken its toll.

Light from the morning cut a swath across storage and work space. The only feet inside this shack recently were of the arachnoid variety. No electricity. There was an oil lamp on the work bench. No light. There was a modern camping lantern. Batteries dead.

Hugo must have inherited his grandmother's propensity for neatness. Simple metal shelving ran along two walls. The third had a workshop-styled wood bench with a few tools sitting out. Salvaged kitchen cabinets were shoved under the bench and hung on the wall above. I opened one of the doors. My eyes were adjusting but it was still hard to make out distinct shapes. Half the cabinets were empty. The others contained crystal and porcelain, tablets and phones, jewelry.

"You just have your fingers in everything, don't you Hugo?"

I left the heavy air of the shack, coughing up a lung. Dust two inches thick. A license plate expired in November.

I didn't like where this was going.

I kept following the path. Could there be another treasure trove? The land rolled down to a stream lined with trees and growth. The path followed the contours of the earth but stayed determinedly aimed for the stream.

"Diamond? Diamond?"

My name was clear but far from strong. If the wind had been blowing the other direction, I wouldn't have heard Carlo. Guess he'd given up on Celina.

"Down here. Follow the path." I shouted, wondering if he could hear me upwind. He crested the ridge and waved, relief on his face.

"Did you search the shed?" He thumbed back over his shoulder.

I briefed him on my findings. "What did Mama have to say?"

"Grandmother. *Signora* Franzetti hasn't seen Hugo since last

May. She didn't know the exact day. He had a job in Rome and came home when he could."

I snorted.

"The last time he visited, he stayed for three days. She remembered because he rarely stayed more than overnight. He was always needed in Rome."

We continued down the path. To the untrained eye, we would just be a handsome couple enjoying a pretty morning, talking about the foibles and idiosyncrasies of life.

Carlo shoved his hands in his pockets. "Do you think Hugo killed Rubchinsky?"

"Hugo was into blackmail and robbery. What connection could he have to Gavriil? Why would he kill him? It could have been an accident, like the police said. A guy like Hugo would run. Or—"

"Or, it could have been the job he told his grandmother about. A hit. And, where is he? His grandmother has convinced herself he's working hard at a job only a man of Hugo's talents could do."

Suddenly remembering the fake badge on my breast, I ripped the plastic off and shoved it in my pocket. "Who did you tell her I was with?"

"Tax collection." He chuckled. "I told her you were a training officer from the United States and I would get fired and she would go to jail if we didn't clear up Hugo's tax bill."

"Death and taxes. The only certainties in life."

"Where are we going, Diamond?"

"Wherever this path goes. Have you noticed the ruts?"

"*Si*, from tires. But they are old."

I nodded. "Maybe Hugo had another store house."

As we neared the stream, the thick line of foliage had an opening about ten feet wide. Low branches on either side hung limply from their bows and the brush between had been torn out. I scanned left and right as I entered the denser woods. Carlo mirrored my movement.

We saw it at the same time. A flat panel, grime over a bright yellow, with the license plate in question.

Carlo took the driver's side, I covered the passenger. In the filtered light, the body was difficult to see. Dressed in black, it was nearly upside down on the passenger side.

Carlo and I did what needed doing.

God damn it. I had the messy side.

The vic was male. Gunshot wound to the left temple. The driver's window wasn't broken so the door must have been open at the time of the shot. The momentum took him into the passenger seat but, to get into the position he was, someone pushed him the rest of the way.

"Keys still in the ignition." Carlo worked from his angle, retrieving the wallet. "It's him."

I opened the glove box. Latex gloves, thank you very much. A knife. Vehicle information. Box of condoms. Five balled up papers—parking tickets. A metal snap told me Carlo worked the trunk. I came up for air then did a quick dive into the back seat. Empty.

"Diamond." The tote bag yawed wide as Carlo held one handle, showing off neat bundles of euros. In his other hand, pinched between his thumb and index finger, was my husband's smiling face. "Two thousand euros hidden in the well where a tire would go."

My hands curled into claws and then fists. A raw, unadulterated need to tear and destroy and rend had me returning to the dead man and planting my boot in his shoulder. "You worthless fuck. You waste of life." My leather boot punctuated each word.

Carlo flicked off the safety and handed me his gun.

In a thunderstorm of acid rain, words of hate and disgust were screamed in an insane rant from a voice I didn't recognize as my own. Every goddamn shell Carlo had went into the corpse of man and car. Then I turned my fury to the heavens. "This is your plan? This is your fucking omnipotent plan? You let a piece of shit like this end a man like Gavriil? And you're supposed to be great?" I ended the conversation with a single finger salute and stalked out the way we came. "Take the bag. Pull the car around. We're taking it all."

"Where are we going next?"

THIS LITTLE PIGGY
WENT TO THE BANK

Hansel and Gretel blindfolded and high on sugar crack could have followed Hugo Franzetti's trail. He had set up a PO box at a mailing store in the larger town near his grandmother's house. Carlo flirted with the girl who'd worked there for only a month and did not know Hugo from Hansel. He walked out with a stack of envelopes and the girl's phone number.

The payout: sixty envelopes with one hundred to one thousand euros each.

Stop number two was Hugo's apartment in Rome. It wasn't in a prominent neighborhood where we would have been noticed if we strong armed our way in. It didn't matter. There was no need for huffin' and puffin' or blowin' anything down. Mama Franzetti gave us a key. When we'd gone back for the deep sweep, she'd cried on Carlo's shoulder and asked us to bring her grandson home.

Mama Franzetti might have looked like a country mouse, but she knew what the cock was doing in the hen house.

Hugo's building was built before the living were born. The trials and tribulations of its occupants were steeped into the plaster walls and periodically painted over to make room for new ones. Hugo lived on the top floor. The three flights in the narrow stairwell had me resting my hand on the butt of the borrowed gun.

Hugo's apartment was a single, large room divided into distinct areas: kitchen, living, painting, playing. The walls held unframed pencil sketches of a baby, the neighborhood, and animals. A small collection of baby toys sat in a box on a sunny yellow blanket. Three doors opened off the main room: bedroom, bathroom, and terrace.

"I got the computer." Carlo beelined for the IKEA-style desk. The desktop sat on the floor beneath, kept company by a milk carton filled with paper. "The password is taped to the screen."

"Nice of him." The space was lived in. A peek in the fridge said this apartment was inhabited by the living. "This isn't Hugo's place."

Carlo thumbed through a stack of mail on the desk. "All of these have Hugo's name."

"He's been dead for a year."

Heavy footfalls in the hall alerted us seconds before someone put a key in the door. I sprinted to a position behind the door, drawing my weapon in route. Carlo turned off the computer screen and flattened himself on the floor behind the couch.

The door opened, a body entered. I planted said body against the hard plaster while blistering Italian filled the room. Carlo was on his feet, shouting at the woman. She was tall, nearly as tall as me, but there was nothing to her. Dixon had felt the same when I took down his trespassing ass.

This was a girl.

"It's a kid. What the hell, Carlo?"

Carlo waved at me to shut up. I guess two pissed off women was more than his Roman ass could handle. I tried to pick up their conversation. Not understanding Italian was getting to be a blister on my butt.

"Her name is Valentina. Hugo lets her live here." Carlo raised a brow to me as he took a firm grip on her upper arm and escorted her to her couch.

"Ask her when she saw him last."

"I speak English." She spoke well, with a slightly British accent.

"Thank God."

Valentina curled into herself, knees to her chest, arms binding her legs. She was in her late teens or early twenties, but her eyes were older. Much older.

Different country. Same story.

I fetched a bottle of pastel-colored soda from her refrigerator and set it on the table next to her. "Hugo was your friend. He let you live here when you needed a place."

Valentina nodded.

"But the last time you saw him was almost a year ago. Haven't you wondered where he's been?" I kept my voice soft, casual. Nonthreatening. Her eyes widened, impressed with my psychic powers. "Tell us about him, about the last time you saw him."

She shrugged, rubbing her cheek against her knees.

"Hugo was into some bad things, right? He was good to you," dramatic pause, "but he stole, he cheated."

"I told him not to do it. I told him I'd get the money another way." Valentina began opening her posture, and her mouth. "He was the only one nice to me. The only one who cared. Not even my brother would help me. Hugo said he would get the money but wouldn't tell me how. I begged him not to do anything wrong. We could find another way. He's not coming back, is he? I wish he would have listened."

"So, do I," I said before I realized it was aloud. "What did you need money for?"

She dropped her head, forehead to knees. I gave her the moment she needed to find her strength. When she lifted her head, there was pain in her eyes. "I had a boyfriend. I thought we would marry and...I found out I was pregnant...then my family." She shrugged, speaking volumes about heartbreak and betrayal with the small gesture. "Hugo." She wiped a tear before it could fall. "He was good to me. I didn't want to be pregnant and I found a man, but Hugo wouldn't let me go. He had heard things. He said we would go out of the country to a real doctor." Another shrug, this time with shame. "Real doctors are expensive. He told me not to worry, but I did."

"Tell me about the last time you saw him or spoke to him."

"He had his own business and worked, what is the expression, odd jobs for the money. It was the middle of the day. He said he finished a job and was going to stay with his *nonna* for a few days. When he came home, he'd have the money we needed." She lifted her head, her eyes were glassy with tears. "He never came home. I called his *nonna*, but she said he had left days before. She thought he was here, in *Roma*. I didn't hear from him again."

"Do you know anything about this job or who hired him?" I moved onto the couch, not touching but close. "How did they find Hugo?"

"Why? It doesn't matter anymore."

How easy it was to believe. For as big as the world was we lived in, we forgot how small it was. I came here for justice for Gavriil. Now it was justice for Francisco Thelan and Mama Franzetti and this woman, Valentina. Pawns and victims in some asshat's game.

"This goes far beyond you and Hugo. Help me find the bastards and I'll make them pay."

Valentina stared questioningly into my eyes. I filled my answering gaze with every ounce of determination, tenacity, and grit I had. She lost the contest, turning to the computer. Her body followed. She didn't show surprise at finding the computer on. She just turned on the screen and opened the file system for Carlo's inspection. While he worked, I went through her kitchen and began cooking. Nothing fancy, but I found working in the kitchen relaxed people. I needed Valentina cooperative, not afraid.

Under other circumstances, Valentina would have been a college co-ed, learning to live on her own. Instead, she sat at her tiny kitchenette and started talking. She talked and talked and talked, to the point I wondered if this girl had anybody in her life she could confide in. Honestly, she was pouring out her heart to a woman who plastered her against a wall and held her at gunpoint. Stockholm Syndrome much?

With her salary from a small shop and the money in Hugo's account, she'd been getting by. Afraid of losing the apartment, Valentina told the landlord she and Hugo were married, and he had joined the military. Her daughter, who was still with the sitter, had Hugo's name on her birth certificate. Thanks to the wonders of the internet, Valentina had been keeping Hugo alive. She paid the rent and Hugo's bills—including the PO box and a safe deposit box.

"This box at the bank," Carlo said. "Do you know where the key is? It would be small, different from a house key." He followed Valentina's gaze to a kitchen drawer.

"I haven't thrown anything away. I didn't know he wasn't coming back. Do you think..." Valentina hesitated. "Do you think *they* knew where he lived? If you found me, could they?"

I didn't believe in bullshitting youth. If anyone needed to hear the truth, it was someone who hadn't experienced enough to tell fact from fiction. "They could, but I don't see it happening. Hugo was a loose end, a thread back to them. They think they took care of it when they killed him a year ago. They didn't care if he had a grandmother, wife and baby then. They won't now."

Valentina blinked rapidly. It just got real for her. It was one thing to say Hugo hadn't been back or she hadn't heard from him. It was another to say he was dead. Time for a change of topic.

"If you could do anything, be anything, what would you do?"

The blinking ended as a slow smile emerged. "Art school. I would like to teach art to children."

Yeah, seemed about right.

* * *

"What do you think is in it?" Carlo asked as we approached our next stop on our Tour de Hugo Franzetti. The corner building was three stories high and built of a sandy-colored stone. The ground floor was the neighborhood bank and keeper of Hugo Franzetti's deposit box. Unpredictable, right? Hugo was a small-time thief and blackmailer, but he put his valuables in a bank.

"Hugo wasn't sloppy. He ran his operations as a business. So where are his ledgers, his list of customers? It wasn't in the computer and not in the apartment. We took that place apart, Carlo, and it wasn't there." We found some cash and more dirty pictures in a hole in the wall. Valentina had been surprised at the find and more shocked when we left the cash. "He has a little black book and we need to find it."

Carlo and I entered the bank and went directly to a very pregnant woman sitting behind a desk. He produced the key and requested access to the box. They chatted as she led us past the tellers and back into a vault room. The sharp scent of metal tainted the still air. Taking the key from Carlo, she opened a two-inch-by-four-inch door and slid out a drawer eighteen inches long. She carried it to a table in an adjacent room and instructed us to press a button on the wall when we were finished. Without ceremony, she left us.

"Let's see what we have." Carlo opened the hinged top. The glossy backside of pictures completely covered the opening. "It's too heavy for just paper." He used care to remove the top layer and revealed a trove of loot. "Rings, watches, bracelets."

I flipped through the pictures, and that's all they were. Dirty pictures. "What about a notebook or log?"

"I am still on the surface, wait, I think—"

The crash of the door reverberated in the small space. Our preggo banker filled the doorway, her head at an odd angle due to the gun pressed to it. There was a lot of Italian yammering but no translation was needed. We were being robbed. "Oh, fuck me."

The gunman waved us out. He pushed the banker ahead of us. Carlo kept his body between me and the robber as we were marched to the lobby. I pressed three fingers to his back. My count of bad guys. He nodded once. One in the vault, one behind us, one in the lobby.

Sirens poured in and the tension in the bank stretched to the point we could walk on it. Larry, the lobby bank robber, shouted in Italian. The people knelt. They were still visible from the waist up to the collecting police and gawkers.

I wondered what his game was. He was better covered with the people standing. With them kneeling, he was open to a sniper.

Curly, the vault bank robber, stepped into the hallway and yelled. Larry responded by grabbing a man by his hair, pulling him to his feet, and shoving him to the vault.

And so Moe was left alone with Carlo, me, and the banker.

Hello, opportunity? Please, come in.

I grabbed the banker's arm, praying she caught on quickly. "It's time?" Damn I wish I spoke Italian. "Carlo! It's time." I put my hand on her surprisingly hard stomach. Then someone in there kicked me. "Holy shit!"

The banker picked up her cue. "*È ora. Mio bambino. Dios. Dios.*"

Carlo snapped his gaze to my hand, his eyes wide. "*È ora?*" He turned to Moe. "*È ora.*"

"*No.*" Moe stopped on a dime, shook his head. "*No.*"

The banker sagged against me, wailing with mock (sweet Jesus I hoped she was faking) labor pains. "*Si. Il bambino. È ora,*" she panted between words.

This rattled Moe. He looked to his partners, his attention away from us. Carlo brought up the fist wrapped around the gun and planted it on Moe's temple. It took two blows, but Moe went down.

The banker stood on her own two feet and looked down with contempt. A short strain of venomous words that I translated as "fuck you, asshole" was followed with spit that landed in the asshole's ear.

The civilians shuffled anxiously, not sure what to do. Carlo dragged Moe out of the main aisle. Another employee stepped out of line and opened the maintenance room door.

"*Loro stanno arrivando.*" A woman hissed.

"They're coming," Carlo said softly to me then issued an order to our conspirator.

"*Mio bambino,*" the banker wailed, her arms wrapped under her extended belly.

Carlo waved his hands like a conductor. Immediately, all the people began shouting about the baby.

More police arrived.

Larry and Curly hurried from the vault as sound rose to the point of deafening. Displeased with the chaos, Curly stalked to us, his gun raised to the ceiling as he barked orders no one could hear.

I stumbled into Curly. At the same time, Carlo grabbed Larry by the sides of his black jacket. We both immobilized the gun hands and then went to the man. I hit Curly where it hurts. Some say it's cliché for a woman to go for a man's balls, but I say work smarter, not harder. Achilles had his heel. Curly had his balls.

Well, I had Curly's balls.

Carlo started with a head butt to the nose. The cartilage folded, spewing blood like a popped water balloon. Larry instinctively covered his nose, Carlo went for the gun. Larry recovered and used his fists. Carlo gave more than he got so Larry ended on the floor, but you see how much faster my approach was? And, I didn't end up with a bloodied lip.

The relieved crowd applauded. Carlo bowed.

So, it was happily-ever-after time. Except for one thing. Talking to a bunch of cops was not on my to-do list.

I cleared my throat to get Carlo's attention and tugged on the banker's sleeve. "We need to go. Now. Ask her if there is a back way out."

"I speak English, little bit. Come." The banker led us back to the little room first, snatching a draw string bag along the way. The woman was brilliant. I held, Carlo poured. We emptied the box into the bag without a thought for delicacy, leaving the carcass on the table. "Fast now. This goes to the old basement. Against the wall is a door into the store next door. It is dark."

Carlo pulled out his smart phone and turned it into a flashlight. "*Grazie.*"

"Thank you," I said. "Congratulations on the baby."

The banker smiled, her hand going to her little honey. "*Grazie.* Be safe."

The temperature dropped two degrees for each step down. The scent of raw earth, lingering decay, and dark mold put my remaining senses on alert. The beam of crisp LED light bounced off odds and ends stored and forgotten. Desks and chairs. Framed portraits. Banker's boxes. It was difficult to see the walls around the crap. Thick, white columns rose in contrast to the dark earth. The vault had to be overhead, the floor reinforced for its weight. There was activity above us now. The muffled sound of boots beating on a wooden floor said the police had entered the building. The stooges would be in custody. Soon, they would be searching for us. The normal people, elated because there will be a tomorrow, will rat us out. Even the banker may have to give us up. That was all right. She did her part.

"Here." Carlo turned the knob and put his shoulder to the door. "It's locked."

"Of course, it is. It opens into a bank. Let me see."

"I can do it." Carlo blocked me out. Somebody was sensitive.

"I'm good with locks." I bodied him up, just for fun.

He didn't move. "I cut my teeth picking locks. Ha." The lock sprang open. He put this shoulder to the door again, but it only opened a half inch.

"Do you want me—"

"No." Carlo went Italian ninja on the door, ripping the latch

114

mounting from the antique door frame. "Let's go."

The other side of the door was filled with more crap, just different. "Help me with the table. We'll block the door." We couldn't relock it, but we could stall anyone thinking to follow us.

The steps opened into a small hallway. We had barely closed the basement door when a woman stepped out from an office. She spoke in a chastising flow of words. Carlo held up his hands apologetically, then took my wrist and pulled me into the store filled with an array of hats, purses, belts, and scarves. We hastily selected a hat for Carlo and wrapped my hair in a scarf. The large store bag concealed the one we carried. We slipped onto the street, glancing casually at the commotion. A stretcher was being brought out the door. We turned in the opposite direction and walked away, just like any other shoppers.

A voice raised and then raised louder.

Carlo grabbed my elbow and pulled me around a corner. "Move. Fast."

We turned one corner, then another. He liberated a set of keys from a young Roman, and we raced away on a Vespa—OJ Simpson style. What's a Vespa? It's the little sister of a Harley, a prissy little thing keeping your knees together and whining when you wanted it to go anywhere.

The Vespa wasn't as much a getaway vehicle as camouflage. There were hundreds of them zipping in and around cars on the streets of Rome. Like antelope on the Savanna, the scooters teased, dared larger (but still small) cars to take a nibble.

My sense of direction in Rome is limited to up and down, pizza and cappuccino, but even that came into question as Carlo took us over the cobbled streets. Pedestrians, dogs, pedestrians with dogs jumped out of our path, cursing us with gestures that translated across languages.

The *wee-wah* of sirens closed in on the *wheeeeeee* of the motor. "They're getting close."

Carlo nodded then cut around a steep dropping right. The

scooter slalomed down a street no bigger than an alley as Carlo pulled his phone from a pocket. He gave an order, pushing the pedal to the metal. The Vespa hummed with the vigor of a hundred enraged bees as we charged down the dead-end street.

One hundred meters (it's the metric system, suck it up), graffiti blurred.

Fifty meters. Doors and windows were hidden behind corrugated metal.

Twenty-five meters. The Vespa didn't balk. I dug my fingers into Carlo's hips, ready to dump us on the street. It wouldn't be pretty. The cobbles would take skin, possibly break bones, but I'd take my chances over blunt force trauma.

Ahead, metal painted black with a white skull and crossbones announced the end of the line.

"Stop, Carlo." I reached around his torso for the hand brakes.

Carlo pinned my arms and laughed, his voice echoing as darkness consumed us.

WELCOME TO THE DARK SIDE, WE HAVE COOKIES

On a rooftop terrace, among potted lemon trees and flowering vines, we sorted through the twenty pounds liberated from the bank box. Carlo drew the jewelry aside. The watches had familiar names, like Rolex and Shinola. The rings and necklaces tended toward big and chunky. I'd give you ten-to-one those gems weren't paste. "I know a man who deals in jewelry. He pays top euro," Carlo said.

I salvaged a dagger from his collection. "I'm keeping this." Well-balanced, made for a woman's hand, the tarnished silver handle emphasized the color and texture of the embedded jewels. A wicked blade was hidden beneath the scabbard. The craftsmanship of the knife rivaled some I'd seen in collections. This was nobody's toy.

Carlo turned over a banded stack of euros and there it was—a small, red, leather book.

I wanted it, oh I wanted it, but Hugo would have written in Italian. First thing I'm going to do when I get home is fucking sign up for Rosetta Stone and learn Italian.

"Can you find Gavriil?" I hung over his shoulder, willing the words to rearrange themselves into something I would understand.

He thumbed through the pages, then stopped abruptly. His

index finger with the gnawed off nail pointed to an entry. "He was to be paid fourteen thousand euros. Four up front, ten after. We only found two in the car."

"What is that there? A name?"

Carlo frowned and called his buddy over. He showed him the scribble.

The mechanic who had opened the graffiti-covered roll-door to avert our premature death studied the entry. "Cristanemo,"

Yeah, it didn't do anything for me either. "Who is Cristanemo? Is there a last name?"

"It is not a who," the mechanic said. "It is a what. A flower."

I fell heavy in my chair. Was it really too much to ask for a blackmailer and killer to just write out the name of his client? What was the need for all this cloak-and-dagger shit? All I needed was a name. Joe Blow. Eric Campbell. Buford Winston. Just give me a name and I'll get on with my life...and his death.

My phone signaled a text. Ian Black was returning my call. A few swipes of the screen and voilà. "What do you know about flowers?"

"A guy buys them when he fucks up. Is that what you called about?" Twenty minutes later, he was singing a different tune. "What is this, Diamond? A honey-do list?"

"Just get it done, Ian. Her name is Valentina Rossifiori. R-o-s-s-i-f-i-o-r-i."

"That's a mouthful. What date do you want on this marriage certificate?"

I picked a date a year before Hugo died, making Valentina "a respectable" woman. The concept was ridiculous, as if a piece of paper could define a woman. Valentina had made herself respectable working her butt off to create a life out of an atrocity.

But appearances mattered. It was my mother's credo and bile coated my tongue when I thought it, but she was right. Society, like Mommy dearest, put appearance above substance.

With a swipe of Ian's magic pen, the scales tipped to balanced.

A single mother in any country would never have it easy, but I took some pleasure helping her show what real strength was.

"Put me on speaker," Ian said. "I need to talk to Carlo."

Carlo had faded to the corner of the small courtyard talking animatedly to his buddy the mechanic.

"Carlo?" I waved him over. "Ian wants to talk to you."

Carlo jogged fluidly across the open space to lean in close to the phone. "*Ciao*, uncle."

"Uncle?" The classically handsome Carlo had as much in common with the very ordinary Ian as the statue of David had with Play-Doh. "You've been keeping secrets, Ian."

Carlo grinned, and I saw it. The family resemblance was in the smart-ass smirk. "He also failed to mention I would be working with the queen of diamonds."

Ian huffed like a horse, dismissing both of us.

I knew how to get to Ian Black. "If you can't set the girl up, just say so. I'll turn the page in my little black book—"

"I didn't say I couldn't do it. Jesus, Diamond. Stand down. Carlo, we're going to need some help getting this marriage certificate filed. Does that priest in Scaperia still owe you a favor?"

"*Si*. Send me the documents. I will take care of it."

"Now for the money." I laid out how the cash would be split. Ian and Carlo were compensated for their troubles. Carlo kept the jewels as a bonus. "I need an account set up for Dixon, seed it with ten thousand. Carlo, you'll take care of Valentina?"

"Consider it done."

"Get her hooked up with Mama Franzetti. She'll spoil the hell out of the little girl and tell Valentina to get the roof fixed."

Carlo nodded. "Sooner or later, Hugo has to be discovered. It would help with the social benefits."

For a fraction of a second, I almost regretted spray painting Hugo with bullets. Almost. "Take care of it yourself. I'll kick in an extra ten k. I need to get home."

* * *

I lost a day. How? Well, it went something like this....“Struck by lightning. Seriously?”

The Italian booking assistant with a perfectly made-up face looked put out on my behalf. “These things happen, *signora*. The plane has to be completely inspected and tested before your flight can leave. Two hours. Maybe more, maybe less. Your connection is the problem.”

God damned me. Again. First Hugo. Now lightning. It’s like she was purposely trying to stop me from solving Gavriil’s murder. Well fuck that.

“Rebook me.”

“Just a moment, *signora*.” Polished nails clicked across the keyboard. “Roma to Atlanta—no, *scusi*, is full. Okay, here is another Roma to Venice to Amsterdam to Minneapolis to Baltimore.”

“You don’t have one that goes Rome to Atlanta to London to New York?”

Her plucked brows furrowed. “No, *signora*. That would not make sense.”

“It makes as much sense as sending me to Minneapolis to get to Baltimore.”

The passion pink lips puckered, ignoring my suggestion. “Your arrival would be twenty-three fifty-five, local time.”

With the six-hour time difference between Rome and Eastern daylight time, I would be getting home twenty-three hours after I left the hotel this morning...and it would still be today.

“If you are willing to do an overnight layover—”

“No. Book me through Minneapolis.”

“*Si, signora*. It will just take a moment.”

“You betcha.”

By the time the taxi dropped me in front of my building, my ass had rug burn from being dragged through five miles of airport terminals. After endless hours of purified, reconstituted, dehumidified air, my eyelids were sandpaper rubbing over eggshells. I stepped into the glowing light of the entryway and raised an arm for protection from the light, hissing like a vampire from an old black-and-white movie. Inside my apartment, the night was dark, the air refreshingly humid and Five Finger Death Punch beat on the walls. "What the hell?"

Most of this building was occupied by seniors. By choice. The bass thumbing on my frontal lobe belonged to someone who didn't belong here. I stalked through my apartment. Empty as expected. Slamming the door open in the kitchen, I stalked through the rooms of my office. Nobody, just lots heavy guitar. Where was it coming from?

The loudest noise was in the hallway connecting my apartment and my office. The sound ramped up a few decibels when I opened the rear door. The apartment sharing the back landing—correction: the VACANT apartment sharing the back landing—was lit up like a Christmas tree and thumped like a nest of rabbits.

"Where's my gun. I'm going to shoot the stereo, and then I'm going to shoot the dumbass playing it." I reversed course, aiming for my kitchen and the "utensils" drawer.

"Diamond!" Andrew Dixon stood on the black-iron porch in bare feet, sweatpants, and a t-shirt that was an homage to the noise beating on my head. A wide, goofy smile filled his face as he bounced from one foot to the other. "You're home."

"I am. What are you doing here? I thought you said you found a place."

"I did. Here." He pointed to the lit window.

"That's my place."

"Well, yeah, but, you know, you weren't using it and I needed a place, and this was close to your place so, well...yeah."

The cabin pressure in my head dropped suddenly. "Did it ever occur to you I wanted it empty?"

Long pause. "Why would you want it empty?" Shorter pause. "You want to see what I've done?" Dix had those expectant puppy-dog eyes and if he had a tail, it would have been going like a propeller.

Shit. Why couldn't I be a cat person?

My head dropped in exhaustion. Giving in would get me to bed sooner than arguing. "Fine. Let's see what you did. Turn the music down. It's been a long ass day." The apartments on the short side of the building had a bedroom, kitchen, bath, and an everything-else room. Dix furnished the space with an assortment of furniture. "Where did you get all this? Is that my kitchen chair?"

"I was just borrowin' it, 'til you got back. Here." He handed me the chair.

I shook my head and walked on. The living room was set with the computer equipment we had salvaged from his father's house. Under the front window was a battered desk I'd seen before.

"Did you go back to your dad's house?"

"Just to get a few things. He was at work and didn't see me."

He'd done alright, making a home out of odds and ends. I turned to find him standing in the middle of it, shifting his weight side-to-side as though he was going to get graded on the result. Something in his face reminded me of Valentina and the home she'd carved out for herself. "This is nice, Dix. This is nice."

I kid you not...he beamed.

"So, I can stay? I'll keep the music down, you know, when you're here and I'll...I'll...I'll watch your apartments when you're gone." Behind those sharp eyes, his brain worked overtime to find the right carrot to get me to say yes. "It'll be faster to work together if I'm close. And—"

"Enough, Dix. Enough. You can stay."

He grinned again and slapped his hands on his sides. He was going to hug me. Maybe. Almost. "Do...do you want to see what I found on Doc? Oh, you're probably tired."

Tired and stiff and so damn sick of being awake, but it was going to take some time to wind down enough for sleep to take me. "I do want to see what you found but I need a few minutes to..."

"Shower?" He wrinkled his nose.

I pinned him with a laser-sharp glare. "Are you saying I need one?"

He blinked rapidly. "Uh...no?" Dix defied my glare, leaning in and sniffing me. "Well, maybe. Kinda. Yeah."

"Stop! Fine. I'll go shower. Turn down the music. This is almost a nice neighborhood."

I am of the opinion the single greatest invention of modern society is the hot shower. God bless the men who pumped water into houses and those who brought in a gas flame and the brilliant SOB who put the two together. I nearly wept as the hot water washed the miles away.

I dressed, refusing to wear underwear. The human body can only endure so much. Still, I had a seventeen-year-old in my house, so I went with the ambiguous baggy sweats and a hoodie. I emerged into the kitchen to find a sandwich, a bag of chips, a glass of milk, and a note.

I drank half the milk as I read: *Meet me in the media room.*

"Media room? Since when do I have one of those?" I balanced the glass on the plate, grabbed the chips, and went to find "the media room."

In my "work" apartment, heretofore referred to as my office, the dining room had been transformed into, well, a media room. Two sixty-inch screens were mounted to the bare wall, one above the other. Wires bound with black ties hung inconspicuously, disappearing behind a computer tower.

"Where did I get the monitors?" I sank into one of three plush seats. The material moved under me, molding to my shape. This wasn't a chair. It was the mother of all bean bags on steroids...with a beer chaser. "Where did these...whatever you call these come from?"

Dix retrieved a keyboard from a table with enough dents to have fallen dozen flight of stairs. He dropped into the chair next to me. "Internet. Express delivery." He stared at me with a little half smile, like Mona Lisa.

He was weirding me out. "What?"

He shrugged. "Just glad you're home."

"Yeah, well, me too. Thanks for the sandwich. Want a chip?" I tilted the bag his way.

"Def. So, here's what I found." He dug into the bag with one hand and typed nimbly with the other. "Doc and the Buford guy emailed a lot." He opened a file with the titles of over two hundred emails. "So, what I got out of it was Doc invented something, some kind of seed, and Doc wanted to give the seeds away, but Buford thought it was a better idea to sell the seeds and use the money to invest in research."

"Gavriil's project was a genetically modified variation of quinoa capable of being grown in arid climates. He was work-ing on the food shortage problem, trying to save populations. Buford wanted the seeds to line his fat pockets."

Dixon frowned. "Are you sure?"

I nodded. "It was in Gavriil's journal. Notes on his progress with seeds of different plants. He focused on crops high in protein, to balance the diet. Buford and his AgNow! lobby were named sponsors of Gavriil's grant and expected him to turn over all the resulting plants to them. Buford was just in it for the money."

"Huh. You think?"

"Trust me. The only 'best interest' Buford cares about begins with a dollar sign."

He brought up a picture of Buford at some golf outing. His full face was lit with laughter, his cheeks and nose rosy from an afternoon in the sun. The argyle pattern of the golf shirt stretched over a hard belly. "Have you met him?"

I finished my milk, wiped my mouth. "No, but I heard about him. He brought out the Russian in Gavriil. I'm going to meet him though. Very soon. What else do you have?"

Those long, lanky fingers tap danced over the keyboard. The bulk of Buford Winston disappeared and *presto*, the petite Quili Liu appeared.

"Dr. Quili Liu received her PhD in biology when she was twenty-four. I guess that's young?"

I nodded. "Most people are twenty-two, twenty-three when then finish their bachelor's degree. A master's and a PhD typically adds four or five more years. Gavriil said she had book smarts. She was one of the hardest-working scientists he had."

"In high school, she was a runner up for the Stockholm Junior Water Prize. I found an article on it. The winner, a kid from Germany, he fell down the stairs in the hotel and broke some of the bones in his neck. I Googled Quili..."

"She Americanizes it to Julie."

"That's way easier to say. So, I googled *Julie* and found a bunch of articles. She's won all kinds of prizes and awards. There was one in the school newspaper saying she took over Doc's project."

I set the empty plate and glass aside and gave the chip bag to Dix. This oversized bag chair just kind of hugged my body. I didn't have to hold my head up, just my eyelids. "She was Gavriil's assistant. I heard her name nearly every day. He said she was good but would never be great. He felt her work lacked a purpose, you know?"

Dixon's young eyes met mine. "Nope."

"It's the difference between doing something you have to do and something you want to do."

"Like how I fall asleep writing a paper for Ms. McGinnis, but I can stay up all night hacking into Doc's email."

My gaze narrowed. "How exactly did we get these monitors and chairs?"

Jessica Fielding, feature writer for *18Σπ Magazine* (pronounced "I Ate Some Pie"), had a lunch meeting set to interview Quili Liu for a series on the top thirty scientists under thirty. I took special care in selecting "Jessica's" attire to ensure Quili saw only "Jessica." Quili and I had met twice. The first year Gavriil

..I were together, he wanted me to come to the department holiday potluck. Quili was finishing her first semester as a full-time employee of the university. We were introduced but didn't socialize. She was more interested in the department chair than her supervisor's girlfriend. Then she came to Gavriil's funeral. I remembered her as one of the parade of faces. If she said something to me, I had long ago forgotten it.

I was taking a big enough risk going myself—I wouldn't be stupid enough to count on her not remembering me. At the time, I had blond hair, but I had my eyes. They always gave me away.

Tilting my head and pulling my eyelid, I slid the contact into place. Voila. Brown eyes. Brown hair. I could have been Carlo's sister—younger sister, of course. I dressed in a black suit. Professional, understated, unremarkable. Sensible shoes. I was dressing to gush over a woman. It wouldn't do to out-dress her.

I sat in the back corner of the trendy restaurant, paying extra for the table with the view of the entire dining room. With twenty minutes until the appointed time, I used a tablet to re-read the material Dixon put together. The kid had good instincts. Give him a few years to get past puberty and he'd have real potential. He had dumped the years of emails between Gavriil and Quili to a single directory and sorted them into folders by topic. I had read through most of the project emails last night. Here's a synopsis...

BORING.

I fell asleep and finished it this morning. Wasn't any less boring but couldn't fall asleep reading it on a treadmill. There wasn't a lot to work with. The messages to my husband were completely professional. His were often less professional, more conversational. Hers never were. Each one began the same way. *Dear Professor Rubchinsky.*

"Ms. Fielding?"

It didn't matter if she was asking for a day off or announcing the results of a months-long analysis. There was one exception.

"Ms. Fielding?"

A folder Dix called "Crybaby." He read them right. The

notes were an eclectic collection of polite but pointed complaints, documentation of injustices, and blatant ladder climbing.

"Excuse me. Are you Jessica Fielding?" A small-framed Asian woman with a round face peered at me through equally round spectacles.

Damn it. How long had she been standing there?

"Dr. Liu." I jumped to my feet, offering my hand and, when she took it, pumped it for oil. "Thank you so much for meeting me. I was just reviewing my background research. You have led such a fascinating life, accomplished so much at such a young age."

She tossed her hair over her shoulder, preening under the attention.

"Please, sit. Did you have any trouble finding the restaurant?"

Quili Liu melted into the vinyl seat, rubbing against the arched back until settling into a position slightly askew to the table. "This restaurant is well known to everyone as the university president frequently dines here."

The chitchat began. We ordered lunch, and I started the interview. Quili straightened her body, folded her hands on the table, and leaned toward me. There was no nonsense in her body language. I quickly learned two things. One, Quili Liu was a name dropper. Proof of her excellence was based on who she had beaten and outsmarted and those who coveted her. Two, Quili Liu did not like to come in second.

"Your magazine is naming the top thirty scientists?"

I played the role as the engaging reporter. "This is our twenty-fifth year. We have five Nobel laureates as our alumni and our past leaders are at leading research institution on five continents. The competition is unparalleled. Nominated scientists go through a rigorous peer review—"

Quili's chin lifted, her eyes sparkled. "Who nominated me?"

"I'm afraid I don't know. I just conduct the interviews on the, well, I'm not supposed to tell anyone this, but I can tell you—I interview the top five finalists." I leaned back, dragging the line, drawing her in. "We are interested in the story behind the scientist. You know, something our readers can really sink their teeth into."

"Am I the top scientist?" Quili took the bait, the hook lodging in her ambitious jowls.

"I couldn't tell you even if I knew." I leaned forward in confidence, conspiracy. "I will tell you the stories count. Two years ago, before I worked here, I heard the top candidate was demoted to number four because he hadn't attended his grandmother's funeral. Everybody wants compassionate science."

"My supervisor died. A year ago." Quili saved me the trouble of tactfully steering the conversation to Rome. "Dr. Gavriil Rubchinsky. I was with him when he died."

Gasp. Who knew? "I'm so sorry. What happened?"

Quili began the story with how excited she was to present her research on an international stage. She described how nervous she was, choosing her dress for the reception. "So many people would be there. People who could make or break a reputation. Dr. Rubchinsky was late. He knew so many and promised to introduce me. I called to his room and he came immediately."

The trained interrogator in me wondered why she chose to start the story here. It was nearly an hour before Gavriil would die on the street alone. She didn't mention Ilsa Duma-whatever.

"Professor Rubchinsky bought me a glass of wine and introduced me as he promised. I hope you can understand, there were no younger scientists there. Department chairs from M.I.T. and Stanford and Case Western Reserve and Johns Hopkins and everywhere else in attendance. I had presented a paper that afternoon and all were congratulating me on my work."

Okay, it was getting a bit thick in here. So thick, it wouldn't have shocked me if she claimed she walked on water. The way I remember it, Gavriil had three papers accepted to the conference. Of course, Quili's name was on those papers—the *second* name. She presented one of them, sharing the load and the credit.

"It was such a special night, an important night...but my head was hurting. Professor Rubchinsky noticed. There was a *farmacia* across the street and he offered to buy medicine. I accepted and... and...when he crossed the street..."

The water works started, but I was too dumbfounded to give the expected reaction. When she sobbed a little harder, I picked up the cue. "Oh, Dr. Liu. How horrible."

"It was my fault." She cried out, her confession turning the heads of neighboring tables.

"Oh, no. No, you can't blame yourself."

"Yes. I know. It does no good. Instead, I have dedicated this year to Professor Rubchinsky. I tell the graduate students, we are not just working to feed the world, we are fulfilling a great man's legacy. Yes, it will be my name on the new varietal, but it will be Professor Rubchinsky's blood in it."

First, gross. Second, narcissistic much? Third, damn straight it's his legacy, and she was warping it to win a prize that only existed on the fake website Dixon set up.

Our lunches arrived and Quili continued to talk unprompted. A picture emerged of a bright child, one pushed by parents and culture to achieve the highest levels of academic success. Where the scientist had thrived, the woman seemed to go unnoticed. When asked about life outside of the laboratory, she floundered. She stammered, pretended to struggle with the words, and then her face glowed like a light bulb had just turned on.

"I have been learning golf. Many famous scientists play golf for relaxation. And, of course, there is the business side."

Business plus golf equaled a big red face. "You wouldn't happen to know Buford Winston, would you?"

Her face shut tighter than a door on a submarine. "Yes. I have met him."

Quili definitely did not like Buford. My guess was she inherited the animosity between Buford and Gavriil just as she inherited the grant. "His AgNow! is your grant sponsor, I understand."

Chatty Cathy had run out of string. "AgNow! provides money for a large number of research grants." She made busy with her beef tenderloin medallions.

"Have you golfed with him?"

She shook her head, going nonverbal.

"Have you seen him recently?"

Quili primly set her fork down and folded her hands on the table. "Is Buford Winston the top scientist under thirty, or am I?"

Having been put in my place, I looked duly submissive. "You are, Doctor. Mr. Winston is a top name in ag. His name opens doors. I thought if you and he were friendly, it might be of interest to the review panel."

Her pointed little nose went up, held, then descended. I had been forgiven. "I have not golfed with Mr. Winston. Yet. But when we do, there will be much conversation."

I asked her again about Rome and the story changed a bit. Funny how those lies get all tangled together. I asked specifically about Francisco Thelan. "It must have been horrible. Two tragic losses in the same day."

Quili selected a cracker from the basket and began breaking off tiny pieces. "I had only met him. He and Professor Rubchinsky were great friends. They teased each other. Professor Thelan taunted about the professor's wife. She is very beautiful and Professor Thelan said the professor would have solved his little dilemma if he was not distracted."

"Had Professor Thelan met Professor Rubchinsky's wife?" Because if she, ur, I did, it was news to me.

"He seemed to know about her. The professor said Professor Thelan would have slowed global warming if he wouldn't be so cheap about paying assistants. It is harsh, but I know was true. I saw Professor Thelan finish a drink the professor had left untouched."

Thelan had picked up Gavriil's drink, the poisoned one. The penny-pinching dope punched his own ticket when he snatched the drink. And yet I had to thank him. If he hadn't, all the evidence would point to Gavriil's death being an accident. Now something else bothered me. Liu hadn't been at the table when

Gavriil ran out. How did she see Thelan take his drink?

Something occurred to me then. Something so shockingly obvious I stood up and gasped. There was a second suspect. Because if Hugo was driving the killer bumblebee, who pushed Gavriil into traffic?

I missed something.

"Is something wrong, Jessica?"

I blinked, bringing Quili's concerned face into focus and, shockingly, had an awareness of me standing in a crowded restaurant, making like the Statue of Liberty. I sat. "Sorry. I just remembered another appointment, but I think I have what I need." I signaled the waitress and readied my credit card. Places to go, things to do.

"Already? So...so soon?" Quili's eyes were wide with surprise. "What about my story?"

"I think I have all I need." The waitress set the bill on the table, I shoved it and my card back at her.

"Maybe you can come to my lab. Plant husbandry is fascinating. Your readers...and the committee...I..." She was grabbing at straws, so obviously hoping to keep me focused on her. "I...I have propagated the last of Professor Rubchinsky's plants. The ones he grafted last year."

Sure, it gave me pause, but the only answer was "no." I needed to be in front of a monitor, finding what I missed. I'd pull Carlo back in. How did we not see it? If Hugo was driving, someone else pushed him and poisoned the cocktail. Someone who was paid the difference between the four thousand euros in Hugo's book and the two thousand in the trunk.

"Ms. Fielding?" Quili cocked her head as if I was a puzzle she was trying to solve.

"I am sorry, but I really do have to run." The words came out curtly but not mean. Not mean enough to make Quili look like I just stole her teddy bear. Take two. "Give me a few days to draft the story. If I have any questions or there are any gaps, I'll give you a call back."

She pressed her lips together tightly and gave a quick nod. "I am sure you will find my work is far above those even at more prestigious institutions."

We walked through the restaurant together. Not friends. Not even colleagues. There was an odd force at work. It felt like when you try to press together the same poles of a magnet. You know, pushing the + side of one magnet to the + side of another. It just doesn't fit.

I understood what Gavriil had meant about Quili and why he couldn't put it in words—English or Russian.

On the sidewalk, I offered Quili my hand. "Thank you again for your time, Dr. Liu."

Hers was small and cold by comparison. "You will call with follow-up questions." A statement, not a question.

"Of course." We parted ways and nearly instantly, I had a knot in my stomach. For a moment I thought it had been the chef's special talking back, but it was my gut instinct. The one responsible for telling me when trouble was too close for comfort.

Slowing my breath, I took measure of the off-campus setting. An urban street lined with shops and restaurants below and apartments above. Younger people plugged into their phones hurried under sagging backpacks to their next appointed rounds. Older people acted as obstacles to the faster moving crowd. And then there was the man sitting at a coffee shop table, not reading his paper, not drinking his coffee. I stopped and followed his line of sight to Quili Liu.

"Damn it. Damn it, damn it, damn it." I hurried back from where I came. "Dr. Liu! Dr. Liu!" I shouted her name, bringing lots of attention to the two of us. Men like our coffee guy thrived on discretion. Nothing kept them at bay like the limelight. "One last thing."

Quili had started walking to me. The simple smile on her face told me she hadn't sensed she was being watched. "You have thought of something additional?"

"Yes. Is your car nearby?"

"I walked."

"Perfect. I'll drive you back to your office. I'm this way." I threaded my arm through hers and led her down the sidewalk. "Have you had any odd happenings since the conference in Rome?"

She tried to slow, but I didn't let her. "Odd? Like how?"

"Oh, I don't know. Anything. Hang-ups. Feeling like you're being watched. Misplacing things."

This time she did stop, her brows pressed together. "Why are you asking this?"

A car trolled by with a driver fresh out of the school of hard knocks. His dark glasses didn't hide his appraising gaze. I read his lips. "Got her."

"Move it." I pulled Quili, giving her the choice of being dragged or keeping up. "I'm not a reporter. I'm an investigator, and there are at least two men following you."

"Me?" She glanced over her shoulder, but finally kicked it in gear. "Why?"

"I suspect because of Gavriil Rubchinsky's research."

"It is *my* research. I have far surpassed anything he had achieved."

"How much have you shared with Buford Winston and Ag-Now!?"

"Nothing." Her words came faster, shorter as she hurried to keep the pace I set. "He pressures over and over, but I tell him the work is not ready."

We rounded a corner and I broke into a sprint. "Run. Now. We need to take advantage of the few minutes of cover. There. The white car is mine. Get in." I pressed the fob button, opening the doors for us. I hurried into the street and the driver's door.

"Is that the man?" From the passenger seat, Quili pointed to where the coffee shop guy stood on the corner searching hard for someone.

"Yep. Recognize him?" I started the car and backed up until

my bumper kissed the car behind me. It gave me enough room to clear the car in front of me. Probably.

"No. I've never seen him." Her voice quivered then she gasped as a black Escalade burst past the coffee guy.

"Buckle up." A break came in traffic and we shot out of the tight spot, paint job intact. We raced past coffee shop guy in the opposite direction of the Escalade. His gaze followed me, his marble face an open book. I resisted flipping him off and got to work sweeping the scene in front of me side-to-side. Left mirror. Windshield. Rearview mirror. Windshield. Right mirror. Repeat. Lots of black SUVs on the road these days. Too damn many. Too damn alike.

I turned right and seconds later, a black Escalade made the same turn. It ate up the ground, growing larger than life in the mirror. Fortunately, I had more than a few ponies under my own hood. "Choke on my performance engine exhaust, asshole."

I put distance between us, but I needed a better plan. Nobody cleared the streets like in the movies to let us race around the crowded university. There were people and traffic lights and cars everywhere. The winner would be the one who thought fastest on their wheels.

Which would be me because I had a plan. A very good plan.

I started to laugh. This was going to be priceless.

Five pins dug into my arm. "Why are you laughing? Are you an insane woman?" Quili's face had gone past white to grayish-green. One hand was dry needling my arm while the other had a death grip on the door.

"Trust me." I slowed as we approached the corner, rolled around the stop sign, and kept turning into a parking structure. "Watch this."

We both turned, watching the street through the rear window. Five seconds later, Cadillac man barreled around the corner and blasted past us.

Quili's gaze snapped to me. "He's gone." She retracted her claws from my forearm.

"Wait for it." I hadn't gotten two words out when a siren blared and raced past. Her eyes widened in awe, maybe she thought I was psychic. "Police station. It pays to know your neighborhood."

I took a ticket to lift the entrance gate and pulled into the secured structure. I found a nice spot on the roof and turned the engine off. It was time for a heart-to-heart with Quili. "I need to know everything you know about Buford Winston and AgNow!"

Yes, Buford Winston had been pressuring her for her work. He scared her with his yelling and screaming and threatening to pull her funding. She had given him some of Gavriil's results last October. He had called two weeks ago wanting more.

She had problems in the lab since taking over. Equipment going missing. A break-in damaged the climate control system. A fungus breakout. Bad luck.

Or was it?

"Find somewhere else to stay." I started the engine and left the roof behind. "Don't be alone, definitely do not go to work alone until you hear from me."

Quili pressed her hand to her throat. "Wh-what are you going to do?"

"What I do best."

"I don't know what to do." Her brown eyes glassed over with tears. "Where can I stay?"

OH, HELL, NO

You are bat shit crazy if you think I'm taking her home. Isn't it bad enough I have a teenager-slash-golden retriever wagging his tail whenever I walk in the door?

I drove Quili to a nearly respectable motel in a place no one would think to look for a professor of agriculture. It was just up the road from The Hideaway. I took a circuitous route as I checked for a tail and, as chance would have it, drove by the house Montgomery Rand once dared me to fuck him in. The motivation I'd created had reduced the wood frame to black ash, increasing adjacent property values by ten percent.

As I rolled down the street, guess who was sitting on a porch smoking.

Inspiration struck, and I swung into the driveway. "Stay," I ordered Quili then left the car. "Monte. Looking good. Everything back in working order?"

Monte narrowed his eyes, his expression wary as I walked up the walk. Recognition was a cold slap in the face. "You."

"Me. Nice place." He smelled of weed and mild body odor. "You live here alone?"

"My uncle lives here, but he's out of town. Don't burn it down. He'll never let me in another house." There was a healthy amount of fear in his voice.

"No worries. I just need a little favor."

He snorted. "Why would I do you a favor?"

"Call it fire insurance. You'll get paid for your time."

The wheels in his genius head began to churn through the drug-induced haze. "What's the favor?"

"Babysitting." I whistled like a construction worker and waved Quili to come out. She did, and Monte's doughy chin hit the porch. I could see the appeal. Quili was delicate, pretty. "Here's the deal. One week at most. She stays inside. Job pays two hundred dollars a day."

She hurried from the car to the house. I opened the front door and ushered her inside. Monte was less enthusiastic as he walked through the door.

"I'll need some money. You know, gas and food and stuff."

Good ol' Monte. "Quili, how much money do you have on you?"

She clutched her purse to her hip. "Forty. Maybe Fifty."

I drained my own wallet of two hundred. "This should get you started."

He took the money with one hand, grabbed my wrist with the other. "What kind of trouble is she in?" He whispered the question, as if Quili, standing only ten feet away, wouldn't hear.

"None if she stays out of sight." He looked at the cash as that genius brain weighed the evidence. I gave him a little bit more to sway the jury. "She was in the wrong place at the wrong time. I'm going to straighten it out but need a safe place to park her. Are you my guy?"

He looked at the bills, then shoved them in his pocket. "I got this."

"I know you do." He preened under my stroke of confidence. With a wave of my hand, I beckoned Quili away from her inspection of a bells from around the US. "Quili Liu, meet Montgomery Rand. Monte's agreed to hide you for a few days. This will be easy. You'll need to call in sick to the university. Make it something good, something that takes a good week to get over. Stay inside. You need something, Monte will go get it." I turned to Monte. "Stay clear of her work, apartment, anywhere she's known. You don't know who's watching. Is there a room she can use? I want to talk to her before I leave."

"The one at the top of the stairs."

I led Quili up the narrow staircase. The house was cut from the same mold as the one that burned. It was in better shape, cleaner. This house was a home, complete with pictures and mementos of a family man. The room at the top was small and furnished in five-year-old girl. The pink walls held thumbtacked posters of unicorns, princesses, and dancing flowers. Hard to be afraid in a room like this. Nauseous, yes. Afraid, no.

"I don't understand what is happening." Quili sank onto the bed neatly made with a pony comforter. "Who are you?"

"Like I said, I'm an investigator. I am looking into the deaths of professors Gavriil Rubchinsky and Francisco Thelan. As you know, both died a year ago at the summit in Rome. My team and I are certain the two deaths are connected and related to Professor Rubchinsky's research."

Quili froze, dumbstruck. She didn't move, didn't blink. Eventually, she swallowed, then opened her mouth to speak. "You know this? You have evidence?"

"Yes, I know this. I'm working on the evidence."

"Who do you work for?"

"Let's just call me a freelance investigator."

She drew her lower lip between her teeth and began to bite at it. She was so small, barely one hundred ten pounds soaking wet. In the child's room, her age and inexperience showed through.

I covered her clenched hands, squeezed encouragingly. "I will get to the bottom of this. It's what I do." She stared at me, right into my eyes. I let my determination and certainty shine through. I returned the probing gaze, seeing a woman who wasn't nearly as confident as she appeared.

Her gaze fell away, resting on the hands clasped tightly on

her lap. "I believe you will."

I left Quili and Monte with the voicemail number in case of an emergency, then raced home, using technology to get a head start on work.

"Please, say a command." My car had a British accent. I called her Bridget, slang for British chick.

"Call Black." I didn't expect him to answer. We had an arrangement. I left a voicemail with just a call back number. His call would be routed to my cell. Done.

"Please, say a command."

"Call Dixon." Him I expected to answer.

"Hello?"

"Dixon, I need those emails you downloaded between Doc and Buford. ASAP. And why are you whispering?"

"I'm taking my trigonometry final. We're not supposed to use phones."

"Then why did you answer?"

"Because you called."

In the distance, a stringy, elevated voice carried through. "Mr. Dixon, I know you are not using a cell phone during a final exam."

"No, Mrs. Gamulkowicz, I mean, well, yes but not for the test. It's my—"

"Probation officer," I said. "Tell her I'm checking if you're in class."

"It's my probation officer. She's just checkin' up on me. Here."

Then Mrs. Gamulkowicz's voice was in my ear. "Who is this?"

Bernice Gamulkowicz and I got along like water and electricity. I could picture her floral muumuu shimmying with attitude. She did her best to zombify my kids by psychically draining every ounce of joy from their lives.

"This is Karen Murray with the Department of Youth Rehabilitation Services." Karen was my friend from the old neighborhood and a legit juvie probation officer. "Andrew was assigned to me last week. His record shows chronic absenteeism from school. I was calling to ensure he was in school as reported."

"He is in the middle of his trigonometry final. It would be to your advantage to understand the student's schedule and to call at an appropriate time." She delivered a fine verbal slap to my face.

"Yes, ma'am."

"In fact, it is completely inappropriate for you to call the student during class time. Call the office to verify attendance. The number is in the phone book." *Snap.*

She hung up on me. No wonder Dixon cut.

A text came in. *Sorry. Will call later.*

"Damn high school." I had skills of my own. I needed to re-screen the security videos and read through all the emails between Buford and Gavriil and book a plane ticket to Bum Fuck Egypt.

Is that what they still call the middle of nowhere?

In my fancy new media center, I re-watched the security footage. When Carlo and I first viewed the film, we were missing one vital piece of information. What Hugo Franzetti looked like. No way Hugo drove the car; he served the poisoned cocktail. Even if the car was idling in front of the hotel, there just wasn't time to get into the seat and hit Gavriil. Plus, he would have been seen. Someone would have noticed the uniformed waiter racing into the street, jumping into a car and then hitting someone. The reports said the car came out of nowhere, not a rare thing in Rome. I backed the video up and played it again. This time, I watched Hugo. He delivered the tainted drink. He crisscrossed the room, full tray, empty tray. On the edge of the screen, he paused, hand to his head. He was on the phone. Then he resumed working. Two more trips between the bar and the flock of customers, then he disappeared through a door. One minute later, he came back into view, hands empty and wearing a jacket over his uniform. He didn't speak to anyone as he crossed the foyer and walked out the door.

Gavriil followed less than ten seconds later.

How could I have missed it the first time? Sloppy. Sloppy. The most important case of my career, of my life, and I was screwing it up. I would have kicked my own ass, but I'm not doubled jointed.

I needed to work smart. I called Carlo Giancarlo.

"*Ciao*, my American Diamond. You have missed Carlo?"

"Not in the mood. I need you to look at the driver again. Hugo wasn't driving the car." I caught him up on what I saw. "Somebody was sitting close by with the car running. Somebody he could call. Talk to Valentina. Find out who Hugo hung with. Find me the driver. God have mercy if it was her."

"I will see her immediately. Good?"

"Good enough."

"Tell me, have you spoken to my uncle Ian?" Ian was not the easiest name to say with an Italian accent. He said it like his mouth was full of marbles and he couldn't quite get his lips around the back-to-back syllables.

"No. I tagged him an hour ago. He hasn't called back yet."

"He hasn't returned my calls. It is not like him. At least he would text me but nothing since yesterday."

"Huh. That's strange." It gave me pause. We were all creatures of habit and the first clue something was amiss was often a breaking of said habit. "Maybe he's just on something hot. I have to go out of town. If he hasn't been in contact by the time I get back, I'll go hunt him down."

"*Va bene*. I will call tomorrow with progress. *Ciao*, Diamond."

"Bye, I mean, *ciao. Ciao*."

Next, I went to flights. My destination: Buford Winston of Tulsa, Oklahoma. I don't like booking my own flights. Too many damn choices and not one of them matched what I wanted. I searched and searched again. Impossible as it seems, you can only go from the Washington, DC area to Tulsa in the morning. I didn't want to go in the morning. I wanted to go this evening but unless I was making the eighteen-hour drive—which I wasn't—it looked like I was stuck until morning.

Booked it. Paid for it. Moved on.

The twin sixty-inch screens displayed the emails between Gavriil and Buford in a font Helen Keller could read. The first came from Buford two weeks after Gavriil secured the grant. It was friendly enough. Congratulations...blah blah blah...excited about opportunities...blah blah blah...sure we can come to an equitable arrangement.

Ha!

From day one, all Buford cared about was equity, liquidity, and profitability. The triple *itys*.

There were a hundred exchanges over the years Gavriil had the grant. Just a few each month. Buford initiated the contact, Gavriil responded, Buford closed it. The messages were civil, even when they had strident differences of opinion. Several emails alluded to voice-to-voice conversations; a few made plans to meet in person at conferences.

Everything was nice and calm and so damned polite my teeth ached.

But I wouldn't be fooled by a wolf in sheep's clothing. Ilsa witnessed Buford verbally dressing down an Italian cop. Quili quivered as she spoke about being intimidated by Buford's loud and over-the-top behavior.

I needed to talk to the man behind the curtain.

How to do it. My first instinct was to piss him off. Burn away the smooth front man in a fiery flare of temper. Course if he was pissed *at* me, he wasn't likely to talk *to* me. I needed him pissed at someone else. I needed to be the messenger he not only did not want to kill, but the one he wanted to confide in.

"I think Jessica Fielding is getting an extended performance."

"Who's Jessica Fielding?"

I bounded to my feet, sliding the knife out of my ankle sheath and making ready to attack.

Dix leapt backward. "Whoa! That was fast, Diamond. Like lightning fast. Like blink of an eye fast. Like—"

"I get it, Dix. I'm fast." Drawing myself to full height, I let the blade fall against my leg.

Dix's long hair swung as he shifted his weight from one foot to another, a ball of pent up energy. "Can you teach me to be fast like you? Because, you know, that was spectacular."

It was on the tip of my tongue to say he'd have to grow out of his puppy phase first. Too much energy, feet too big for his frame. But I didn't want to crush him. He'd had enough of that in his short life. "We'll see, Dix. How did the trig final go?"

"I don't know. Do you have anything to eat?"

The boy ate like a mammoth. "I think there's still cereal left."

"Sweet." And he was gone.

I followed at a more human pace, then leaned against the door frame as he poured half a box of cereal into a mixing bowl. "Did you know the answers to the questions on the final?"

"Oh sure. That stuff is easy. I mean, it's just angles and curves and stuff. And they use those Greek symbols. I like those. I'm thinking about using one to, you know, sign things."

"Like a signature?"

"Yeah. If they couldn't read, they would sign with an X. I'm thinking of using Ξ, the Greek letter Xi, which this table on the internet said is like the American letter X."

"We use the English alphabet. It's a descendent of the Latin alphabet."

Dixon settled at my little table, spoon in one hand and leaning on both elbows. "So the Greeks have a letter that looks like 'X' but sounds like *ch*. And it wouldn't be very interesting if I signed with an X. It would just look like I couldn't read, you know?"

"I suppose. Why Ξ and not A or Δ? For Andrew or Dixon?"

A single finger came up, prompting me to wait as he inhaled enough for a baseball team. "Alpha is pretty cool as a lowercase letter, but the capital just looks like a A. Boring, right? Delta is a maybe, the triangle thing is kinda cool but the lowercase one, whew, I'll never learn to make the squiggly thing. Maybe you should use Δ, for Diamond, right?"

"I like using C, the symbol for carbon, which is what dia-monds are made of. I'm like you, I don't go for obvious. D for diamond is kindergarten stuff. But C for diamond, that makes you think."

"I like it." He drank the milk, set his empty bowl in the sink, then went back to the refrigerator.

"You can't still be hungry." Maybe I sounded more exasper-ated than I felt because Dixon suddenly blushed. Really, I was impressed.

"I was just looking out for dinner. The snack will hold me over for a while."

"Let's take a look through the emails and I'll take you out to dinner."

"Deal." He blitzed past me, doors bouncing off the walls. And the kid thought he was slow.

"I'm going to have to buy sugar-free cereal." But Dixon was good as his word and in his skillful hands, we moved through the emails like a bee in a flower garden.

"So, here's what I don't get." Dixon shifted in his oversized bean bag chair to face me. "I hear you saying the Doc and Buford didn't get along but none of these emails are, you know, bad. The ones from his assistant lady, the ones in the 'Crybaby' file were worse than Buford's."

"That's the genius of Buford. The man is slicker than a greased pig."

"They're slippery? I've never seen one. Well, I've never seen a live pig, except in a zoo, but it wasn't greased."

I pinched the bridge of my nose. "Black ice slippery. You know, the kind you can't see and then *wham*, you're on your butt. Buford acts like a cultured cowboy when he really is pig shit."

Dixon cocked his head. "You have a thing for pigs, don't you?"

"Forget it. The point is, no matter how friendly or professional

Buford's emails are, the man was determined to use Gavriil's research to line his pockets. With or without Gavriil's cooperation."

We worked well together. I had to explain a few terms to Dixon, a few concepts he hadn't come across yet in his young life, but he paid attention, and he learned fast.

Gavriil had become obsessed (like only a scientist can) with quinoa after a trip to Bolivia. The fact it was a five-thousand-year-old food still consumed today blew. His. Mind. Then he found out even back then there were hundreds of varieties of the plant and all parts—roots, leaves, and seeds—were consumable. Zero waste. Quinoa was a complete and balanced protein, and it had antioxidants, and it was a good source of some very important minerals. Gavriil about wet his scientific panties. Then, then came the pièce de résistance...quinoa had a remarkable tolerance to different growing conditions. Thin cold air, hot sun, little rainfall, salty or sandy soil, name your adverse condition, and there was a quinoa varietal to thrive in it.

Gavriil started growing it in our suburban DC neighborhood. If anyone was foolish enough to ask about it, they were treated to the above lecture on quinoa...the long version. In the beginning, we had quinoa about once a week. As his obsession grew, so did its appearance on my dinner plate. It's not that I didn't like quinoa, it's like this...I went to private school, K to twelve, back in the day when plaid filled a school girl's wardrobe. I've been out of school for over thirteen years and I still won't wear plaid. Can't look at the stuff without feeling claustrophobic. I'm the same way with quinoa.

A guttural cry of a feral cat had me reaching for my knife again. "What the hell is that?"

Dixon sheepishly examined his oversized feet.

"Don't tell me you brought a cat into my house."

He blushed. "It was my stomach."

The time in the corner of the screen said six o'clock. Time flies when you're reminiscing about quinoa. "Come on. I know a place."

The mom-and-pop Italian restaurant didn't have a name on the front of the building. The old sign fell apart, leaving just the red and green stripes of the awning to indicate where the best meal in the neighborhood could be found. When lack of a sign didn't hurt business, Marie and Tony Longo saved the money. Dixon bounced as we walked down the street. The kid acted like he'd never been taken out for a meal. He grinned ear-to-ear, saying hello to anyone brave enough to make eye contact.

"Table for two?" the pretty young hostess asked.

"In the window. Can we sit in the window?" Dixon pointed to a dirty table in front of the big picture window. The world outside appeared as if on one huge, high-definition television screen. Of course, Dixon wanted to sit there.

"Just let me clean it off," the hostess said with a smile.

"I can help."

I snagged his collar. "Down, boy. Let her work." The hostess got busy then signaled us over. Dixon bolted forward, his collar snapping from my fingers.

It was fun being out with Dixon. He had no filter. If he thought it, he said it. If he wondered about it, he asked. If he didn't agree, he argued. Our conversation started with breadsticks and ended with a slurp of pasta and the Treaty of Versailles. You can figure out how we got there.

My phone chimed with a text. "Oh." My disappointment had been verbal.

"What's wrong?" Dixon craned over the table to read the screen.

"Nothing. Just the airline confirming my flight is on time."

"What were you expecting?"

"Ian Black. He should have called by now." I checked my texts and messages again. Still no Ian.

"Yeah, I talked to him the night you came home from Italy. He wanted to talk to you, but you were in the air somewhere. He helped me with some of my things—he knows some really cool shit—but then he had to go. He said he'd call back in ten minutes, but he didn't."

Newsflash. "Ian called looking for me?"

"Yeah. He said something about phones and numbers and not having time to wait."

I leaned forward until I could look in his eyes. "Think hard, Dix. Did he give you any clue to what was going on?"

Dixon tightened his mouth, his face still with seriousness. "He said he needed to talk to you. He said something about an order, and he'd do what he could to keep you out of it."

"Keep me out of it?" Again...dead woman. What was there to keep me out of? Besides hell. "Anything else?"

Dixon shook his head. "He was interrupted. He said he'd call back—"

"But hasn't." It was out of character for Ian, tripping yellow flags and warning sirens. "We're going for a ride."

The last piece of bread went down Dixon's gullet while I paid the bill. We walked back to my car, him bouncing like an unleashed puppy, which had me thinking...did I really want to take a seventeen-year-old to Ian Black's house? I stopped in my tracks, figuring out the fastest route past my building and then into the city.

Dixon leapt in front of me and planted his big paws on my shoulders. "You are not dumping me."

"Dix, you gotta understand, the world Ian and I live in is dangerous. He's gone off the grid when he wasn't planning to."

"How do you know he wasn't planning to?"

"Think. You said he was interrupted, and he would call you back. You didn't think he meant in a week, did you?"

His brows pressed down into thinking mode. "I thought, like, maybe fifteen minutes. Soon as he got done bein' interrupted."

"Right. Carlo expected the same thing. If Ian was planning to disappear, he wouldn't have said anything."

"So, let's go." He galloped, yes galloped, another two store-fronts, then stopped. "What are you waiting for?"

"Dix, man, I can't take you with me." I felt like I was crushing his puppy spirit. His face fell, his eyes went all sad. Then the little shit grabbed the keys out of my hand and ran. "Oh no, you did not!"

Dixon's long, loping gait ate up ground faster than he ate pasta. I pumped my legs hard. Those three slices of pizza were working against me, but like hell some snot-nosed twerp was going to beat me. One. Two. Three, and I leapt on his back.

"Give me my keys." I locked my legs around his bony hips.

"Take me with you." He spun in a circle, my weight carrying him onto a grassy knoll.

"What are you? Suicidal?" My arm wrapped around his throat. Sleeper hold.

"I just want to help." He croaked like a frog as he ran me into a tree.

I relinquished my grip on his throat, grabbed on to the tree and, using my legs, brought him down. "You wanna help, give me my god damn keys."

"Excuse me young man, do you need help?" An octogenarian stood at the very edge of the concrete border curb, a cane in one hand, purse in the other, and a disapproving glare on her face. Next to her was her sister, spry at seventy-five-ish.

Dixon locked eyes with me and smiled. "Yes, ma'am."

I dove for the keys buried in his outstretched hand as a barrage of old-lady whoop ass hailed down. "Damn it. Stop right now."

"Leave the young man alone," sister said with authority. Ex-school teacher? Ex-prison warden?

"Ouch!" The plastic corner of the pleather purse rang my bell. Self-preservation dictated I abandon the keys and seek shelter immediately. "Stop it!" I rolled to my back and used my feet. The best damn defense was a relentless offense. "Fine. You wanna play?"

The next swing of the brick-laden purse met my foot. I snagged it, locking it down while I kicked with my other foot. Yeah, I kicked an old lady. "Dixon!"

He ran while my back was turned. "I'll get the car and pick you up!"

I flipped back into a sprinter's stance, but my legs went out from under me and purses came down hard on my ass.

"You run, young man. We'll hold her here!"

"Dixon!" I glanced up to see him running, roaring with laughter as he reached the parking garage and disappeared.

"You should be ashamed of yourself. A woman your age chasing a boy. It's disgraceful." Elder sister pitched forward from the hips, wagging a finger in my face.

Younger sister clucked her tongue and took a final, half-hearted swipe. "It's those feminists! First, they burn their bras, then they straddle boys in a park. Whew. I gotta sit down."

On my feet and out of range, I pulled my hair out. "Are you two crazy? You don't go accosting people with fake designer purses." I twisted my arm to look at the throbbing spots turning into bruises. "What do you have in those? Bricks?"

"Bibles," younger sister said.

"Never doubt the power of prayer," the elder added.

Tires squealed, and my car took the corner out of the garage on two wheels. The car stopped on a dime, ten feet from the sisters. Dixon's grinning face appeared in the open window. "Need a ride."

I pointed to the sisters. "Stay." I sidestepped to the car, my eyes never straying from the bible whumpers.

Soon as I closed the door, Dixon leaned out the window. "Thank you."

"Are you certain you're safe with her?" the younger asked.

"Yeah. She's not as bad as she thinks she is."

Insult! On top of injury! "Just drive. Turn right, head down to the docks."

"K, K." The car rolled past the Italian restaurant to the intersection. "Left here?"

"Yeah." We came to a very complete stop in the intersection before turning sharply. The speedometer hovered under the posted speed limit. "Didn't figure you for a 'by-the-book' driver, especially after you peeled out of the garage."

Dixon's gaze flickered to the rearview mirror. "Well, I figured I better be legal on account of I don't exactly have my driver's license."

Fingers to my twitching eye. "What does 'don't exactly' mean?"

"I have my learner's permit. I did all the classwork at school and started on the sixty hours of supervised driving."

I don't want to know. I don't want to know. "How many hours have you completed?"

"Twenty. Technically."

"How many actually?"

"Four. My dad wouldn't take me out, but he was drunk and signed off on the others. He thought he was signing up for a jelly-of-the-month club." He turned those puppy-dog eyes on me. "You'll sign off on this, right? You qualify as a supervising. Oh! And if it's dark on the way back, it'll count toward the ten hours of night driving."

And I thought life would be easier when I was dead.

"So, will you? Sign off?" He looked like a little boy, hoping a friend would come out and play.

"What the hell." One of my aliases had to hold a valid driver's license. "Make the next right and take the on-ramp. Tell me you've driven on a highway."

"Sure, I have. Well, not technically, but I've done it hundreds of times in *Grand Theft Auto*."

Twenty minutes, ten horn blares, and five curse-outs later, we rolled down an industrial street frequented by rats and river vermin. The street was wide to accommodate the daily truck migration. Headlights reflected off the glass fragments pushed against the well-used curbs. The sidewalks on either side floated above the street, broken and dislocated. Beyond were warehouses and flex spaces and reclaimed artists' pads. Our destination was the dark building on the river side of the street.

"Pull over here."

Dixon put on his turn signal, coasted to our right, and bounced off the curb. "Sorry. It was closer than it looked." He curled his chest onto the steering wheel. "What are we looking at?"

"Ian Black's home. Three floors of reinforced walls and bulletproof glass." There was a ridiculous amount of square footage in the structure Ian called both home and office. I was jealous the first time I saw it. He had a three-hundred-sixty-degree view of the surrounding street and an escape chute off the back to a hidden platform behind his dock. It was a sweet setup and inspired my own takeover of a building.

"How are we going to get in? Do you have, like, rope and a grappling hook?" Dixon rubbed his hands together in anticipation.

I rolled my eyes. "We're going in the front door."

"Oh. Well. Okay." Disappointed, he got out of the car.

I chased after him. Again. "Dixon, stop."

"Awe, Diamond. Don't make me wait in the car. I can be helpful. It's, you know, a big place, right? So, two heads are better than one, right?" His head hung low, his eyes on my shoes. "Pleeeease?"

I regretted bringing him. I would work faster alone. I wouldn't have to worry about anyone alone. "The rules are: one, you stay behind me and two, you run like hell if I say to. No waiting for me. No trying to help me. Listen to me Dixon when I tell you I'm trained for this. Are you hearing me?"

"Yes." He hopped like a pogo stick. "Yes, yes, yes, yes."

All I could do was shake my head. "Let's go."

Ian's security system was state of the art. The door's lock used a passcode. Any breach of the door or windows activated a blow horn of an alarm and flooded the perimeter with lights strong enough for a stadium. The stairs inside were rigged with pressure sensors. Stepping on them without deactivating the system would have you making like Peter Pan across the storage space.

I had the code from Gavriil's poker days. The penthouse was the favored place for debauchery in general. I punched in the code.

The damn light stayed red.

I tried it again. Same result. Sometime in the last year, Ian changed his code.

"Shit. We're not getting in." I pounded on the door. Nada.

"Lemme try." Dixon shouldered me out of the way. "Yeah. Yeah. I know this model. Last summer I was into security systems."

This kid was an enigma wrapped in a puzzle tied with genius. "Into security systems?"

"You know, hacking into them." He used my car keys to pry off the cover. "They look tough because of the interface, but it's just another computer. Once you learn how to talk to it, it'll do what you want." The door latch slid open.

Inside was too dark to see your own hand. The weak light of dusk couldn't penetrate the tinted windows. No problem, I turned on the lights.

"Should you do that?"

"What? Turn on the lights? We aren't trying to sneak up on Ian." To prove my point, I called out. "Ian! It's Diamond and Dixon. You here?"

The first floor stretched a long way. Bare concrete, stained with oil, time, and things better not known, was slippery under foot. Each floor of Ian's humble abode rounded to ten thousand square feet. The ground floor was an acre or two of garage. Ian had ten vehicles, three motorcycles, two boats, and an ATV arranged around the roll-up door. Yellow tape on the floor marked the designated parking spot for each vehicle.

Dixon followed me across the open floor. The 9mm I'd taken from my car hung at my side. I wasn't expecting trouble; I could see nearly all of the room. I took a knee, looking under the vehicles.

Dixon mirrored me. "I don't see anything. This is the cleanest garage I've ever been in. All the cars and stuff are here, aren't they?"

I nodded. The tenant for each yellow square was present and accounted for. "A place for everything and everything in its place. Let's go upstairs."

Three staircases and an elevator led to the second floor. One was near the main entrance and was officially the front stairs. The black metal staircase was four feet wide with stone steps. Its twin was tucked into the corner behind the boat. The "back stairs" was off-limits to all but a select few. Yours truly excepted.

In the center of the water-side wall was the elevator. The third staircase crept up the elevator like an anaconda, twisting and rising until it disappeared into the patterned ceiling.

I led the way back to the front stairs. This door was least likely to be locked and would put me in a position to see the space laid out in front of me. Ian's home felt empty, but I wasn't going to take any chances with Dix. I motioned him to a position hidden from the second-floor door. "Stay here until I call clear. If I tell you to run, get the hell out of here, back to the car, and away from the river. Go to the nearest police station and wait there. If I don't call you in one hour, bring them in, guns drawn. You got it?"

His long face fell. Understanding had dawned. "Don't go up there, Diamond. Call the cops now."

He still didn't understand who I was. "I'll be fine. You make sure you are."

Gun cradled in a two-handed position, I soundlessly ascended the stairs. The door to the second floor was open. This was Ian's office. The space was divided into six distinct areas by furniture, equipment, and more floor tape. Here, again, there were few hiding places. Which made it obvious we weren't the first to come through. "Shit." I went back to the door. "Come on up."

"Did you find him? Holy crap, someone was pissed." It was an understatement. The office space looked like Boggle dice after being given a tumble. Desks sat on their sides or tops. Legs of chairs poked in the air. Paper covered the floor like confetti.

Back to the front stairs and up to the third floor.

The place felt dead, empty. Whatever happened here was done. "Dixon, come on up."

His entrance was slow this time, looking before he leapt to the space by my side. The third floor wasn't in any better shape than the second. "Do...do you think whoever did this, you know, like, got Ian?"

The kid was a mind reader. "Nobody gets in here without Ian knowing about it."

"We did."

Point. Counterpoint: "Ian didn't get where he is by being stupid. If someone came in while he was here, he knew it. He'd be ready. He'd have a plan and a backup plan." I completely believed the crap I spewed. Had to. Because the alternative was..."Stay behind me. We're going room to room."

We began in the kitchen. One hell of a mess but no people—breathing or otherwise. Next was the living area. A screen designed for a theater dominated the interior wall while two rows of man-sized couches sat in homage. Bullets had ripped a line across the soft leather of the front one.

Half-bath. Clear, no damage, but really, there wasn't much to break in it unless you had a thing for porcelain.

Middle of the floor was the game room. Pool table, card table, bar. All matched with green felt and chocolate brown leather trim. A sharp knife had been dragged across the leather while angry stab wounds marred the soft felt.

The door to the master bedroom was wide open, the setting sun casting shadows that didn't belong. "Dixon, don't—"

"Is she dead?" His voice trembled.

I didn't answer the rhetorical question. The woman laid across Ian's bed, her head off the bed at an uncomfortable angel. She was very naked and totally dead. I had to walk to the river side of the room to see her face. A single shot to the forehead had thrown her across the bed. Following the dictates of gravity, blood had drained to the lowest point, her head. "Don't come over here. Is this your first dead body?"

"Second, the first one wasn't naked. Look at the chair. Is that her blood?"

Grabbing the edge of the bed spread, I pulled it over, covering her body before following Dixon's gaze. The upholstered chair aimed to a television screen was stained with blood. Whose blood? I'd need a laboratory for the answer. I wouldn't bet on it being our dead lady. The only visible cut on her body was the one on her forehead, and everything I saw said she died where she fell.

"Probably not."

"You think it's Ian's?"

The scene began playing in my mind like a movie. The front bell rang. Ian used the security system and recognized the woman. He let her in and one thing lead to another. Either he forgot to reactivate the system, or she deactivated it. While they were getting busy in the bedroom, enter our shooter. He shot the woman and got busy working Ian over. Or maybe he started working Ian over and the woman objected. *POW*. Objection overruled. He went back to Ian...but something happened. "If he has Ian, why destroy the apartment and the office. It takes time and it takes anger to do this. If you have Ian, why not just leave?"

"Maybe there was more than one of them. Maybe there were even three or four, downstairs and up here at the same time." Dixon's gaze flickered to the body, still seeing what the blanket hid. His face had an unhealthy green undertone.

"Bathroom, Dix. Now."

He covered his mouth as he ran and bounced immediately out. "There's another one. In the bathtub. Another body."

"Is it Ian?" I didn't wait for his answer, racing past him to see for myself. Not Ian but an ugly man in black with knuckles raw to bleeding. His head had connected with the bathtub spigot and stuck there. He considerately bled down the drain.

The bathroom resembled ground zero for a World War III battle. Bullets and casings and shards of porcelain littered the marble floor. Streaks of blood stood out in sharp contrast to the white tiles. But there was more, if you understood what you saw. The streak brushed across two tiles and ended abruptly before the tattered laundry basket. The basket was empty. I jiggled it. Lifted it. Shook it. It was just a basket.

Then I noticed one tile was raised a fraction of an inch above the others. I stepped on it and one of the white panels making up the ornate wainscoting recessed. I pushed it in to reveal a chute.

"Dixon?"

"Yeah?" He leaned in just enough to see me.

"Don't follow me." I sat on the floor, scooting until my legs were in the black abyss.

"W-wait. What should I do?"

"Stay by your phone." I shoved off.

I took Gavriil to a water park once. They didn't have them when he was a kid and had been "too old" once he arrived here. My "too old" man loved it, racing ahead of children to line up for the tube rides. His favorite were the enclosed ones, completely black so you had no idea what was coming.

Add cobwebs and "pellets" and you know where I am.

Forty-five-degree slide, sharp turn to the right, drop, sharp turn, drop. With each drop, my stomach rolled. With each turn, my head felt like a pinball. My legs hit something hard and I spilled out onto a rough concrete mat. It took a second for the marbles to stop spinning and my eyes to adjust to the dim light.

"Nice of you to join me." The voice was more air than sound. Ian's lips were cracked, a bloodied towel bunched under his head, his body hidden beneath a Mylar blanket. He tried to push to sitting with hands bound by plastic cords, but he fell back to the concrete. The blanket dropped off his shoulders and pooled around his bare hips. Bruises the size of fists littered his chest and ribs. There wasn't a part of his face and upper body free of abrasions.

"Must have been one hell of a party." I dug out my phone. "Dixon?"

"You're alive. Thank God, you're alive. I heard you scream and I thought...I thought..." Between the gasping breaths, Dixon cried.

I did not scream. And if I did, it wasn't my fault. Even Indiana Jones would scream if he was getting a face full of spiderwebs and spiders and things spiders eat in spiderwebs. "Just a weird echo. Maybe my gun scraping against the pipe. Call an ambulance. I have Ian."

Ian shook his head adamantly. "No. No ambulance. Just you." He closed his eyes, his body sagging back to the concrete. "All I need is you."

"Fuck. Move the car to the front entrance," I said to Dix. Stowing my phone, I pulled out a knife to cut the ties. Ian swayed at the tugging on his wrists. "Suck it up. You're not hurt bad." I snapped out the lie to keep him conscious. "I hope you don't expect me to play nurse. I already got plans."

BUFORD WINSTON LOVES HIS ASS

A stubborn man can drive a good woman to drink. Hence, I stood in the door way of my own bedroom with Grey Goose on the rocks. "Do you have to make so much noise?"

Ian, the stubborn man, refused to go to even an unqualified health facility. "Yee-oww." The sound squeezed out between gritted teeth. His chest heaved in shallow breaths under the attention of Brunhilda, the nurse. "That fucking hurts." Spittle flew from his cracked lips.

"Without X-ray, this is the best way to know if the bones are broken." Brunhilda spoke with a faded, no-nonsense German accent as she pressed her fingers along the ridges of his ribs, pressing on skin purpled and swollen.

Ian tore my pillow case apart at the seam. "God damn it. Knock me out, Diamond. Just do it."

"Damn it, Ian. My pillow. I should pop you."

Brunhilda shook her head, unimpressed with our banter. "I need him responsive."

I grinned at Ian. "She needs you responsive."

Ian gave me a one-finger salute as he glared at Brunhilda. "Where the hell did they find you? The Flying Dutchman?"

Brunhilda looked at Dixon with maternal affection. "Andrew and I are long friends."

Dixon bounced in his position next to the bed. "Mrs. Gunther works at the animal emergency room. The one open all night."

Ian's head shot off my pillow. "Animal hospital?"

"Ah, ya. We see car accidents all the time with injuries like yours. I usually have to muzzle my patients. It is nice to ask 'does this hurt'?" She worked a puffy area on his cheek.

Ian yelped and scooched away as manly as possible. "Yes, damn it, it hurts."

Brunhilda pointed to the warm spot on the bed. "Stay put. I have muzzles and leashes in my bag."

Ian sheepishly slid back into the divot he'd made. "Gimme some, Diamond." I gave, he took, then drained the glass. He closed his eyes, inhaled deeply twice. "Your bedside manner sucks."

It was a toss-up who he was referring to. "You're the one who didn't want to go to an urgent care." I took the glass back, refilled it, and drank. "So, how is our patient?"

"Mr. Ironsides is a very lucky man," Brunhilda said. "Maybe a few cracked ribs. Mostly bruises. He will be colorful for a few days. Moving will be painful but is good for you." She spoke to Ian now, patting his leg like he was a good boy. "If you have sharp pains or they do not lessen, be a smart man and go to the human emergency room."

With Ian warm and dry, color returned to his face. Sure, there were blues and reds and purples, but underneath was the rosy glow of someone among the living.

"You sleep now, Mr. Ironsides. Sleep is the best medicine for dog, cat, or man." Brunhilda Gunther left quickly after imparting wisdom. Her job was done, her patient out of the woods, so she moved on. Dixon and I sat on the edge of the bed, watching Ian.

Ian's gaze flickered between the two of us. "Don't tell me you're going to sit there all night. It's creepy."

"It's my bedroom."

A pervert's smile adorned his chapped lips. "You planning on sleeping with me?"

Dixon snickered. I rolled my eyes. "I'm taking the couch. I'll be close enough to hear you if you call. I want to review the file on Buford again. I have a bright-and-early flight for Tulsa and want all the ammo I can get to take him apart."

Ian sat up, signaling Dixon to adjust the pillows. "Go and get your computer. We'll do it together." Ian watched Dixon walk out of the room, then turned his attention fully on me. "There's a recovery order out for you."

"Get real, Ian. I'm dead, remember?" The idea somebody would put up money to have me captured and turned over alive was ludicrous. "Ridiculous."

"A hundred thousand ridiculous."

Bright and early refers to the sun's position and the time on the clock, not my disposition during said period. I was happy to bypass the chirpy ladies at the airline desk for the stern and no-bullshit faces of the TSA.

"Flight seven-eight-five-nine with service to Chicago now boarding premium platinum members with our company logo tattooed on their person. Please queue on the red carpet and be prepared to show your tattoo."

I checked my ticket. Not me. I don't know why I bothered—I didn't have the tattoo. Still, I abandoned the mass-manufactured blue chair for the amorphous swarm of people anxiously awaiting the call of their class—or lack thereof.

Four hours, two cups of coffee, and one plane change later, I tooled across Oklahoma's open roads. The temperature was about the same as in the greater DC area, but the scenery couldn't have been more different. Once outside of Tulsa, outside of Sapulpa, and away from the I-44 corridor, I could see. Like, really see.

Sometimes I forgot how beautiful our country was.

The farther off the beaten path I got, the narrower the roads became. The asphalt driving surface faded into the adjacent earth. It was difficult to tell where one ended and the other began. Driveways emptied to the road every now and then, truck-wide worn paths of dusty earth marked by a mailbox and the occasional garbage can. Nature going where it wanted to go, doing what it wanted to do.

The GPS in the rental car brought me to the entrance of Buford Winston's ranch. I expected the larger-than-life AgNow! chief to live in a high-end estate with as much in common with a ranch as a raindrop has with a monsoon.

I'll woman-up and say it: I was wrong.

Buford Winston lived on a working ranch. From the long line of fencing stretching in both directions, it was a big ranch. Some fields were planted; others had cows. One side of the driveway was a long pen with mules. A lot of mules.

Couldn't say I'd ever seen one close up before. They were oddly attractive creatures. Intelligent eyes and a spring in their steps. They followed along as I rolled up the driveway, kicking dust even as slow as I was going. They trotted ahead, knowing where I was going better than I did.

The driveway headed straight for a sprawling ranch house with a low porch running the full length. I stopped and parked where the gravel path turned along the house. At the fence line, the man of the hour stood in deep conversation with one of the asses. Buford Winston wore jeans up to the widest point of his big belly. A plaid shirt was tucked into the pants and everything was held in place by a pair of beige suspenders. His head was covered by a cowboy hat the same color as the suspenders.

I stepped out of the car to face the man who'd likely arranged my husband's death. I felt naked. Not with respect to clothing—Jessica Fielding's professional suit, sensible heels, and blond wig were impeccable—it was my personal safety. I didn't have my gun on me. The bulge would ruin the lines of the suit and tip off the experienced hunter I wasn't just a lil' writer from Chicago. I was sure Winston had guns around, but none were on his person. The only bulges were home grown. I planted a big smile on my face and started the game.

"Mr. Winston. I'm Jessica Fielding with *American Science Quarterly.*" I came around the car, extending my hand.

Winston took my hand, though, by the expression on his face, it was out of the habit of manners. "Jessica Fielding from *American Science Quarterly.*" He shook my hand slowly, his head moving at the same rate. "I don't recall having anything on my calendar for a face-to-face meeting."

I imagined how Jessica would feel which, as intended, brought a blush to my face. "We don't exactly have a meeting scheduled. I worked with your secretary to meet at your office, but it didn't work out. I learned you were here today and, well, I took a chance." Cue irresistible grin.

Buford took a small carrot from his pocket and fed it to the ass. "Who likes her carrots? Does Buttercup like carrots? Yes, she does."

"I realize this is...unconventional—"

"Young lady, it's downright rude. I have an office specifically for the purpose of conductin' business. I have a home specifically for the purpose of livin' my private life. Give me one good reason why I shouldn't throw you off my property?"

Plan B. Cue pathetic eyes. "I'm a freelance writer, just starting out. *American Science Quarterly* is interested in my article, but I need you to be able to finish it. You're right, it is rude of me to just come here. But I'm a desperate woman."

"What is your article about?"

"It's called 'Old Mother Earth's Cupboard,'" I spoke fast, the way people do when they're overly excited about something. "Get it? Like Old Mother Hubbard from the nursery rhyme? So, it's about how, with global warming, our food-producing capabilities are not going to keep pace with population growth, especially in desert climates. I did a lot of research on Professor Gavriil Rubchinsky's work in the field. You sponsored his work...so you must have supported it. I have so many questions and you're the only one who can answer them."

Winston stroked Buttercup's long nose. "Why aren't you talkin' to Professor Liu? She took over the work."

Good question. "I did, but she didn't...she explained the science but not the, you know, humanity of it." Oh God, I was talking like Dixon.

"No. She couldn't." Winston measured me up, head to toe. "You look as out of place as a fish riding a bicycle."

Cue smile number two. "I would have worn jeans but, you know, wanted to look professional. Because I am professional, I mean a professional writer. Not like a professional professional."

"I know a lot of folks who think being professional is about the way they dress. What watch they wear, what golf clubs they own. A professional does what they do for the better of the society they serve. Put on your jeans, Ms. Fielding, and we'll talk about feeding the world."

Winston showed me to a bedroom in the ranch house. Spacious rooms blended one into the other, giving a sense of freedom and space matching the Oklahoma setting. The bedroom was designed to make a guest comfortable. I made use of the attached bath to relieve myself of the previously mentioned coffees, then dressed in jeans and a performance tee. A lightweight jacket hid my holster and the 9mm it carried. A knife slid into my ankle sheath and covered with bootcut denim. Fully attired, I rejoined Winston in the main room.

Winston ended a call when I walked in.

"Sorry, I didn't mean to interrupt. Your call I mean. I know, my just being here is an interruption." I hoped he was enjoying my impression of an insecure neophyte. For myself, I think my IQ dropped a few points.

"More comfortable?"

I nodded, queueing smile three. "Much. The suit comes with the job. But this is the real me."

He nodded. "Where you from, Miss Fielding?"

"Please, call me Jess. I grew up outside Chicago."

"Cubs or White Sox."

"Cubs. Twenty-seventeen was just the start. I see a dynasty in our future."

"Ah, the relentless optimism of a Cubs fan." Winston headed toward French doors, opening to his rear acreage. "You shoot, Jess?"

"A little. I once had a boyfriend who enjoyed shooting. I went with him a few times. Why?"

"I was going to take target practice before you rolled in. We can chat out there."

Perfect.

The back of the house had a wide deck sectioned by purpose. There was the eating area with tables and chairs for twelve. There was the cooking area with a grill, smoker, and two burners. There was the sunning area with six lounge chairs, cocktail tables set in between. Finally, there was the pool area with a small zoo of inflatable animals. None of them were mules.

"You have a great house," I said as I followed Winston down the steps to the grass. "You must have great pool parties."

"Pool parties? I don't know about that, but the grandkids do enjoy it." Winston climbed behind the wheel of a golf cart. "The shooting range is on the other side of the ranch. We'll get there faster this way."

I rounded the cart to the passenger seat, noting the cases for handguns already stowed in the cargo area. Winston took us out to the road, down a quarter mile, and onto a dirt path with ruts custom made for the vehicle. Winston and I didn't speak on the drive. The chugging of the golf cart and crackling of the gravel made conversation at a casual decibel impossible. I studied the big bastard. He had the look of a hardworking, good old boy. Someone who grew up getting his hands as dirty as his boots. He didn't look like the player he was.

We bounced over ruts until we reached a mound of earth three times as tall as me with targets line up across the front. Some were purchased, probably made somewhere in China and shipped here for rich folks to put their money into. Most were random. Tree stumps worked as pedestals holding objects of various shapes and sizes. Glass. Plastic. Ballistic material. Half a desk lamp. An old car door with a white number 8 in a blue circle. A scarecrow with no arms and one leg. The space was a cross between a graveyard, a junk yard, and a hot mess.

"So, ask me your questions." Winston slid out of the cart and began moving the gun cases to the table set permanently in front of the shooter's position.

My question? Why did you kill my husband, you son of a bitch?

I went through the list of reporterly questions I had developed on the plane. When did you become interested in the food shortage crises? What were your goals in funding a project such as Professor Rubchinsky's? Were you satisfied with the progress?

I asked a question. I fired. He answered a question. He fired. Gradually, I brought the topic to what mattered.

"I understand you were there, the night Professor Rubchinsky died." *Bang, bang, bang.*

Winston sighed heavily. His shoulders sagged for an instant then he brought his hands up. "Yes." *Bang, bang, bang.* "One of the worse nights of my life."

Right there with you, buddy. "What happened? What *really* happened. I read the police reports but, well, there has to be more." *Bang.*

"Nice shot."

"Thanks." I had been careful to miss the target, shooting like the rookie I claimed to be. But I'd been focused on his answer, not my cover, and nailed the bull's-eye.

Winston transferred his gaze from the target to me. "You read the police reports? In Italian?"

Something in those sharp eyes made me swallow hard. "In English. Translated. My Italian is limited to mozzarella and fettuccini." I shrugged. "What can I say? I'm thorough."

"I bet you are." *Bang, bang, bang.* "I was there alright. Drank a beer with a leech who wanted to attach to my wallet. One minute, Gabe was enjoying a drink, the next, he's dead in the street."

Gabe? GABE? Oh, no he did not.

"The leech died that night, too."

"Professor Thelan? He was hitting you up for money?"

Winston chuckled as he reloaded. "Nothing so nefarious, Jess. He wanted his own project grant funded. His concept wasn't bad, but his scope was too limited. Not to speak ill of the dead, but the man was as cheap with his ideas as he was with his money."

"Why did Professor Rubchinsky leave the hotel?" *Bang.* "I'm out of bullets."

"Good. Now tell me who you really are."

Winston held a .44 capable of making a hole in me big enough to see daylight through. He was a big man, an old man. I could outrun him but not the bullet. I slowly raised my hands, empty gun and all. "I...I don't know what you mean."

He cocked his head. "You don't want to lie to me. You're not a reporter. Not with a magazine or anyone else. You're not as young as you pretend to be. Not as stupid, either."

"It's not what you think." I feigned scared. Then I round-house kicked the gun out of his hand and landed in a shooting stance with my barrel aimed at his heart.

"I take it you have one bullet left? You're full of surprises, aren't you Jess." He shook the sting out of the hand I'd kicked.

"The name is Diamond." With the ruse gone, I spoke in my voice, letting the cold show in my eyes. "I know you killed Gavriil—"

"I did *NOT* kill, Gabe." Armed or not, Winston was dangerous. Those thick hands flexed as if ready to break something or someone in half. "Let's get that straight between me and you right now. Didn't kill Thelan either." He turned his back on me, as if he didn't have a loaded and deadly weapon trained on him. And I wasn't talking about the gun.

"After you two butted heads, did you send him a drink?"

He snorted as he turned. "If that's the best you got, go back whcrc you camc from." Hc stood his ground, as I stood mine. "Who do you work for?"

"His wife."

Winston lowered his eyes. Emotion drained from his face until only a brutal sadness remained. "Gabe was one of my best friends. He was passionate about his work. He was passionate about his wife. How is she?"

"She's dead."

"Oh. No." He staggered, catching the table for support. "When? How?"

"A week or so ago. She fell asleep and a candle fell over." There wasn't a need to finish the thought.

"This may sound wrong, but I'm glad Gabe died first. The way he loved his woman, he wouldn't have survived her passing on first." Grief carved new lines in Winston's full face. There was nothing laughable about the curve of his mouth. His red eyes had been trampled by crow's feet. "If she's dead…why are you here?"

I lowered the gun and put Jessica Fielding away. "Because I made a promise." As Winston stared, I removed the wig and the netting containing my own dark hair. "You knew he was killed. Why didn't you press the Italians to investigate?"

"I did. Damn near ended up in jail myself." It likely was the scene Ilsa had witnessed. "They were so focused on Thelan they wouldn't listen. Never made sense to me. Why him? Nobody kills mediocrity. It's its own punishment."

"The cocktail Thelan drank was served to Gavriil. When he left it behind untouched, Thelan helped himself."

"The cheap bastard would be alive today if he'd bought his own drinks." He swore under his breath. "Why was Gabe killed? Do you know?"

It should have been easy to stay hard-ass on Winston, but he was so pissed off, it took the edge off me. "I was hoping you could tell me." I laid out what went down, in general terms.

His face turned beet purple. I thought he was having a heart attack. As I was trying to figure out how to find his sternum for CPR, he stalked back to the table, picked up two guns, and unloaded them into the rest of the scarecrow. Casings flew in a scene straight out of the freaking old west.

When both clicked empty, he turned to me.

"Feel better?" I asked.

"For all the good it did." His face was back to human color, though his heavy brows were still pushed down. "Let's go to the house. I have some things you need to see. Those last few weeks, Gabe was acting bipolar. We'd chat, and he'd be normal. Then he'd send me an email completely out of the north pasture. We got into it a few times. I'll admit it, I went cowboy on him, but he went all Russian on me."

The emails recovered from Gavriil's account showed few emails to Winston. It surprised me, but if they spoke as regularly as Winston said, they would email less. Gavriil had been frustrated by Winston those last few weeks, getting as loud as Winston had just done. He was angry Winston was losing confidence in his work and put the blame squarely on Winston's shoulders.

"Were you going to pull out of the project?"

"No." Candid. Definitive. I believed him. Then Winston removed his hat and ran a hand through thinning hair. "I may have threatened it but just to sober him up. Gabe was nearly finished with the first phase and we were getting ready to move into field testing. It was just...he'd come out of left field with ideas. Costs would double, maybe triple. The money didn't exist, and the benefits couldn't justify the extras." His fingers danced over the keyboard. "Read this. You'll see what I mean."

Winston brought up an email I had never seen before. The "from" stamp had Gavriil's email address. The subject referred to the grant project. The body of the email was formal. It referred to specifics of plant data and projections and made demands on modifying the scope for the next phase.

The word choice was off. My husband used a very formal English in emails, one reflecting a textbook education in the language rather than growing up in it. There were a few exceptions. He used the word "chat" for "talk" and said the word in the same accent Winston just did. I had wondered where it came from. He used the word "on" instead of "about." He would think on, talk on, dream on, etc. There were other examples, nuances of language that pointed to the author's identity. "Gavriil didn't write this."

Winston raised an eyebrow. "Know him well enough to be sure?"

I didn't answer. Instead, I scrolled down the email. "Are there others like this? I want to send them to my guy."

"I'll bring them up."

While Winston worked his computer, I called Dix.

"Andrew Dixon's phone." The voice wasn't Dix's but someone older, more cynical.

"Ian?"

"Diamond? How's Missouri?"

"Oklahoma. Where's Dixon?"

"He's here. Hold on." Ian screamed for Dix at the top of his lungs. "He's coming."

"Holy hell." I shoved the phone arm's length away. "Jeeze, Ian. I was using that ear."

"Sorry."

"You doing better?"

"Yeah. The kid knows a thing or two about treating bumps and bruises. He can cook, too." He snickered. "Heats up a different can of soup for each meal and makes these monster sandwiches. Damn, but the kid can eat for a skinny shit. Did you know his birthday was a few days ago? He wouldn't say, but I think his old man gave him the black eye."

"You'd be thinkin' right."

"Hell of a way to grow up. Here he comes. I'm putting you on speaker."

"Hey Diamond." Dix sounded a kind of happy and carefree his life didn't have. Or maybe it was in spite of what his life didn't have.

"Hey Dix. I hear you're making a pretty good nurse. Don't let Ian talk you into wearing a uniform." They groaned and chuckled. "Dix, I need you to dig back into the emails. I'm here with Buford Winston. He exchanged emails with Gavriil, but they weren't in the ones you gave me."

"Give me a few dates." Dixon was all business, taking the dates and the subject lines.

Winston leaned toward the microphone. "Well, boys, it was a series of emails called 'Quinoa Phase 2 Scoping.'" He read the dates of the email exchanges. "There may have been a few others, but those got me hot and bothered."

The clicking of computer keys came through the speaker. Dixon grunted, then Ian. They chirped in geek at each other over whatever they were seeing.

Finally, Dix spoke in English. "The series isn't here, Diamond."

My mind flipped through possible solutions. "Could you have missed it in the download?"

"No. I didn't pick and choose the files, I snatched the whole enchilada." Dix turned away from the phone. "Oh, let's get tacos for dinner."

"Guys? Focus. How can Winston have emails with Gavriil's address, but they didn't come from his account?"

"We need the emails," Ian said. "I have a few ideas, but we are going to need the emails to get behind them."

"I can link into Winston's system and download them," Dixon said. "I'll get everything from Doc's to run a comparison to what we already have."

"Now, hold your horses, boys." Winston held out his hand as if my dynamic duo could see him. "I have confidential information in my email. I can't have you just rooting around like a pig for truffles."

"What's a truffle?" Dixon asked but plowed forward without waiting for a response. "Candy, right? A kind of chocolate?

I bet they would go great with tacos. I can be in and out in like…ten minutes."

Winston scratched his head. "Is he talking about truffles, tacos, or emails? I can't keep up with the boy."

"Few can," I said. "Dix, remote into this computer and identify only emails from Doc. You hear me? I come home and find anything else and your ass is dropping three floors the fast way."

Winston raised a brow in my direction. "Those boys live with you?"

"Yes," they answered simultaneously.

I tried not to laugh and failed, the tension I hadn't noticed fell away. "They're like cockroaches. They stay, no matter what I do."

The twinkle came back into Winston's eyes and he let Dix have his way with his computer. From what I could see, Dix minded his manners and didn't take more than he was supposed to. The four of us worked past dinner time. I left them to the emails and tacos and joined Winston on the deck for steak. Serenaded by crickets and cicadas, we drained a fine bottle of bourbon. As the moon rose, I came to accept Buford Winston not only wasn't an ass, he was a friend.

Damn it. I needed another suspect.

THAT'S SWAT
I CALL AWESOME

My five a.m. flight out of Tulsa landed in DC around eleven. Well, I assume it did. I wasn't on it. I woke up with the sun solidly above the horizon and some jackass deciding now was the perfect time to hee-haw at the top of his lungs. I stumbled out of bed wearing the clothes I'd worn last night, parts of which were fused into skin and bone. Extraction was an outpatient procedure performed without anesthetic.

"Ms. Fielding? Jessica? This is Lois Winston. You all right in there?"

My hand was pressed to the gorge in my hip. "Yes ma'am. Just...waking up." Yeah, I was that lame.

"All right, then. There's plenty of towels and hot water. I'll have breakfast waiting when you're ready."

I brushed my teeth twice to scrub off the fur coating my tongue. The shower rinsed away the dried bourbon sweats and had me smelling like a girl again. I dressed in Jessica's carefully coordinated separates and only hesitated when I lifted the wig. Jessica was flying today, and she was a blond in her ID picture.

My flight was landing as I sat to tackle a chick coop's worth of eggs plus bacon and potatoes. Lois was a goddess. Buford contributed Bloody Marys. "Hair of the dog that bit you?"

I took the offered glass. With a salute, I drank. Good dog.

With a lot of fast talking and a burn to the credit card, I got on the last flight to DC. It gave us time to look at Dr. Liu's proposed scope for the Phase 2 grant. Revision five.

I had proofread many grants and papers for Gavriil. This one was well written even if, in my opinion, the promised outcomes were very pie in the sky. Grants were competitive; you had to sell yourself and your ideas to the grantor. Even in science, it pays to be sexy.

Buford dropped the paper he'd been reading on the table. "It's been a year since Gabe died. I don't know. Maybe I'm just old and crotchety but that young woman puts me off. Gabe had confidence in her. That should mean something, shouldn't it?"

"It should, but the fact that it doesn't means something, too. You live by your gut."

He chuckled, rubbing his protruding belly. "Always have and it's never been wrong." He was quiet for a long moment, staring at the proposal. "I'll approve it, I suppose. The theory is solid, and it builds on Gabe's work. I transfer the grant now, and we start over. This is too important." He covered my hand with his. Squeezed it. "We better get you going."

I sat in my seat, jostled by the taxiing plane, feeling hollow. I thought of my own relationships with my coworkers and what Gavriil knew of them. Some days, I spent more waking hours with coworkers than I did with my husband. It was natural to know details of each other's lives. I was close to the people I worked with first at the agency and then with the kids. Hell, one was squatting across the fire escape from me. I could forgive myself for misreading Buford. His blow up with the Italian cop? Grief. Loud, boisterous, booming grief. The argument with Gavriil at the conference? It was the culmination of the emails. Two good men, two sharp minds on completely different pages like some high science Abbott and Costello routine.

WHO's on first—that's the World Health Organization.

WATT's on second—as in kilowatt hours of power.

I don't H2O's on third—no water, no life. At least on this

173

planet.

Buford's emails bothered me. A lot. Dix got into the details enough to confirm they were not sent from Gavriil's university account but a masked phantom account. Could my husband have done it himself? Could? Yes. Would? No. This is the difference between working in the abstract and knowing your victim.

Gavriil devoured the theory of science but was totally disinterested in technology. He procrastinated getting a smart phone until his students' phones shamed him. In the division of household chores, setting up new devices fell on my side of the line. Home computer, DVR, Netflix, the radio on this new car, etc., etc., were my areas of responsibility. (More than a fair trade as he took the laundry.) Gavriil *could* have figured out how to send masked emails to Buford, but he *would never* care enough to spend real time at it when he could be doing something productive. It was even less likely he wouldn't have mentioned it to me at some point.

So who sent them? Everything leaves a digital thumbprint, no matter how faint. It was the little bits of information buried deep within the file structure that could help someone with the rights skills and tools find the needle in the haystack. Dix had the skills. I had the patience to let those skills work.

I needed Dixon and Ian to generate a lead because I was running into a dead end. Buford Winston didn't hire Hugo Franzetti. Carlo Giancarlo was still looking for the driver of the yellow car. Next step would be to resurrect the conference list and scrutinize every name for connections to Gavriil. There was little to work with on the attack on Quili Liu. I hadn't gotten a plate or a picture. It was on Dix's to-do list to tap into the traffic cameras and get an ID. I had to presume the events were all connected until I could prove that they weren't.

What other options were there? That wasn't a rhetorical question. I was running out of suspects, out of theories, and out of energy. I wasn't ready to go home yet. I drove without a destination, hoping inspiration would find me. The area became familiar.

I parked on the grassy respite in the middle of a metropolis.

"Hey, baby." Squatting down, I plucked the tender weeds growing over my husband's resting place. "Sorry it's been so long." Next to him, the earth had been mounded over where my body lay. "I went to Oklahoma. You should have told me Buford wasn't an ass."

My butt settled on the cool grass. I leaned against the headstone. I'd come so far, learned so much but still felt miles away from the end.

I didn't know my next move.

Gradually, I became aware of the light...or lack thereof. Night had descended. I lifted my head and, ow, my neck rebuked me. My back was none too pleased, and my hips refused to get into the game. I rolled to all fours and crawled up the headstone until I stood upright-ish. My phone fell from my pocket. I bent to pick it up thinking I would have to pass this on to the CIA as an interrogation method.

I pressed a kiss to the stone. "Save me a seat next to you. Remember to put a good word in for me at the gate. I love you."

I moved slowly across the uneven ground, shuffling my feet until my hips thawed. My phone had stayed quiet throughout my visit. It wasn't respect or even good luck. It was still in airplane mode. I swiped the necessary digital buttons and brought it back to life.

Dixon and Ian had called and texted. Twenty times.

Ian answered on the first ring. "Where the hell have you been?"

My time with my husband was private. "I'm on my way back to the building. What's going on?"

"Your boy genius and I just figured out who put the recovery order out on you. It's not good, Diamond. It's Sam Irish."

"Well, shit." I was shocked when I shouldn't have been. His behavior at my funeral was bad news. He didn't buy my charred corpse routine. "Did you get a number for him? An email?"

"Better. The kid got an address."

I snorted in disbelief. "Like I believe Sam Irish could be found that easily."

"It wasn't easy, Diamond." Ian's voice hardened in defense of Dixon. "He's using an alias, Patrick O'Malley. And we verified. I called him myself from a clean phone, pretending it was a wrong number. It was him."

"Where?"

"Baltimore." He read the address.

"My own backyard. What a tiny, messed up world we live in. Well, it would be rude not to—"

"Don't go there, Diamond," Ian said hastily and with authority he didn't have.

Irish and I had a long, sorted, sometimes steamy, sometimes violent history. Ian had been on the fringe a time or two. He had reasons for his opinion of Irish, but he didn't know him the way I did. "When did he post the job?"

He sighed dramatically, a none-too-subtle reiteration of his disapproval and acceptance of the inevitable. "The day of your funeral."

I laughed. There was nothing else to do. "Irish had made me worth more alive than dead." And then something clicked in place. "Ian, you never told me the details of what happened to you. Could it have been Irish?"

He sucked wind. "I don't see how. I met Tamara in France years ago. Whenever we were in the same place, we got together. I wasn't expecting her but, well, was happy to pick up where we left off. We were reconnecting when two men entered the living floor. The primary alarm tripped but it had been glitching and I was distracted. A secondary alarm tripped but not early enough. It got ugly, fast."

"We saw the end result. What were they after?"

"They never told me. One asshole came at us with a sap. Knocked me stupid. Tamara was out cold. They worked me over. She woke up and went after them. She was naked and screaming and drew them away. It dawned on me she knew the score. While she had them distracted, I limped into the bathroom, to my escape route. One of them came after me. I had a backup gun hidden there. The asshole didn't want to kill me. He had a gun but used his fists instead. I put him down then went for the hatch. I heard a gunshot as I closed the door behind me."

"You and me have history together," I said. "If I was searching for me, you'd be on the top of my list."

"Fuck me," he said in agreement. "Do you think they staked my building out to see who came for me?"

"Not impossible. It took a while for us to put the pieces together."

"I noticed."

"Maybe you should wear one of those life alert bracelets, then I'll know when you get the shit kicked out of you." I smiled when he told me to do something physically impossible. "If they staked it out, they could have gotten the plate for my car, which is registered to a vacant lot under a real dead woman's name. It's possible they followed us to my building. Keep your eyes and ears open and security on."

"I'm taking it seriously. What are you going to do?"

The type of people attracted to a hundred K aren't dissuaded by a little thing like a death certificate. "Fulfill the order."

"Think, Diamond. Irish doesn't fuck around. If he put an order out with big money behind it, he's expecting to get something out of it. What are you trying to get out of this?"

"A hundred grand." This was going to be fun. "And bragging rights. I'll call you later." I ran to my car—hips be damned—started it, programmed the GPS, and peeled out of the cemetery. Ian was right, Irish played for keeps. Here I was, a woman with nothing to lose.

I didn't have time to finish the thought before a text came through. Someone had left a message for me. After more key strokes than I'd like, Quili Liu's voice floated into my car.

"This message is for Jessica, uh, Miss Fielding. This is Dr. Quili Liu. I am hopeful you will call me back. I feel I am being watched." She left a number.

I dialed the number. "Hello, Quili. It's Jessica."

"I am so sorry to bother, so sorry. It was nothing." She spoke quickly in her accented English. "There was a cat and Monte sometimes feeds him." She prattled on from there. There was no trace of fear in her voice.

After her third apology, I interrupted and asked to speak with Monte. "How goes it?"

"Good. Very good. I'm teaching her to play the video game *AnnihalNation*. She's got killer instincts." It was cute, Monte had a playmate.

One hour and thirty-six minutes later, I parked on a street around the corner from Irish's cul-de-sac. The neighborhood was high-end, with big houses on bigger properties. Still in Jessica Fielding's favorite outfit, I strode down the sidewalk with the confidence of a woman who belonged on these exclusive streets, even if it was just to visit a friend. I rounded the corner and walked smack into a party alit with the bright red lights of the boys and girls in blue.

"Son of a bitch. What did you do, Irish?" I whispered to the night as I avoided a group of neighbors on a lawn. The cul-de-sac was crowded with a Baltimore SWAT truck and no less than six cars with spinning lights. More unmarked cars filled the curb line back to the main road. Men and women in full gear were in ready positions at strategic posts. No one joked or chatted. Radios crackled and echoed in the still night. This was the real thing.

I just didn't know what kind of thing.

I sidled up to a young police officer at the back of the action, hoping to overhear the radio chatter. As I approached, the stand-down order was given. Tension snapped like a rubber band as a man in his sleep pants was marched out of the house, hands behind his head.

Sam Irish had the body of an MMA fighter. Hard angles and flat planes, looked damn fine in a suit, a pair of jeans, or his underwear. His auburn hair was long and unruly as it'd been at the funeral. His dark eyes were narrow and swept menacingly across the gathered multitude. With his hands behind his head, the muscles of his chest and abs were pulled tight, the lights of the police vehicles painting his body.

The air blistered with Irish's curses as he was walked over to a cruiser and was placed in the back seat.

"I'm the fucking victim, you idiots." Then the door was closed.

The officer stood at the door for a few minutes, Irish swearing at his back, then spoke into his radio and walked away.

I approached from the opposite side, opened the door, then slid into the stingy back seat and a torrent of expletives. "There's no point in playing the victim, Mr. O'Malley." I used a drawl infused with Oklahoma, just because it was fun. "This will go much faster if you just tell me your side of the story."

"My side of the story?!?" His head spun on a swivel, black eyes slashing with fury. "My side of the story is you fuckers have—Jesus Christ! It's you!"

Over his shoulder, the officer was returning. I slid back out the door. "Don't make this harder than it has to be." I winked, then closed him in.

Oh, Irish was not happy. His fist connected with the reinforced, shatterproof glass. His face was twisted and cruel; his mouth promised retribution of biblical proportions.

"What? I can't hear you...the glass...I can't understand what you're saying. Do you know sign language?"

"You'll want to step back, ma'am." The officer inserted himself in front of me. "This is an active scene."

It was cute how he cared for my safety. Obediently, I took several steps backward. "He does look a bit rabid. What did he do?"

"Nothing, ma'am." There was relief on his young face. "It's over. It's safe to return to your home."

"Oh, I'm not a resident. Jessica Fielding, reporter. I picked it up on the scanner." I leaned in conspiratorially. "Can you help me out a little? My editor has been on my case to make me prove I can handle the crime beat. He thinks I'm too young." The cop had a baby face. I played the odds "too young" would be something he could relate to.

He glanced around, then lead me into a shadow. Irish pounded on the window again, shouting inarticulately. "A call came in reporting a hostage situation at this address."

"Who owns the home?"

"Patrick O'Malley. When attempts to contact Mr. O'Malley were unsuccessful, the Baltimore SWAT team mobilized." The cop was into it, adrenalin fueling his running mouth. "Following all department protocols, we attempted to engage with either the homeowner or the suspect. Eventually, we were able to make contact with Mr. O'Malley and the call was determined to be a hoax."

"A hoax?" Funny how a prank of this type would come on this particular night. "Then why is he in the back of the squad car?"

"A precaution. For Mr. O'Malley's safety."

It was work not to laugh. He had no idea there was a lion penned up in that cage.

My phone chimed. A text from Dixon. *Stay away from Baltimore for a while*. He ended it with an angel emoji. My sweet, stupid, put-gas-on-a-fire angel.

"It's called swatting," the cop said, continuing. "People call nine-one-one and convince the operator a hostage has been taken or other violence is ongoing. The SWAT team responds, and well, scares the hell out of the unsuspecting victim before the hoax is revealed. It's a crime local, state, and federal agencies take very seriously."

"Do you know why it was done?"

He shook his head. "It's usually a case of revenge for some social slight. It's fun and easy for gamers and online societies. A girl won't meet you, you SWAT her family. Some guy destroys your level fifty-seven village, you SWAT his family. It's rarely about money."

"What are the odds you'll get this guy?"

"That's above my pay grade." He pointed with this thumb over his shoulder. "Do you have any idea how much money is sitting on this street right now?" His radio burst to life speaking in a code he didn't know I understood. "I gotta go."

"Can I quote you on this?"

He glanced over his shoulder again. "Better not. Good luck with your editor." He jogged back to his car, preparing to release the lion.

I found a crowd and blended in. Irish's narrow gaze searched for me, but I was just one in a sea of professionally bleached blonds. I texted my person with exceptional cyber skills. *Tell me you did not use your own phone.*

Instant response: *No. I'm not 14*

Me: *Keep your head down. You don't want to fuck with this guy.*

Dix: *He shldnt fuck with u.*

Oh, my little cyber criminal was being gallant. Me: *Ian know?*

No answer. No answer. Dix: *Does now. Dropped dinner. Big mess. Gotta run.*

People milled about, walking in all directions around the ten-house cul-de-sac. The street had the hustle of a neighborhood block party despite the day being minutes away from turning into tomorrow. Irish stood on his front walk glaring at the crowd, not giving a flying fuck he was a few ounces of cotton away from buck naked. The neighbors noticed. Responses varied with gender and proclivity. Irish was a fine piece of eye candy.

I fell in behind a family walking past me, making myself invisible. Two houses away from Irish, I used the shadow of a hedge line for cover to the rear yards and quickly crossed to his. The back door was unlocked after I picked it; I accepted the invitation in.

The house was brightly lit, modern and tasteful. I walked through to the half bath in the center hall to observe Irish.

Through the open front door, I saw him in a Superman pose, powerful against the dark night. I stepped back and began removing the pins holding the wig. His accent grew thicker the more pissed he became. The door slammed shut.

"SOME DUMB FUCK SWATTED ME. DEAD FUCK. HE IS ABSOLUTELY A DEAD FUCK." Irish switched to Gaelic but continued shouting in capital letters. He wasn't far. In the living room. The kitchen.

Dix didn't know what he got into with the stunt. Sure, even if he knew, he wouldn't have believed it. That's what being seventeen is about. I was going to have to nip this in the bud.

"I WANT THE FUCKER RIGHT HERE. RIGHT FUCKING HERE." Commence foot stomping. Irish was going to burst a blood vessel if he didn't relax.

I removed another pin and dropped it in the sink. Then another. A sweet little *clink* was made by metal on porcelain.

And then a different kind of click sounded, and the working end of a pistol pointed at my still-blond head.

Irish followed the gun to stand fully in the doorway.

The last pin fell, and I removed the wig, then the netting holding my hair. "Dark brown. My natural color. Surprise."

"I always knew you weren't a blond." He took his finger from the trigger, then scratched his chin with the barrel. "I knew it. I fucking knew it. A candle, my ass."

"You didn't have to be so dramatic at my funeral."

His eyes flashed with approval. "I knew you were there! I felt you."

I glared at him. "But you didn't figure I had a reason for killing myself."

He shrugged. "Only one thing mattered. You didn't say goodbye." He reached out, non-gun hand, fisted my hair, then pulled me to him. The kiss reflected the man, hard and dominant. Irish and me, we had passion between us from the first, crazy assignment. But never love. I reciprocated the kiss because if he'd pulled a Lazarus on me, I'd be fucking thrilled to see him again.

Then he bit my lip.

"Hey." I shoved him. Hard. The taste of iron hit my tongue. "What the hell."

"Don't you die on me. Ever. Again." He shoved me back, then soothed my lip with his thumb. "What are you doing here?"

A cocky smile grew across my face. I wasn't afraid of Irish. Never had been. You don't have to be afraid of a dog to know it's not a good idea to kick one. "Heard you were looking for me."

"Sit. Make yourself comfortable. I want to know everything." He waved a gracious hand toward the couch, a gesture I once welcomed.

But I wasn't up for a trip down memory lane. Better to keep this impersonal...kissing aside. "I'm in the mood for a drink. Why don't you find some pants and I'll buy you a pint?"

Irish swore at the expanse of skin he wore, then an unholy smirk settled on his face. "Does it bother you?"

I openly assessed his body. When one has a work of art in front of them, one should appreciate it. "If there was a vote for the eighth wonder of the world, I'd nominate you. But there isn't and I'm thirsty." I headed for the front door. "You coming?"

The bar of his choice was barely a mile away. Irish had his hand on my back as he steered me to what had to be his table. Back of the room, in a corner so dark even the shadows had shadows. He sat facing the room, forcing me to either sit next to him or trust him to watch my back. He was still working his way toward forgiving me for the whole death thing, so I gave him my back.

A waitress way too perky for the time of night came to the table with Irish's Guinness in hand. She handed me a menu, but I went with the drink of the night: a widow maker.

Sometime, karma was a cruel, twisted freak.

Irish reclined against the booth like a king, regal and confident. "You always had amazing eyes but with the dark hair, they're brilliant. Can't say as I care for the baggage under them."

I narrowed said amazing eyes. "Excuse me?"

"You've lost weight. You're practically scrawny. I bet I can count your ribs." He reached across the table for my shirt. I slapped his hand away. "So, I know you're married, you're a scarecrow, and you're dead. I presume you killed yourself to escape the bastard?" His face contorted into an ugly mask. "Did he hurt you?"

"No," I said instantly. "My husband is dead. 'We regret to inform you' and 'a tragic accident' and 'we all mourn his loss.'" I slammed my hands on the table. "It was bullshit, Irish, pure bullshit. He was killed, and it was too inconvenient for the police to believe his death was anything but a traffic accident."

He leaned back and held court. "Tell me."

I did. I laid it all out. Every road block. Every dead end. Every stone unturned since I died.

"I'm so close." I held my thumb and index finger an inch apart. "I can feel it. If I can just get there…"

"Then what?"

"Then I'll nail the bastard." My hand clenched into a fist waiting for a target.

"I know you will, but my question was what will you do *after* you nail the bastard?"

"I'm focused on here and now. This mission. You can't look to the next game until you win the one in front of you."

"You've always relied on your instincts to get you through. You've got good instincts, so you've gotten through, but for this, you need a plan."

"I have a plan, weren't you listening? Nail. The. Bastard." It's been a debate between us for years. Irish is a hothead, but he's a planner. Me? I prefer flying by the seat of my pants. I enjoy the ride.

He shook his head, like he always did when I won an argument. "What do you need?"

"First, close the contract. I can't work with every Duey, Cheetam, and Howe getting in my way. Second," I paused for dramatic effect, "pay up. I found me and delivered myself.

184

Payment due in full."

"In the morning. One hundred thousand dollars for one night?" He cocked his head, then shook it, laughing at himself. "I'm a fucking idiot for thinking it's a bargain."

"I'm not staying the night." Arrogant bastard. Is it any wonder why we make a great team? I took a card from my pocket, conveniently prepared with a bank account. "I'll make it easy on you."

He had one of his perplexing smiles on his face as he dialed, almost as though he were enjoying spending his money on me. He greeted someone in French, leaving the table with my card in hand. It was comfortable in the dark bar with Irish. I almost felt normal. An ordinary woman meeting a friend for a drink.

My phone rang; I answered. The voice was male and likely called from some other bar. "Lori? Is this you?" He slurred the *esses*, stretched out the *ooo*.

"Sorry buddy, wrong number."

"Yeah, well, how do you know?" Ah, the wit of drunk logic.

"You're right, I'm sorry. I have the wrong number."

"Damn straight." And he hung up on me.

"Dumbass." The waitress placed a platter on the table. "Not you," I said when she seemed put out. "We didn't order this."

"I did. I'll see some meat back on those bones." Irish stepped in behind the waitress. He sat, going straight for the stomach ache waiting to happen. "The banking is done, the time is mine."

"Maybe. What are you doing here in the States?"

His eyes sparkled with mischief. "I'm on loan."

I snorted. "The last time you were on loan, a congressman, a defense contractor, and a trapeze performer lost their jobs after a scandal."

"Lies!" He pounded his fist, roaring with laughter. The years melted away in the wake of heavy food, good beer, and better stories. Age was creeping in, though, afflicting him with a version of Alzheimer's causing him to misremember the times I saved him from a lion (feline variety), a cougar (human variety), and a jealous husband with an itchy trigger finger. Of course, my retelling of the lasagna incident, the banker's bisexual (and enthusiastic) wife, and an African coup were spot on.

The lights came up, and the waitress began mopping the floor.

"Somebody's trying to tell us something." I blinked to get my eyes to adjust. We walked out, arms around each other, both reluctant to part. It was an awkward kind of silence, broken by my phone. The screen glowed like a beacon in the starless night. I recognized the number. It was dumbass again. I declined it, wishing I had blocked the number. "Do you think—"

"Down. Down." Before he got the second period out, Sam had me on the ground. Three blasts of gunfire preceded the shattering of the car window next to us. Tires squealed, and we were both on our feet.

"My car," he shouted, running across the nearly empty lot.

"No. Take my car." I pressed the fob, flooding the space with light.

"Bloody hell. Don't argue. I'm the better driver. I've *always* been the better driver. Get the fuck in."

I did because his car was closer. He was *not* the better driver. "Don't lose them. Move, move."

He peeled out, accelerating up the empty road like a dragster. Our target was the piece of shit two blocks ahead, driving on both sides of the road. As he calmly closed the distance, I felt around for the weapons he would have stowed. I checked the loading on a handgun, then gave it over to Irish.

I kept the sawed-off. It matched my mood. "This is your fault, you son of a bitch."

"In what world is this my fault?"

"Your stupid contract. He's getting on the highway. Don't lose him."

"I'm not going to lose him, Mother, and this has nothing to do with me."

"Bullshit, Irish. This is just the kind of crap I've had to put up with. I should shoot you on principle." The highways were empty by Baltimore standards and our dickhead was swerving around like he was playing a game of Mario Kart.

"I don't hire bush-league amateurs. Do you really think anyone I hire is going to drive a Saturn Ion?"

I squinted to see the tail. "Seriously? I didn't know there were still Saturns on the street."

"There'll be one less after tonight." The pedal went through the metal, hitting the proverbial ground. Cars honked as we passed them like they were standing still.

I pressed a few buttons on his roof and eventually the sunroof opened. "Hold her steady." I climbed onto my seat.

"Not yet. I want them off this road."

"Me, too." The exit coming up emptied into a commercial and industrial area with wide roads and few people. Perfect. Bracing myself, I went Major Tom. The wind stung at a hundred miles per hour. I aimed, fired, and the sideview mirror exploded. The car fishtailed before regaining control and taking the exit. I slid into my seat and reloaded. "Take the exit."

"You missed," Irish said with juvenile delight.

"I hit what I was aiming at. Take the exit."

"Christ, woman, stop with the backseat driving." He cut across the lanes, our quarry seconds ahead of us. The ramp arched smoothly to the right, depositing us on an empty one-way street.

"No one out but us rats." A warehouse screened our rat from sight when the road turned sharply. Irish slowed only enough to maintain control.

"Where is the fucker?" Irish's question was rhetorical but... where was the fucker?

"There!"

I braced myself as we put the brakes to the test. Out my window, headlights glowed on a gravel road next to railroad tracks. An engine revved twice, then gravel flew.

Irish roared with challenge, whipping his seven-passenger,

reinforced Suburban juggernaut onto a collision course. White light flashed from the passenger side, bullets glancing off like gnats. "He's pissing me off."

"You see?" I punched his shoulder. "You see the bullshit you sowed?"

"Get out there and get this asshole out of my way."

Back through the sunroof. First shot. Front grill. Second shot. Windshield. The boxy car meant for runs to Taco Taco Taco was no match for the heavy gravel railroad embankment. It tripped over the rails and did the mechanical equivalent of a slow fall down the other side. It went man-to-man with a storage shed and the shed won.

Irish and I alighted. (I've always wanted to use that word.) With a hand, he had me holding position behind the front of the vehicle. He went to the back door and returned with enough fire power to face down a zombie insurgency.

I took the vest, gun, and extra rounds. "How do you want to play this?"

He palmed his gun and stepped out. "The usual way..."

BAD COP,
BADDER COP

"Out of the car. Hands where I can see them." I channeled authoritative badass as I gave the orders.

"Out, you fuckheads. Give me a reason to end this now." Irish circled the car, shouting in an American accent better than mine.

The fuckheads inside were white, male, and young. Both shook their heads like the Hulk had gone to work on the few brains they had.

"You shoot them, Dagger, you gotta do the paperwork." My weapon trained on the driver's head, I searched for their piece. It wasn't in the driver's hands. Those were wrapped anaconda-style around the steering wheel. "Keep those hands right there." I stepped wide and examined the face. Stringy, blond hair was tied at the back of his head. Blue eyes, slightly dazed, sat on a long face. He was no one I knew.

"I don't think so. I cook, you clean. That's the deal." Irish peered over the roof, shaking his head to say he didn't have an ID either. He pulled the passenger out the missing window, banging his head on the doorframe. "That's what you get when you don't wear your seat belt."

I swung my door open and introduced Ponytail to my friend pavement. I patted him down as he squirmed on the ground. "A shame those airbags didn't deployed, with a pretty face like yours."

Irish's fuckhead swore in ascending tones as he was relocated to the back of the car. Mine couldn't tell up from down, literally. After much prodding, he made it to his feet, where genius decided to make a break for it and rammed his head into the tire wheel. Knocked himself out cold.

I blinked rapidly...because I could not laugh. Thanks karma, I owe you one.

Irish paced in front of the fuckhead, ten years older, fifty pounds heavier, one hundred percent meaner. Fuckhead was smart enough to keep his gaze on the ground. "This was a mistake. Sorry, man. Real sorry."

I leaned against the car, ready to follow Irish's lead. "I'm not feeling it. You, Dagger?"

"I'm feeling it, Cookie. Oh, I'm feeling it." He grabbed the fuckhead by the throat and shoved the barrel in his mouth. "I'm feeling it. You feeling it?!?" Fuckhead's screams competed with Irish's shouts for airtime. "Shut up. Now. I'm going to ask you one time. Who was your mark and who is paying you?"

Fuckhead gaggled on the barrel.

"Pull back, Dagger." I walked into fuckhead's field of vision. "You're gonna tell us what we want to know. Aren't you?"

His hands were up now, eyes closed, head nodding. A pool of piss spread around him. Irish withdrew the barrel slowly.

"T-target was a blond bitch. I-I got a cell number and an address for that bar." His gaze flickered to me. "You aren't blond."

It wasn't worth a response. "Who's paying you?"

"I don't know."

Irish stepped forward. "They all say that. The first time."

"I don't, I swear." Fuckhead practically rolled under the car. "I-I needed cash, so I called a connection. Two days ago, I got a message from someone with some fucked up name paying ten g's for a drive-by. Today I got a message to be ready, then came the deets."

A deadly quiet fell.

Irish paced away and then turned. "How stupid do you think I am." He stalked back to fuckhead.

"It's the truth, I swear. I fucking swear on my sister's life." His voice was hoarse, his face colorless except for the blooming welt left by the dashboard. Desperate blue eyes clung to me. "Tell him. Tell him it's the truth."

"What was the name?"

"Chrissy something. It was long. I don't know, but it was long. It's in my phone." He went for his back pocket. Irish dragged him from under the vehicle, put him on his face, arm twisted back to the breaking point. Fuckhead's voice broke, edging on hysterical. "It's in there. Check for yourself."

He didn't have a password on the phone, but he did have five texting apps. The seconds it took to find the right one probably felt like hours with your face doing an impression of a waffle on the gritty pavement.

"Chrysanthemum," I said.

"Like the flower?" Irish removed his weight from fuckhead's back.

"Wanted the woman dead. I don't ask why."

Three hours before sunrise, we were back at Irish's house. For those of you concerned about the fuckhead twins, we left them where they were. If they didn't manage their way out in another few hours, the early-shift workers would find them. Irish was as surprised as you are when I dragged him out of there ASAP.

I needed to talk to Ian and Dix and considered going back to my place except for two complications. One, Irish would follow me. Two, I didn't want him to kill Dix.

"More coffee?" He stood behind the gourmet kitchen counter, coffee pot in hand, every straight woman's wet dream.

"Yeah. You changed your recipe, right?"

"About two years ago, after a little visit to Ethiopia."

"It's good. Really good. Sam?" I waited until his gaze came up. I had a question I needed an answer to. "Why did you put a hundred grand out to find a dead woman?"

His face was a mask, giving nothing away as he stared back. Then he turned away, going to the refrigerator and pulling out a carton of eggs, milk. He wasn't going to answer.

"Sam—"

"I knew a girl once. Aibreann." The Irish name was pronounced "av-rawn." "April. She was as sunny and sweet as the month she was named for." He cracked eggs into a bowl, his eyes on his work.

"You loved her."

"When she passed, I felt it." He looked over his shoulder, his gaze forbidding. "Say what you want about the Irish and our ghosts, but I felt it. I know what death feels like." The eggs when into a pan, the sizzle the only sound in the room. "When I opened that lid and saw the charred flesh within, I felt nothing. I waited for it, told myself it was the shock of seeing you laid out, as it were, but it never came. I left that church pissed because you left me, left my life so thoroughly that I couldn't feel you. Then I saw Ian Black with that smile he always wears. Why would Diamond's pet be smiling at her funeral, I asked myself. Only one answer."

"Jesus, Sam, why didn't you leave me alone? You had to know I had a reason."

He shrugged as he divided the eggs between two plates. "I only cared about one thing. Finding you."

"For a man who claims to be logical, that's fucked up." My phone rang, returning my page. "Ian Black. Do not call him my pet," I said to Irish before answering it. "Ian. I have you on speaker. Irish is here."

"Morning, Ian. Long time no see." Irish said, brogue back in residence.

Ian grumbled. "You get the money, Diamond?"

Irish crossed to the table, plates in hand. "Aye. Your Diamond is a richer dead woman." He refilled my coffee from the pot on the table, no regret discernable on his face.

"Tell me some good news, Ian."

"Carlo found the driver. It's none other than Valentina's older brother, Franco. Carlo found him in a seminary and pressed him. Franco said he raced down the street when Hugo shouldered a man into the path of the car. Franco fled to Hugo's flat, hiding the car. He fought with Valentina, walking out when she demanded to know what he had done. Franco decided to turn himself in. He waited for Hugo to tell him what he was going to do. We both know why Hugo never showed."

Another shot from my blindside. Valentina's brother.

"Franco asked Carlo to pass a message to you, the widow. Franco said he's made his peace with God but doesn't expect you'll be as forgiving." Ian sounded like he was reading the statement, his voice flatter than normal. "He regrets the evening more than he can say. He was arrogant, brash, and took your husband's life. Nothing can undo his actions, but in that horrible moment, his life changed. He found his humanity."

"After."

"What?" Ian asked.

"*After* that horrible moment, not *in*," I said. "If he'd found it in, he would have turned away." My head dropped back and landed against Irish's stomach. His hand squeezed my shoulder. "What's the point of his message?"

Papers rustled across the line. "He's sorry? Hell, lot of good it does us."

"I assume he doesn't know who hired Hugo?"

"No," Ian said. "All he heard were euro signs. He said Hugo was paid four thousand upfront. They split it."

"Fucking sucker. Hugo lied. His little black book showed fourteen thousand for the deed. Four before, ten after." It burned my biscuits Gavriil was killed for so little. I know how wrong it sounds, as if someone had put a hundred-thousand-euro hit on him it would be somehow, I don't know, less bad. But really?

Fourteen thousand? Cars cost more. "The math adds up now. The two thousand is the trunk was Hugo's share of the advance. The balance was paid in lead."

"The client used an alias and had texted Hugo to set it up."

"Let me guess. Chrysanthemum?"

"Yeah. You already knew? The deposit showed up in cash in an overnight envelope from a flower shop in DC."

I filled him in on our evening. "I have the phone Chrysanthemum called and texted to and the passwords for the recipient's account. Do you think Dixon can weasel out the contact?"

"He started on it, then he got sidetracked." Ian snickered. "I got him a hooker. Sort of a belated birthday present."

Irish shouldered me aside. "This kid, Dixon, is he the one who swatted me?"

I cursed my blunder while Ian choked on his laugh, answering Irish's question without saying a word. "Let it go, Sam. Your contract put a big price on my head. Ian was beaten and left for a popsicle. If the roles had been reversed, you'd have done a lot worse than swatting. Dixon's mine. That makes him yours. Let it go." I invaded his personal space, inviting him in.

"I already got Dix on the emails. We'll get there. Need to know what you want to do with Valentina's brother. Carlo's waiting on your directions." Ian swore softly. "Diamond, Carlo believes the guy's on the up and up but, you know, he's Italian and raised to think priests walk on fucking water."

Here I was, in the gray area. My mission was justice for Gavriil. I didn't care what form or by who. I had the man who killed my husband, who hit his body with a car so hard, he'd crushed his chest. He literally broke his heart. I had the man...and he was becoming a priest.

Could I forgive him? No. Not if I lived to be a hundred.

Could I tell Carlo to take him down?

I'm thinking...

Well, if...

Maybe...

As much as *I* wanted to, it wouldn't be what my husband would've wanted. So, I was damned if I did, damned if I didn't.

Karma hated me.

"Tell Franco to feed the starving." Gavriil would want people cared for first. "Franco has to pick up the baton he knocked out of Gavriil's hand. I'm not talking about organizing can food drives. I'm talking about getting that church of his to teach people how to fish and use drip irrigation, how to build wells and plant quinoa." I dropped the fifty-pound weight posing as my head into my hands.

Just because it was right didn't mean it felt good.

Irish's arm snaked across my collarbone.

"Good call," Ian said. "Especially the damn quinoa. Next, the kid's made progress on Winston's emails. It's a sweet hack mimicking a host email while still allowing the host access to a portion of the account. The address has a blind tag built in so a reply to sender is routed to the placebo account. It's been blamed for security breaches in every industrialized nation. Hold on a minute, Diamond."

Ian's voice became muted as he spoke away from the phone. He and Dix were having another geek-to-geek conversation. Dix's tone was triumphant. Ian shifted from skeptical to hot-damn. "He's got him, Diamond. Dix has a picture of the hacker. Not great images but good enough. He's texting them to you now."

My phone chimed, confirming the download. With the swipe of my thumb, the grainy image of my husband's killer filled the screen. A telephoto lens had been used to capture a hooded figure at a computer. Five images, taken in rapid succession as the target turned.

"Fuck!" I exploded up, knocking Irish away from me and spilling my chair onto its side. The back of the chair was in my hands. The legs cut through the air as I whipped it from over my shoulder, smashing them on the table, then against the floor. Over and over until splinters flew like missiles in all directions. Spinning like a shot putter, whatever I could wrap my hands around was launched across the open space. "Fucking bitch. Fucking psycho cunt from hell." The vicious words stripped my throat raw, so I shouted louder. An arm came around me. I caught it and threw it, too.

Ian's tinny voice rode atop the racket. "Irish, what the fuck are you doing?"

Irish rolled with the toss, landing on the balls of his feet, hands at the ready. "Me!?! She's the one on the rampage."

Obliteration. Annihilation. The gates of hell burst open and I was the demon birthed. Books flew. Glass crashed. Furniture rolled. Anything not nailed down got thrown. Anything nailed down got the crap beaten out of it. Nothing escaped my fury.

The room spun, flying by until the coarse carpet was scraping the skin from my face. "Stay down, Diamond. For fuck's sake, stay down." Irish's knee was in my back, his heavy ass keeping me where I was.

"Never." I used my head, my feet, elbows and teeth. The man was a human octopus, countering every move until all I could do was scream my outrage.

Irish shouted over me. "Who the hell is in the picture, Ian? I'm going to rip them apart myself."

"Chrysanthemum. That's all I have, Irish."

"Quili Liu. It's Quili fucking Liu. Gavriil's assistant." I fought until my arms ached. Breathing like a thoroughbred after a sprint, I stopped fighting. Rational thought pushed front and center, leashing the last of the unbridled energy. Breaking Irish, turning his house into kindling, would only piss me off more. I needed to think, to plan, like Irish preached, and then, only then, would I act. "You can get off, Irish. I'm not going to hurt you."

I heard his derisive snort as his weight lifted off. He offered me a hand and pulled me to my feet. The upscale living / dining space had been remodeled by a Tasmanian devil. Tornados did less damage. Crap. When I stood face-to-face with Irish, I said, "I'll replace it all."

"Sorry I didn't get it for you faster, Diamond." Dixon's

young voice was heavy with self-disapproval.

"It's not on you, Dix. It's on me. I didn't go there, not after the near-miss on her. Why would she plan such an elaborate rouse to throw suspicion? I wasn't on to her."

"They weren't after her," Irish said, still holding my hand.

The wheels turned. "Then they were after…" I lead with my left. He pulled back. My knuckles burned from the brush with his morning beard. He grabbed my wrist, turning me until he had my back pinned to his chest. "You ass! Fuck your furniture. I'm not replacing a stick of it. How am I supposed to solve this when you throw red herrings in my lap?"

He leaned back, lifting me so my feet kicked uselessly in the air. "If I knew what you were up to, I could have spent my money helping you." My elbow connected with his ribs and he spun me away from his body.

Going in low, I swept his feet out from under him. "Don't you dare make this sound like it's my fault. I killed myself for a reason."

He leapt over me. "You should have contacted me."

I thrust my hand up, disrupting his graceful landing. "I had a job to do. I didn't even know you were in the country."

He rolled and came to his feet again, facing me. Coming at me, he moved through a sequence of blows readily defended. He wasn't trying to hurt me, and I'd stopped trying to hurt him. He tied me up, arms over our heads, face-to-face. "It didn't matter where I was," he snapped into the scant inch between us. "For something this important to you, you should have called me. You called Black." He spat Ian's name out as he shoved me away.

The choreographed hand-to-hand was no less physical for the lack of intent to kill. It ran the temper out of both of us. He was sweaty, disheveled, and irritated. Beneath it was something else. Disappointment? I hadn't called him for help. Before, he would have been my first call. Even before my official network. But my life changed. In accepting Gavriil's world, I walked away from the one Irish lived in, closing the door and throwing away the key. I never intended to come back to this underbelly world where there were no good guys. Yet, here I was, and I needed help. "I'm calling you now. I'm taking her down. Help me."

A cocky smile grew on the devil's face. "You don't have to ask."

"Jackass." Still, he made me smile. "I want to know Liu's secrets and her mistakes. Dixon, Irish, find her connections to these Chinese hacker stories. I've got a hundred thousand of Irish's money to spend on information. I want to know if any other 'deadly accidents' have happened to Americans or on American soil. Dixon, get a better picture of Liu and send it to Carlo. Ian, have him press Valentina, her priest-to-be brother, and Hugo's grandmother. Tell him to hit the doorman and staff at *Il Leone*. Somebody saw her. She's not half as good as she thinks she is."

For myself, I took the task of calling my new friend, Buford Winston. After the requisite small talk (on his part, not mine), I laid out our suspicions.

"Gotta tell you, that fires on all cylinders for me. Guess I didn't think whether or not it sounded like Gabe. Too busy bein' pissed to pay attention to details. I went straight to thinking he mighta been hitting the vodka." His outrage grew as the pieces fell into place, until he blasted from the pulpit, "There's a special hell for connivers, backstabbers, and two-timers."

I believed he was ready to send Quili there with his bare hands. So, soon as I hung up with Buford, I called Lois and gave her the heads-up. She hid his car keys.

Assignments made, the team scattered. Irish to his office. Ian and Dixon to their holes in the wall, which left me alone in the ravaged room. I righted an arm chair and sat. Realization sank in. We'd solved it. We knew what happened to Gavriil and to Francisco Thelan. In a matter of hours, we'd be able to prove it. And I had the murderer sitting on a pink bed in protective custody.

Hindsight is amazing. What was an unsolvable mystery from the outside became remarkably simple from the inside out. This one came down to an unquenchable thirst to be at the top.

Quili Liu arranged for Gavriil's death to assume his position. She was not a woman to come in second, nor wait for her time to come. Why bother when, for a few thousand euros, she could be on the top now? The top ag producers could clamor for her attention today.

I gotta tell you, I thought this moment would be so much more...epic. I expected to be jumping and fist pumping and whooping it up because good had prevailed. After all, we solved a crime that authorities said didn't happen.

But the satisfaction wasn't there.

Things still felt...what? Undone? Incomplete?

Justice hadn't been served.

A text notification came through. I had a voicemail. Seconds later, Montgomery Rand was in my ear. "Don't get mad, but your woman is gone. She just left. I tried to talk her out of it. She said the danger was all clear. I asked if you'd called, and she blew me off. I tried to stop her, but she pulled a karate move on me. I think she cracked my back. That's got to be worth—" Delete.

Quili Liu left the safe house. Well, somebody was feeling cocky.

Of its own accord, the seed of a plan planted itself in my brain. It wasn't nice but it was good, in the bad kind of way. All I needed was a realtor, an electrician, and a king.

I'LL TAKE THE COUP DE GRACE
WITH A SIDE OF FRIES

Gray clouds boiled with the fury of the gathering storm. Thunder rumbled in the distance, a low, growling threat sending animals with any sense to shelter. Rain closed in, the scent heavy in the wind that tore across my newest property. I walked the perimeter one last time, Ian and Dixon in my ear.

"Exit camera three aaannd enter camera four," Dixon said in my ear.

"That's less than a two-second gap between camera angles," Ian added. "She brings company, we'll see them coming."

"Maybe we should come in there with you." Dixon had been puppy-dog enthusiastic about setting up the warehouse for the final act but had been giving me sad eyes since learning he and Ian would be in a van a half mile away. After finding Ian in his building, Dixon had lost some of his fearlessness when it came to where Ian and I were at any given time.

I kept reminding him I was dead.

"This is between me and Liu. You did your part," I said. "Time for me to do mine."

"Trust Diamond, Dixon." Ian sounded as though he didn't have a care in the world. "Hey, did I ever tell you about the time she hijacked a ferry?"

Again, with the stories. "Borrowed, Ian. Sheesh. I gave it back to the captain just as soon as those river pirates were under arrest." The teasing balanced out the tension. I didn't interrupt as Ian told a highly exaggerated version of a tiny incident Dixon swallowed hook, line, and sinker.

The sky darkened, bringing night on two hours ahead of schedule. A flash of white lightning and a roll of thunder announced the storm's arrival. Heavy drops of rain fell, splattering on the weed-infested parking lot.

I entered the warehouse. The cavernous space was too dark to see the ceiling. Only when lightning flashed could the true size of the room be appreciated. This had been an assembly facility. Gears and tools, twisted sheets of metal, and half-assembled machines littered the waist-high tables. It was as if an entire crew had gone home at the end of a shift and never come back. White LED lights set within the castoffs created shadowy monsters, hungry and lurking.

I walked the path my quarry would follow to the raised platform, approving of the ominous atmosphere created by the black-on-black motif. The stage held only a wide-armed chair resembling a throne that held court over the dilapidated ruins. Here I reigned, the queen of Diamonds in a fucked-up Wonderland of my own concoction. I dressed for the occasion, continuing the monochromatic theme. Lycra pants finished in boots made for fast moves. A corset allowed free arm movement. A leather coat flowed like a cape, a twin to the one Irish wore at my funeral. My eyes were the stalking green of a cat about to dine very well. I painted my lips to match.

I sat and allowed the stillness to take me. At last, everything was ready.

In the two weeks since this plot of mine hatched, I debated if I was going overboard. Wouldn't I be satisfied with a straight up end to this story? In a moment, it could be over with the sting of a bullet, at the end of a rope, or the bottom of a glass.

I watched Quili Liu die a hundred times since that day in Irish's house.

While the fantasies were cathartic, they were too fast. Quili

Liu did not deserve fast and it wasn't because Gavriil's wife was pissed. It was because Liu deprived an entire population of the good that the geeky scientist was doing. In killing him, she murdered a population.

Since fast and easy were out, I stuck with plan A. Slow and terrifying.

Ian tapped into his connections and fed information into the closed Chinese network. The Chinese liked order and predictability. Doubt and suspicion made them nervous, and nervous made them dangerous.

Dixon hacked into things I didn't know could be hacked into. He messed with Liu's computer, the control system on her greenhouse, and her Stitch Fix account. He giggled as he imaged her hard drive, cancelled appointments, insulted the university president's wife, instigated an ice age, and had her clothing delivery include only orange articles.

Irish had become a regular at my kitchen table. Ian and I both kept an eye on him, expecting retaliation against Dixon, but it didn't happen. Guess Irish was a dog lover, too. Dix won him over with his boundless energy, loose morals, and a bottomless stomach. The black eye finally faded but not before Irish saw it. Dixon didn't rat out his old man.

For myself, I'd been stalking Liu. Nothing horrible, just enough to put her on edge, to wobble that cocky attitude. Then I blackmailed her. Ten thousand dollars for the records that proved she hired Hugo Franzetti to kill.

Tonight, at dusk, she would pay the ransom, in person and alone.

All the i's were dotted, all the t's were crossed, and so, I waited. Minute by minute, our paths came closer to resolution.

Rain pelted the roof, sounding as though the sky dropped marbles. Lightning flashed, flooding the industrial space. Still, I waited.

The air smelled of petroleum, dust, and rain. Nothing to be afraid of.

"Car approaching," Ian said in my ear. "The car is slowing in front of the building and turning onto the circular drive."

I left my throne for my starting position, a recess near the entrance. Screens ran the length of the room, invisible to the naked eye in this light, enabling me to play puppet master with impunity.

"Three figures exiting the vehicle. Open the door in three... two...one."

I pressed a button on the remote Dixon had built for me. The front doors opened.

"Confirmed, Liu with two men. She and one of the men jumped. The third was cool, the taller one. Both men are armed. Assault rifles. Approaching door two."

Another button on the remote and a recording began to play.

"Halt. Thou art about to enter the next dimension." The booming voice of R&B's next superstar echoed off the concrete floors. King was happy to help with my escapade, and maybe he thought the mind control juice hadn't quite worn off. "This place is for the pure of heart. Enter with reverence; leave with bounty. Enter with dishonor; leave in a casket." He stretched the syllables of the last three words, painting a picture of an endless hell.

The effect was even better than I hoped. King didn't just read the script I'd written with the help of Jose Cuervo—he performed the fucker.

"They stopped," Ian said. "They looked spooked. That weird shit you had King say actually has them nervous."

When we talked about my death, that is my first death, I told you I'd have gone out epic if I could have.

This is me, going epic.

"Choose now," King's disembodied voice directed.

The disconcerted chatter of my quarry came through my ear piece, overlaid by Ian's chuckle. "She's pissed, Diamond. One of the men does not want to—shit, take cover!"

I covered my ears, patiently awaiting the result of the assault rifle versus the industrial door. In the end, the gun was exhausted, and it still took a hand to open the door.

The small figure, our dear Dr. Quili Liu, led the incursion, tossing the spent weapon aside. King's voice played on a loop, a recording of slow, melodic nonsense that birthed unrest. Liu barked an order in a Chinese dialect; the men fanned out. The complex arrays of light and shadows before them were designed to warp perception of space. Liu staggered to the left, a hand on a machine press stabilizing her. She walked past me, followed by the man I came to think of as Extra #1.

From a selection of weapons within my alcove, I selected a sap then stepped out from the screen, a shadow moving among shadows. The weight in my hand was an extension of me, cutting through space and hitting true. I caught Extra #1's dead weight, slowing his descent to the ground, eliminating sound. He carried a handgun and two knives, both of which were now mine. Covering him with a dirty tarp, he became another forgotten relic in the warehouse.

"What the fuck?" Liu asked. Okay, I don't actually know what she asked, not understanding a word she said, but she had a what-the-fuck expression on her face. Extra #2 responded. Probably said, "I have no idea, but the lights are fucking toxic." When Extra #1 didn't comment, the parade stopped. Both turned and looked to the spot where I used to be. Liu walked backwards, edging toward the center of the room, finding nothing. She wasted more bullets on the walls and ceilings. Still the bassy chanting droned on. She barked orders to the last man standing.

Lightning flashed, and thunder echoed as though I had cued their lines. Snapshot images of their faces showed fear in the wide eyes. She did not like the soundtrack custom made for her arrival. I'm not going to try to spell the jibberish King recorded. Insert whatever you think demons crawling out of hell sound like. With another button on the remote, a weight dropped. Extra #2 whirled, firing over and over and over until there was nothing left to shoot. The second rifle hit the floor.

Liu ordered Extra #2 to the offending area. He walked with a stride that was determined, ruthless, fearless when someone was trying to scare him. You know the kind. There's one in every horror movie. Until they get eviscerated.

Behind the cover of the screen, I came up behind him. He called to Liu, signaling all clear. She turned her back on him. Neither saw the garrote reflect white silver in the flash of LED light. It cut through skin and muscle, a blood-red pool tainted the colorless floor. Pained and desperate shouting rebounded across the vast space as the man fought for his life and lost.

And then there was one.

"Who is there?" she said, finally deciding to try English. "I am here to make a deal. I have the money."

Right. I almost forgot about the ruse. Staying to the shadows, I retook the stage and my throne.

It was almost fun, triggering the surprises engineered along the corridor. She jumped like a frightened cat, spinning in the air, screaming like some nineteen seventies horror star. With a flash of reflected light, bullets hit the scraped metal, dangerous for the random angles of the shrapnel.

I wasn't behind protective cover. I wasn't layered in Kevlar. But I wasn't scared. Tonight, retribution was my armor.

Pause the looped satanic ramblings and play the grand finale. "Stop." The recording gave the order and Liu obeyed. "Go no further. You have reached...the end." King laughed then, climbing the scale. Do-Re-Mi-Fa-So-Fuck-You. Electronics elongated and twisted his voice into a maniacal sound that could never be mistaken as sane.

"Stop this. Stop I said." Her accent was stilted, afraid when she tried to be commanding. "Who are you?"

The laughter abruptly stopped, the silence in its wake was the crack in the gates of hell. Something wicked this way comes.

Oh, shit, that's my cue. "I'm the one you've been waiting for." I played my part, the calm, bored deity.

"I've been waiting for? You set this up. I am here to explain you are wrong about Italy."

It was a cute ploy. I brought the stage lights up enough we could talk face-to-face. Her eyes widened. "Jessica Fielding?" She raised her gun.

Mine was already trained on her. "You want a chance of walking out of here, drop it. One-time offer."

She thought about it. Her decision was in her eyes. I shot the gun out of her hand. Hard for me to tell if I hit her hand, her arm, or the gun itself. All I cared was the gun was now on the ground.

"I'm unarmed. You cannot shoot an unarmed woman. It's the law of the American."

Wonder what movie she got that from.

I cocked my head. "But then, I wouldn't be shooting an unarmed woman, would I? I'd be shooting a killer."

With wide eyes, she vehemently shook her head. "I not killed anyone. No one." Her grammar was falling to pieces, just like the rest of her.

"Hugo Franzetti."

Liu looked like I was speaking Greek.

"You remember Hugo. Italian. Small-time con, looking to make a few bucks. Don't tell me you don't remember the man you hired to kill Gavriil Rubchinsky? He did your dirty deed and you rewarded him by filling him with lead and driving his car into a ravine. You must have been dancing in your quinoa when Gavriil was killed by the car and Francisco Thelan died by the drink. Talk about throwing off suspicion. Don't worry. I won't blame you for Francisco Thelan, after all, you weren't trying to kill him." Sarcasm dripped like syrup from a pancake.

"He...he try and kill me." She tripped over her own feet as she moved back toward the only door visible.

I adapted a visage of sympathy, a therapist coaxing their

delusional patient to reality. "Of course. You needed to do something drastic to protect yourself." I leaned in. "You had no choice. When the emails you sent to Buford Winston did not succeed in Gavriil's funding being pulled, in him being fired so you could step into his place, you had to do something physical, something permanent. You had done it before. The winner of the Stockholm Junior Water Prize. The chair of the botany department. The roommate. They were all hurdles, impediments, road blocks."

Liu didn't move, her dark eyes glossy in the fractured light.

"Just like a little rabbit, frozen in the headlights. Don't look so shocked. You did well. Really well. You only made one mistake."

Liu did not take criticism well. Her eyes narrowed, her brows pressed together. "Mistake?"

I fired the gun to the ceiling, the skylights exploded as the explosives I'd planted were denotated. Glass and rain poured down.

"You.

"Killed.

"MY.

"HUSBAND."

With each word, I stalked toward Gavriil's killer. With each step, I fired the weapon and triggered another explosion.

Liu retreated, tripping over God knew what. She scrambled across the concrete floor covered in glass and shell casings. I felt the power of a very unholy hell coursing through my body. I sprinted the distance between us, catching her by the back of her collar and hoisting her to her toes. "You've been a bad, bad scientist."

Her attempts to free herself were feeble. A few girly kicks. A swipe of her nails. She actually tried to go boneless and slide out of the shirt I held.

I pressed the gun to her head and just kept it there, letting the anticipation build.

When nothing happened, she slowly looked to me, daring to ask the question. "Are you...are you going to kill me?"

I grinned. A Cheshire Cat, wide-ass, big, toothy smile. "I was hoping you would ask." I released her neck and picked glass from her hair. "Only someone with your moral depravity could appreciate my plan. Killing...killing is easy, wouldn't you agree? In a fraction of a second you'd be gone. Oh sure, there would be some satisfaction that the scientific community would forget your name in less time than it takes to boil water. That is, if they even noticed you are gone. The problem is...I kill you, then I become the bad guy. I can't be the bad guy in my own story. No one would take my side if I did. They'd all be sad for the poor little scientist who didn't have the benefit of special ops training. Couldn't let that happen. Had to be another solution. Instead of thinking of you only as a cold-blooded murderess, I took a look at another role you star in. Spy."

Her face tightened with insult. "I no spy."

"You know all those cloaked emails you've been sending to China? Got 'em. Oh, and the hack you hired to break into Gavriil's email and clone it? Well, the feds can't touch him as long as he's on Chinese soil. You on the other hand." I looked down at her little feet, standing on concrete that stood on American soil. "Not so much."

She knocked my hand away, scrambling to put space between us. When I didn't chase, she reached blindly to the table behind her. She threw anything she could at me, well, in my general direction. Her pitching arm sucked.

Hidden amid the bric-a-brac was a device of my own creation. It looked innocuous, like a miniature tire pump.

"What is that?" she asked.

"The grand finale. Run." I pressed down the small T plunger. Fountains of fire and light raced along the walls, further distorting the space. Liu screamed and sprinted for the door, only to run into a table. The run was long, the fire was fast. Even with the open skylights, the air was thick with smoke.

I walked the other way to the rear door hidden by a screen. Outside, I got a running start and snatched a ladder rung. One hand slipped on the slick metal but the other held true. On the roof, I sprinted to the front of the building, curious if Liu would escape the maze.

"We got three cars closing in. Your friends are joining the party." Ian paused, then said, "Sure, kid. We can do that."

From my perch over the front door, I watched three black SUVs park across the front of the property. Men and women spilled out, hurrying into covered positions. A woman screamed, and our villainess shot out of the building. Shouts of authority rose. Liu spun in a circle, her hands in the air, her voice no match for the agents surrounding her. Flames licked the building walls, casting the gray evening in a deathly orange, as Liu laid on the ground, hands behind her back.

"Holy fuck, Diamond! What did you do! What was with the fucking explosions? That was not part of the plan!" Ian continued to shout in exclamation points as his van drove half on the sidewalk. I removed the earpiece, dropped it, and ground it into the roof.

I recognized the man in the lead. Enrique Torres. I knew him by the way he moved. He secured his prisoner, then handed her off to another agent. He stood in a Superman pose, surveying the beauty of my work. He threw his head back and laughed in homage.

The next day, nothing happened. In defense of the day, there was nothing to happen. Not from my point of view. I'm sure Quili "Killer" Liu was busy lining up lawyers and crying to ambassadors. Her conniving little mind was probably working so hard smoke was puffing out of her ears. I can imagine her cellmates leaning over her, snorting in the China prime grade.

Everybody else worked. All I could do was imagine.

The day after that, nothing happened again. I got out of bed,

got dressed, and then just stood in the front window waiting for
something to happen, looking for a reason to...to do something.

Anything.

Third day, I met Irish for lunch at a small restaurant. I retold
the splendor of that night. He complimented me on the planning.
Our lunch continued long after most people came and went. I
asked what he had going on. Thought I could be useful, in a
dead woman kind of way.

That's when he dropped the bomb. He was leaving for an
assignment. The work: confidential. The location: confidential.
Likely return date: maybe sooner, but probably later.

I had this weird, hollow feeling in my throat. Life was moving
on...without me.

He said goodbye, and it really felt like goodbye. He told me
to get some sleep and ordered me to eat—as if he could order
me to do anything—then he left.

Ian had moved back to his place. Dixon split his time. Ian
and I argued about who got to feed the bottomless pit each day.
We both wanted him. Hell, we both needed him.

I wasn't sleeping well. I spent my nights inspecting the ceiling,
one square inch at a time. My mind drifted to the outtakes from
my life. My biggest mistakes, worst humiliations, loneliest moments. Gavriil was featured nightly.

If only I'd gone to Rome with him.

Day four, nothing happened.

Day five, I didn't bother getting out of bed.

Day six, I was getting the picture. Today, yesterday, tomorrow. What's the difference?

Day seven, the illustrious technicolor extravaganza I created
felt like a year ago. Ian came over, bringing pizza with him for
dinner before a movie with Dixon. Ian relented and said Dixon
could drive. The latter bounced with anticipation; the former
rattled off rules like a prison guard.

They asked me no less than a dozen times to go along, but I
wasn't up for a movie. I had no reason to be unhappy. Ian

brought word the Department of Justice filed charges rivaling the Encyclopedia Britannica in word count.

Let's take a look *Family Feud* style...

The charges were surveyed, the top three answers are on the board. Name the crimes Quili Liu was charged with.

Operating as an unregistered agent of a foreign country? Number one answer. You are not having a good day when the feds write that one down.

Murder in the first degree for Gavriil Rubchinsky and Francisco Torres? X. Sad, but true. With Hugo dead and the Vatican's newest priest on a mission in Sub-Saharan Africa, first-degree murder didn't stick.

Attempted murder for Jessica Fielding? X. Strike two. Can't murder someone who doesn't exist.

Conspiracy to commit murder? Number three answer. Total of five counts after all the evidence was in.

Fraud and other finance-based crimes? Number two answer. Turns out those grants Buford administered came from the US Department of Agriculture. When Liu cheated Buford, she cheated Uncle Sam. Both were pissed.

Ian heard from a guy, who sleeps with a woman, who is a secretary for Enrique Torres's department, who heard that Liu cried, feigned bad English, ordered her own release, then had a breakdown. For a woman like Liu, a few decades in a prison, isolated from the intellectual fanfare of a university, branded a fake, stripped of her accomplishments, that was her seventh circle of hell.

"Come on, Diamond. Come with us. I've been practicing, a lot," Dixon said.

His endless energy drained me, but I mustered a smile. "Told you once, told you twice, video games don't count."

"It's a driving simulator. It counts. That's how they teach pilots to fly."

"That explains a lot. Lightning, my ass." I gnawed on a pizza crust. It was as hard and bland as my life.

"You sure, Diamond? We don't have to see *Carnage and Entrails 2*," Ian said. He winked at Dixon. "There's other movies out. You know, ones girls like."

I snorted. "When have I ever been accused of being a girl? Appreciate the offer, but I'm going to hang here. I have work to do."

Ian looked at his watch. "Come on, kid. We should hit it."

Dixon bound to his feet, snatched the keys from Ian's hand, and ran out the back door.

"You want a bulletproof vest," I asked. "Helps with impact."

Ian chortled. "He's getting better."

I put a hand on his arm as he passed. "You're a good friend. You were to Gavriil and me. You are to Dixon."

The fucker blushed. "Yeah. Thanks. You, too."

Alone in my castle, I cleaned up after dinner. There were no leftovers to put away, just a few plates and a couple glasses to wash, a box to throw away. No point leaving a mess.

I did one last walk through to be sure I didn't forget anything. I stuck a Post-it to my "special" utility drawer with Ian's name. Papers were also in there. Ian and Dixon were now president and CEO of Diamond Cut Enterprises.

There was a time when I thought the world was better off because I was a part of it. That time had passed. I was nothing more than a shadow. A memory. It was time I was forgotten.

The day was overcast, the clouds heavy with a rain that would soon fall. Black birds swooped past my windows, racing tree to tree like frantic addicts looking for a fix.

Everything was just as it should be.

In my bedroom, I took off my boots. The hardwood floors were cold on my heated feet. I picked up the silver-plated frame with my wedding photo. I touched the face of the man smiling out at me. I picked up my gun. The three of us went into the bathroom where we all climbed into the bathtub.

No burning down the house this time.

It was just me and a bullet. Diamond and lead.

Ian knew how to take care of a body. I wished I could have figured out a way to get into my coffin. I wanted to be buried next to Gavriil. I knew it didn't matter where my body was. Six feet deep, bottom of the river, burned to ash, it was all the same. I was going to meet him where bodies didn't matter. Still, it would have been nice.

This time I wore my favorite sweatshirt, the one with the holes at the wrist cuffs my thumbs fit through. My favorite yoga pants in the soft, comfortable cotton. The bullet was for my heart. Broken as it was, it would still bleed while it beat. The blood would wash down the drain. That's why I didn't go for a head shot. Big mess. I didn't want Dixon to see me like that.

I touched my husband's face, remembering how his stubble tickled the palm of my hand. "I hope you put a good word in for me." My voice broke. "You know I—"

The back-gate buzzer sounded like a National Weather Service warning. I jumped, smacking my head on the spigot. Fuckin' A that hurt. The buzzer sounded again, and I fumbled Gavriil's picture. He fell out of the tub and landed with a smash on the white tile floor.

"What kind of world is this coming too when a person can't get fifteen minutes of peace and quiet!" I climbed out of the bathtub and shoved the narrow window as high as it would go. "What! What could possibly be important enough to lay on that buzzer like a whore on a broken mattress?"

"I? What? I'm not a whore!" The blond outside my gate clucked like a hen, then pushed the damn button again.

"Bitch!" I elbowed the screen until it popped out, then shoved my gun hand out. "Do it again. I dare you." The screen hit the pavement with a crash. Her hand reached for the damn buzzer. "What do you want?"

"I'm looking for Diamond. Please tell me you're not her." She wore designer black pants and an elegant white shirt. Her hair was wild in the breeze, her face one I'd never seen before.

"In the flesh. Doesn't tell me what you want."

"I have a problem." Her gaze swept around the parking lot.

"Welcome to the club. Try Jack on the rocks." I started to pull back.

"I got a note," she said hastily.

"Good for you. I'm sure your mommy's proud."

"He...he said you had to read it."

This was getting old. "Who?"

"His name is O'Rourke." Her voice drifted. "He wants to help."

"Then go lay on his doorbell."

There was bite in her voice this time. "He told me *you* could help me."

"He was wrong," I said, showing bite of my own. She tore open the letter. "Did you say that was addressed to me? You can't open it. It's against federal law!"

"Arrest me." She held the paper between both hands, her brows tightening. "This doesn't make sense."

Don't ask.

Don't ask.

"Well, what the fuck does it say?"

"It's an IOU from you to someone named Sam Irish. Good for, and I quote, 'One favor you can call in anytime, except the hours of two a.m. to four a.m., anyplace, except Malta, the Yucatan Peninsula, and Gary, Indiana, for any reason, unless it's stupid.'" She looked up at me. "It's only seven, we're in Washington, DC, and it's not stupid."

"Ha! Of course, it is." I waved the gun triumphantly, knowing I caught her in an ipso-facto. "It's all stupid!"

"My husband's been kidnapped," she shouted, her voice breaking on the last word. "He's been missing for two days. The police don't believe me. They think he's run off with a mistress."

I froze, my arm, head, and shoulder out the window. "Fucking Irish," I muttered, looking to the sky. A crow circled overhead, swooping lower on each turn. "We're not going to let him mess this up, are we?" A maniac robin appeared out of no-where. The streak of orange raced between the buildings, banked right, hung left, and crapped on my gun hand. "Fucking karma."

ACKNOWLEDGMENTS

This one was for fun, but as always, no story is a work of imagination alone. First, my thanks to those who made Diamond into the woman you read today. Chris Rhatigan, editor extraordinary, my thanks for all your hard work, advice, and conversation. Thank you to Matt, Karen, Denny, Kristen, Jane, Traci and Johnny, my reading team, for suffering through the typos to make Diamond sharper. And deepest thanks to Eric Campbell and everyone at Down & Out for being great to work with.

Many websites were utilized in the research on quinoa. Two of my favorites were the Harvard T.H. Chan School of Public Health (1) and The World's Healthiest Foods (2). The research on Rome and the Italian countryside was during a first-hand experience called "vacation." The hotels, streets, people, Vespas, countryside, etc. Diamond encountered were the souvenirs I brought home, infused with imagination. The lighting hitting the plane and being re-routed through Minneapolis was true, though. No elaboration needed.

Finally, thank you, dear reader. As I said, this story was written for fun. Mine in writing, yours in reading. I know you have many choices of where to spend you free time and appreciate you spending a little with me, Diamond, Ian, Dixon, and Irish.

Until we meet again,
TG Wolff

(1)   https://www.hsph.harvard.edu/nutritionsource/food-features/quinoa/
(2)   http://www.whfoods.com/genpage.php?tname=foodspice&dbid=142

TG WOLFF writes thrillers and mysteries that play within the gray area between good and bad, right and wrong. Cause and effect drive the stories, drawing from twenty-plus years' experience in civil engineering, where "cause" is more often a symptom of a bigger, more challenging problem. Diverse characters mirror the complexities of real life and real people, balanced with a healthy dose of entertainment. TG Wolff holds a Master's Degree in Civil Engineering and is a member of Mystery Writers of America and Sisters in Crime.

tgwolff.com

On the following pages are a few
more great titles from the
Down & Out Books publishing family.

For a complete list of books and to
sign up for our newsletter,
go to DownAndOutBooks.com.

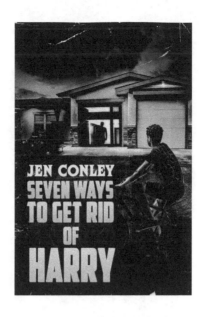

Seven Ways to Get Rid of Harry
Jen Conley

Down & Out Books
June 2019
978-1-948235-93-8

Danny Zelko, needs to get rid of his mom's boyfriend, Harry. The guy is a creep. Of course everyone blames Danny. It's his fault he gets into fights at school. It's his fault he can't control his anger. Danny isn't such a bad kid—he has his own lawn business, makes his own dinner, even takes out the garbage and closes up the house without being asked. All he wants is for his mom to be like she used to be—a real mother who acted like one. Because Harry makes her stupid. And the prospect of spending another day with this man makes Danny feel helpless and broken.

Danny, never the one to cower, decides to do something.

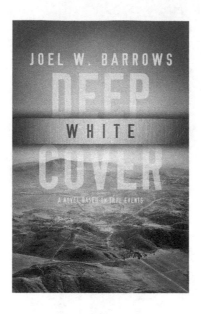

Deep White Cover
Joel W. Barrows

Down & Out Books
May 2019
978-1-948235-81-5

Extremist anti-immigrant groups and white-supremacist hate-mongers have begun to combine resources, and ideologies. These new hybrids of hate pose a rising threat, not only to the country's immigrants, but also to national security.

ATF Special Agent David Ward, undercover as a disgruntled veteran of the Army's Special Forces, works his way into *The Nation*, befriending its leaders and learning its secrets...or so he thinks. In truth, the organization's reach exceeds anything that the seasoned agent could have possibly imagined, something he will learn only when it seems too late to stop the revolution they seek.

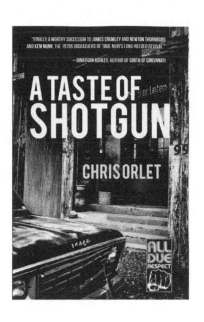

A Taste of Shotgun
Chris Orlet

All Due Respect, an imprint of
Down & Out Books
978-1-946502-92-6

A local drug dealer has the goods on Denis Carroll. That shooting at his tavern five years ago? Turns out the cops got it all wrong. Now, after five years of blackmail, the Carrolls have had enough. When the drug dealer turns up dead, Denis is the prime suspect. As more bodies pile up, they too appear to have Denis' name all over them. Is Denis really a cold-blooded killer or could this be the work of someone with a grudge of her own?

In this darkly humorous small-town noir everyone has something to hide and nothing is at seems.

It's Not My Cult!
A.X. Kalinchuk

Shotgun Honey, an imprint of
Down & Out Books
978-1-948235-71-6

Anthony Dosek, after unwittingly creating a flying saucer cult he would rather forget about, goes to live with his cousin and his wife. Anthony's ruthless second-in-command would rather Anthony not forget his followers, and in trying to create a founder-martyr that will increase cult donations, this wannabe Iago dispatches a cynical former veteran and his naive sidekick to make that martyrdom happen.

In the meantime, to make amends, Anthony tries to reconnect with the mother of his child that he fathered while leading the cult.

Praise for *Widow's Run*

"Tina Wolff's novel is for crime-fiction fans who like it action-packed and hard-edged. Written with feisty panache, it introduces Diamond, one of the most aggressive, ill-tempered, and wholly irresistible heroines to ever swagger across the page."

—David Housewright, Edgar Award-winning author of *Dead Man's Mistress*